PRAISE FOR
Charmed & Ready

"Havens's writing is snappy, instantl̲____ ____ ̲____ and down-right charming."

"I'm thoroughly charmed and read̲ ____ ____ If only the [TV] networks could ____ their new comedies as delightful a̲s ____
—Susan Young, *The Oak____*

"A delightful ride from the first page to the last . . . the action is immediate and lightning fast."—*Romance Reviews Today*

"Wonderfully witty . . . Readers are sure to enjoy this second book in the Charmed series. It's magically delicious."
—*ParaNormal Romance Reviews*

PRAISE FOR
Charmed & Dangerous

"Simply bewitching!"
—*New York Times* bestselling author Jodi Thomas

"From assassination attempts to steamy sex scenes to the summoning of magical powers, Havens covers a lot of ground. Weaving together political intrigue, romance, and fantasy is definitely tricky, but Havens makes it work in this quick-paced, engaging story with unique and likable characters."
—*Booklist*

"Mix the mystique of all three Charlie's Angels, Buffy's brass and scrappy wit, add the globe-trotting smarts of Sydney Bristow, and you might come up with enough cool to fill Bronwyn's little witchy finger."
—Britta Coleman,
author of *Potter Springs*

"Smart, sexy, and sinfully wicked."
—*USA Today* bestselling author Ronda Thompson

continued . . .

Like a Charm

CANDACE HAVENS

BERKLEY BOOKS, NEW YORK

THE BERKLEY PUBLISHING GROUP
Published by the Penguin Group
Penguin Group (USA) Inc.
375 Hudson Street, New York, New York 10014, USA
Penguin Group (Canada), 90 Eglinton Avenue East, Suite 700, Toronto, Ontario M4P 2Y3, Canada
(a division of Pearson Penguin Canada Inc.)
Penguin Books Ltd., 80 Strand, London WC2R 0RL, England
Penguin Group Ireland, 25 St. Stephen's Green, Dublin 2, Ireland (a division of Penguin Books Ltd.)
Penguin Group (Australia), 250 Camberwell Road, Camberwell, Victoria 3124, Australia
(a division of Pearson Australia Group Pty. Ltd.)
Penguin Books India Pvt. Ltd., 11 Community Centre, Panchsheel Park, New Delhi—110 017, India
Penguin Group (NZ), 67 Apollo Drive, Rosedale, North Shore 0632, New Zealand
(a division of Pearson New Zealand Ltd.)
Penguin Books (South Africa) (Pty.) Ltd., 24 Sturdee Avenue, Rosebank, Johannesburg 2196,
South Africa

Penguin Books Ltd., Registered Offices: 80 Strand, London WC2R 0RL, England

This book is an original publication of The Berkley Publishing Group.

This is a work of fiction. Names, characters, places, and incidents either are the product of the author's imagination or are used fictitiously, and any resemblance to actual persons, living or dead, business establishments, events, or locales is entirely coincidental. The publisher does not have control over and does not assume any responsibility for author or third-party websites or their content.

PRINTING HISTORY
Berkley trade paperback edition / February 2008

Library of Congress Cataloging-in-Publication Data

Havens, Candace, 1963–
    Like a charm / Candace Havens. — Berkley trade pbk. ed.
        p. cm.
        ISBN 978-0-425-21926-3
    1. Women librarians—Fiction.   2. Witches—Fiction.   3. Texas—Fiction.   4. Chick lit.
    I. Title.

PS3608.A878L55   2008
813'.6—dc22   2007032671

PRINTED IN THE UNITED STATES OF AMERICA

10 9 8 7 6 5 4 3 2 1

Like a Charm

Prologue

⚜

Sweet, Texas, is just like any other small town, except that it's a magical place. A coven of witches protects it, and generally everyone gets along. It's also quaint; beautiful, in fact. With its gothic architecture it could be a small village in Eastern Europe.

I'm Kira Smythe, and I never felt like I fit in there.

Other kids at school could cast spells or turn themselves green. Of course none of the magic is overt. Most outsiders seldom take notice of the odd occurrences around them— like a small child being whipped out of the way by a gust of air before an oncoming car could cause harm.

Except for an imaginary friend or two when I was five, there was nothing remotely magical about me. In a place where everyone is extraordinary, I've always been perfectly ordinary.

I left my hometown at the tender age of seventeen for college and only came home when I had to see my parents on holidays. My goal was to climb the corporate ladder and go after dreams that had nothing to do with magic.

I never wanted to live in Sweet again. It was my past, and I had new worlds to conquer.

Plans change and sometimes an ordinary person is called upon to do the extraordinary. I've learned something important in the last month, a lesson I'll remember forever.

Only idiots say *never*.

Chapter 1

Just breathing isn't living!

POLLYANNA
By Porter, Eleanor H. (Eleanor Hodgeman), 1868–1920
Call #: F-POR
Description: 236 p.: ill.; 22cm

When Melinda Jackson leapt from the roof of the Zeb Corp. building in Atlanta and landed fifty stories below, my life changed forever.

I'm the reason she jumped.

I'm Kira Smythe, a contract attorney with Zeb Corp., one of the largest companies in the world. I've spent most of my life trying to do the right thing, to follow the good path and to stay away from trouble.

That didn't keep trouble from finding me.

A week after Melinda jumped, I woke up in a hospital room in Atlanta. Bright lights shone overhead and I squeezed my eyes against the intrusion.

A disturbing dream, one where it was me on that ledge, had brought me out of a long sleep. The last thing I remembered before the dream was working on the Bedford-Meade merger contract in my office. Chaotic snapshots of me help-ing Melinda with her sexual harassment case against a nasty fellow at Zeb Corp. flashed through my head. I was the pros-ecution's best witness, and everything had seemed to be go-ing our way. That last day in court played out in my mind. The judge had an odd smirk on his face as he relayed the verdict. I should have known.

We hadn't counted on the power of old Atlanta wealth, which the defendant had on his side. We lost the case. An amazing woman, Melinda was strong and calm throughout.

By the end of the day she was on the edge of the build-ing, and that's when everything went dark in my brain.

I knew she was dead, but I didn't recall what she had said or how I made it off the roof that day. I only knew I'd been there.

I closed my eyes again, and when I opened them my fa-vorite paralegal and best friend, Justin, hovered over me wearing his crazy baseball jersey that reads, "Pink Sheep of the Family." I wanted to smile, but didn't have the energy.

There was also a woman sitting on my bed. My eyes were still bleary. "Mom?" I wondered if I might be dreaming. She lived more than a thousand miles away in Sweet, Texas, and I hadn't seen her in two years.

"At least she knows who I am," she quipped to Justin.

They both smiled.

"So, sleeping beauty decided to wake up." Justin winked at me. "Thank God, that nappy-ass hair of hers needs a scrub. Shampoo, anyone?" He made wiggly motions with his fingers.

I rolled my eyes, but it hurt my head and I winced.

Mom squeezed my hand. "Justin, hand me that tea." She was wearing her trademark T-shirt and hip-hugging jeans.

Her feet were bare, and she sat on the bed with her legs crossed as if she'd been meditating. Her long blond curls, identical to mine, were pulled in a loose ponytail at her neck. It sounds strange to say it, but my mother is beautiful. Most women my mom's age spend a fortune on moisturizers and wrinkle creams. Not her. She makes her own soaps and creams and she can pass for forty, even though she's pushing fifty.

She guided the straw from the cup of tea to my mouth and I sipped the peppermint concoction. Calmness settled into my body for a few seconds.

Then the memory of the stairway to the roof and an image of Melinda on the edge, the wind whipping her hair around her face, filled my head.

"It's my fault," I whispered when Mom took the straw away. "I don't know exactly what happened, but I feel guilty so I know I did something wrong. I'm the reason she jumped."

She handed the cup back to Justin and smoothed my hair away from my face. "No, honey, it wasn't you. The police tell us you were trying to help, that you were getting through to her. If anything you're a hero. That young woman was troubled and she made her choice. There's nothing you could have done."

My mom is one of the brightest people I know. Unfortunately, she was wrong about this.

"If I hadn't—I don't know." The words jumbled in my head and I couldn't get them out. "I can't remember what she said, but she was there on the ledge."

"Your mom's right, girl. We know who is to blame and so does everyone else in that office. Time for you to concentrate on getting better." Justin moved around and sat on the other side of the bed.

"What do you mean?" I stared around the room. My arms were hooked up to IVs and a monitor beeped in the background. "Am I in a hospital? What day is it?" My confused brain couldn't quite get with the program.

Mom frowned and I saw one tiny wrinkle at the corner of her mouth. That would mean an instant trip for Botox to most of the women I work with, but my mom sees wrinkles as something people earn. "You fainted on the roof of your office building, and the paramedics brought you here. You've been unconscious for a week. This is the first time you've been able to speak. The doctors say you are suffering from exhaustion and some very serious bacterial and viral infections. Justin tells me you haven't had a vacation in two years, and that you've become a workaholic." She said the last word as if it were poison.

I shot Justin my most evil glare. He only grinned.

"So I'm taking you home with me for a few weeks."

"What?" I tried to scream. It came out as more of a hoarse whisper. When I moved to sit up, the effort made the muscles in my back and arms ache and burn. I fell back on the pillow.

She sighed. "I know hanging out with your father and me isn't on your top-ten list of favorite things to do, but you need some rest, and you need someone to look after you."

"No. I've been looking after myself for years. I'll be fine," I said in my stern lawyer voice. It's this tone that makes Justin say, "Okeydokey, girlfriend, I'm going to run and get you a chocolate chip Frappuccino, cuz you need some mochalicious love."

It didn't exactly work with my mother, either.

"Yes," she said in her mom voice, which is about two

levels above my lawyer voice and comes with a really mean look. Usually Mom is about peace and love and let's all get along, but I could tell she wouldn't back down this time. "I don't want to point fingers, lovely daughter, but you haven't exactly taken very good care of yourself." She waved a hand around the hospital room.

"I won't go." I sounded like a petulant child. I couldn't help it.

"The doctor says you need to take these." Justin interrupted to give me two pills in a little plastic cup.

"What are they?" I held them in the palm of my hand, eyeing them warily.

"Um, something to do with the infection. You have mono, which is why you can't come back to the office. You're totally contagious, and that combined with the bacterial infection makes you socially unacceptable." He put his hands on his hips. "So, you might as well go home with your mom."

I raised an eyebrow. "She wore you down, didn't she?"

"Your mother is a beautiful, lovely woman who only wants to take care of you." Justin bit his lip. "She says they have a great place and you can get plenty of rest. In fact, it sounds so cool, I might come for a visit." He crossed his arms.

"No. I'm not going. I can take care of myself at my condo. In fact, that's exactly what I'm going to do." I reached for the cup of tea, but I couldn't lift it. "What the hell is wrong with me?" I demanded.

"It's the mono doing battle with the upper respiratory infection." My mom sighed. "Take the antivirals." She lifted the straw to my lips again. "Get some rest. Justin and I need to pack a few of your things. The doctors said that as soon as you opened those beautiful eyes of yours, we could take you home. I'm checking you out of this place, and we're leaving first thing in the morning."

I knew I should have argued more, but I didn't have the strength. "Mom, I don't want to go home. I'm sorry." I thought about being in Atlanta, alone with my dark memories of Melinda. "But maybe it's not such a bad idea. Maybe for a few days." At least my parents would be a distraction. I'm the kind of woman who always has a plan for everything, but my mind wasn't up to connecting the dots, and I needed my mom, even though I loathed admitting it.

I grabbed Justin's hand. "Don't forget to pack my briefcase with the contracts and the Blake merger research, my laptop, and make sure you change the meeting set for two weeks from . . . I guess it's one week now." I'd been out of it for almost seven full days. I hadn't missed a day of work in . . . well, ever, so I was due at least this small vacation. "Tell them we'll do a conference call. Dobson better have those numbers ready—tell him I said so. And . . . Why are you looking at me like that?"

Smirking, Justin patted my arm. "The boss lady is back. Listen, you're on a leave of absence. You don't have to do any work until the docs give you the okay. So no worries, chica." He leaned down and kissed my cheek.

"Justin, just do what I said, okay?"

He shrugged, and I let out an exasperated breath. "If you don't, I'll call someone else at the office to do it for me."

"Whatever." He rolled his eyes. "You rest, I promise to take care of everything, including sending you back to your hometown looking like a true diva. Oh, yeah, I love being Kira's personal stylist. Sweet isn't going to know what hit it."

I'm going home. A week ago the thought of returning would

have made me sick to my stomach, but now . . . now I wanted to be there. I might not fit in, but at least it was far away from what had happened here in Atlanta. Fresh air and a few days' rest wasn't such a bad deal. At the very least I could assuage some of the guilt I felt over not visiting my parents for the last two years.

My eyelids grew heavy and I drifted off on a drug-induced cloud of whatever it was they'd given me. Just as I relaxed, an image of Melinda flitted into my brain. I knew no matter how far away I went, the nightmares would continue.

Chapter 2

❧

Think you're escaping and run into yourself. Longest way round is the shortest way home.

ULYSSES
By Joyce, James, 1882–1941
Call #: F-JOY
Description: vi, 239 p.; 25cm

I woke up two days later in a room where everything was white. The bedding, walls, and furniture were all in the same monochromatic tone. The curtains had been pulled back, and a huge expanse of glass-filtered sunlight warmed the room. At first I thought they had taken me to another hospital, and it took a few minutes to realize I was at my parents' ashram in Sweet. I recognized the view. You don't ever forget that wide-open expanse of the West Texas prairie. Even in November, it was a beautiful landscape of low shrubs and rocky hills.

I took a deep breath and coughed on the clean air. I swear a body gets used to pollution.

Bits of the fifteen-hour drive with my mom came to me as my brain clicked into gear. We had only made a few stops, and mom had driven straight through. I tried to stay awake and keep her company, but the drugs and the mono made that impossible. I'd managed to walk into the room on my own two feet, but at the time I'd been so out of it I hadn't noticed my surroundings.

My parents' place is a huge, modern building they built on their land two years ago. For most of the time that I lived with them while growing up, we had a trailer on the 220 acres of ranch my dad had inherited.

About ten years ago they went into the lavender business, and it had been so successful that they now own three ashrams, including this one. It's a place where people come to hang out and get spiritual. There are yoga, meditation, and basic how-to-get-your-Zen-on classes. I hadn't been home in a little over two years, and the place wasn't finished when I left. I'd been keeping up with their progress over the Internet.

Even though it felt like I'd been asleep for forever, I was still tired. I resisted the urge to climb back under the covers and instead went in search of a bathroom. I finally found it behind a sliding panel worthy of Star Trek. It was one of those things where you wave your hand in front of the sensor and it opens. It was small, with just a sink, toilet, and shower, and decorated as sparsely as the bedroom. The towels and tile were white, while the fixtures were brushed nickel.

This is really rotten, but I never thought of my parents as having much taste when it comes to decorating. The three-room trailer we had lived in when I was growing up was a hodgepodge of garage sale and thrift-store finds. My dad sculpted metal parts into his version of art—which he then left strewn all over the yard. Mom called their "style" Early Bohemian. I, the snob, called it Hippie White Trash.

But this place was modern, visually pleasing to the eye, and, well, sterile but calming.

After a hot shower, which made me feel immensely better, I checked out the bamboo armoire in the corner. I found my clothes, but the choices were limited. Justin must have done most of the packing. He has this idea of what women should look like at all times, and it's right out of *Vogue*. There were my striped D&G black trousers, a skirt that matched, and a few button-down blouses with a jacket. I opened the drawers below and found three pairs of shoes, all with four-inch heels. My La Perla sets of bras and panties were in another drawer. For a moment I wondered who had unpacked my belongings, and for some reason it embarrassed me that my mom knew I wore expensive, sexy lingerie and that none of it was cotton.

I sighed. All I really wanted were my well-worn button-flies and my crimson Harvard sweatshirt. A woman needed some comforts in life.

I couldn't find my makeup and tried not to stare into the mirror too much. I'd lost weight, and the dark circles under my eyes looked like they'd been put there by someone's fist.

I made use of the clothes available and slid on a pair of Christian Louboutin pumps I'd drooled over in September. It seemed like a million years ago, but it had only been two months. If I stayed here more than a couple of days, I'd need some more comfy clothes.

I have to call the office, but first I need food.

The bedroom sat on the first floor. I walked out into a large common area with bamboo floors and white couches.

There was a series of hallways and I wasn't sure which one to take. It was quiet and I didn't see anyone.

I desperately needed food and a cup of coffee. *Standing here isn't going to get me anywhere.* I headed toward what I thought might be the front door. My joints and muscles ached and I moved slower than normal. I heard a voice behind the third door on the right and stopped to listen.

"George, we're booked here until June, hon. Yes, La Jolla too." It was my mom. I knocked lightly and opened the door a crack. She was behind a large glass desk, sitting in a big white chair made of cloth. My mother didn't believe in wearing or sitting on animal skins. Of course she'd never slipped her foot into a nine-hundred-dollar pair of Manolos. She might change her mind if she did.

She waved me in. "Look, I'll see if Cathy can get you into Palm Desert in January, but that's the earliest. Oh, don't worry about it. You know we'll make room if we can. I know you need your peace on earth."

Pushing a button on the phone, she slipped her headset off. "You have color in your cheeks." She smiled and came around the desk. Taking me in her arms, she squeezed me tight. "I was worried about you, my Kira."

"I'm better. Hungry, but better." I let her squeeze me, partly because it felt good and partly because I didn't have the energy to make her stop.

"Well, goodness, let's get some food in my girl." She pulled out a tiny cell phone and pushed a button. "Joe, she's awake. Yes, meet us in the kitchen."

That's when it dawned on me. *Oh my God, my mother has a cell phone—and an office.* I looked back at her desk. *And a Macintosh.*

"Mother, I think I'm hallucinating." I was serious.

"What's wrong, honey? What do you see?" She pulled back and stared at me, worry furrowing her brow.

I pointed to the computer. "What's that?"

She turned to see where I gestured, then faced me again with a smirk.

"You know it's a computer. Don't be a snob."

"And this?" I pulled the cell phone from her hand.

"Fine, we've come into the twenty-first century, are you happy? You can't run a business these days without a bit of technology here and there. Your dad has discovered some BBC America show called *Doctor Who*, and now we are overrun with gadgets. It was his idea to do all the door sensors."

I giggled. "Dad watched television?" The laugh turned into hysterics. *My parents*, the ones who would never pander to The Man and get a telephone when I was a teen, or let me have a television.

One of my rebellious acts as a grown woman with a job was to buy a forty-two-inch plasma with my first bonus check. I watched it for forty-eight hours straight one weekend. Geez, now my mom and dad had cell phones and a computer. Pure absurdity.

"I think you need to eat." Grimacing, she pushed me to the door.

She led me to a large room with several dining tables. They too were made out of bamboo and in all different shapes, with accompanying low bench seats.

"Is there anyone staying here?"

"Yes. We have a corporate retreat this weekend. They are up in the hills on a hike. They won't be back for hours."

I followed her through silver swinging doors and into

one of the most beautiful kitchens I'd ever seen, straight out of *Architectural Digest*.

"Holy crap, Mom, this is gorgeous." I swept my hand along the cold, black granite counters. Everything else was stainless steel and glass. There were two industrial stoves and three Sub-Zeroes in the enormous space. Windows lined the north wall.

She pulled out a bar stool at one of the two large islands. "Have a seat, and I'll see what I can find you to eat."

Dad walked in dressed in a big gray sweatshirt and jeans. Some things never changed. His long blond hair had a few white streaks, but he was as handsome as ever. "Puddles." He hugged me hard. I hadn't heard that god-awful name in years.

"Hey, Daddy." I hugged him back. Puddles was a nickname he gave me twenty years ago, and, well, it had to do with my fear of the outhouse we had to use when the toilet broke in the trailer. I'll say no more.

He sat down beside me. "I'm so glad you came to visit." He acted like I hadn't been dragged here against my will, or that I hadn't seen a woman teetering on a roof just before she leapt to her death. I wondered how much my mother told him.

She put a plate of food in front of me along with some chamomile tea, and I eyed the meal warily. "I'm glad too," I said absently, wondering if she actually thought the sliced tofu and avocado on my plate was real food. I cut into the avocado and took a bite.

I made a solemn oath the day I went off to Harvard that I'd never eat tofu again, and I was sticking by that. I didn't care how hungry I became; I wouldn't cave.

Last year I'd been home alone in my Atlanta condo for Thanksgiving and ate nothing but Hot Pockets and corn dogs with mustard for four days. I loved it. Anyone who has had multiple servings of Tofurky will understand.

"If she's up to it, maybe you can show Kira the new vineyard, and your sculpture garden."

Dad clapped his hands together and the popping sound almost made me fall out of my chair. "Oh, sorry, Puddles, the nerves must still be bothering you."

"Joe!" my mom admonished.

"Sorry, kiddo. You know we're going to get you fixed up. You'll be ready to rule the world in no time."

Mom touched his arm, and he shrugged.

"It's okay, Dad. I've just been under the weather. I'd love to see the vineyard and the garden."

Mom's phone vibrated on the counter. "I'll take this in the office. You two have fun, but don't do too much. It's her first day out of bed."

Dad patted my shoulder. "I'll take care of the kiddo."

After my meager lunch, I followed Dad out the back of the complex. "What did you guys name the place?"

He laughed. "Peace Agenda."

I chuckled. "Really?" That was the name of the list my parents made up every time they were getting ready for a big fight, which wasn't often. In fact, I only remembered them raising their voices a few times.

They were hippies twenty-five years after it had been popular. Everything we ate was organic; we recycled before anyone in Sweet had even heard of it, and they approached problems intellectually, including their *discussions*.

They met at Wesleyan while doing their doctoral studies

and have always said it was a perfect match from day one. The only time I'd ever heard raised voices in the house was when they were discussing me, or something I'd done.

I'm actually a list-maker myself, though I seldom do it before I argue with someone. Some people do needlepoint, I make lists.

And I couldn't be more different from my parents. I like the luxuries of life—nice clothes, great food—and I don't mind working hard to get them.

The air was brisk and the wind, which never stops here, whipped my hair around. We walked into a courtyard filled with an array of flowers and plants, along with huge bronze and other metal sculptures. One, in the center, looked like a giant V taking flight. It was as if it floated above the ground.

"Daddy?" I pulled my jacket tighter around me. It was overcast and the wind bit through my thin clothing.

"Yes, it's mine."

"It looks like it's ready to fly away. I love it." I smiled and it was genuine. These weren't at all like the pieces of junk that had graced our yard years ago. Or maybe they were, and my perception had changed.

"I actually designed the landscaping and the house too, though your mother helped with some of the interior design." He said the words nonchalantly.

The art took my breath away. I'd never known my dad was so talented.

My thoughts churned and whirled, and suddenly I felt dizzy. A hand touched my shoulder, but my dad was in front of me. I turned to see who had joined us, and no one was there. I shivered.

"Do you mind if I see the vineyards tomorrow? I'm—I don't know. I think I need to sit down."

"Oh, no." He frowned. "Let's get you inside. You need some of your mom's lavender tea to warm you up. And I'll find you a better jacket for tomorrow." He looked down at my shoes. "Perhaps we should take a trip into town and get you some walking shoes. The vineyards are in the hills, and I don't think they'd be kind to those."

He led me back to my room and I sat down on the edge of the bed. "You rest, now," Dad said as he shut the door.

It had been a strange afternoon. I knew the shivers I had felt didn't have a darn thing to do with the cold. It felt like somebody was watching me. *I'm going insane.* I would have bet big money that someone stood next to me in that garden. A hand had touched my shoulder, but I hadn't seen a soul.

Reasons My Parents Drive Me Crazy

1. They are nosy
2. Tofu
3. They are bossy
4. Tofu
5. They are odd
6. Tofu

Chapter 3

Friendship is certainly the finest balm for the pangs of disappointed love.

NORTHANGER ABBEY
By Austen, Jane, 1775–1817
Call #: F-AUS
Description: vi, 176 p.; 21cm

After three days of tofu and veggies, I decided to take a trip into town. While her food choices leave me hungry, Mom does have a way with herbs, and my energy levels grew each day. The doctor in Atlanta had called and said it was time for some follow-up blood tests.

Mom told me a new doctor had come to town and that he'd moved here from one of the larger hospitals in Dallas. I scheduled an appointment for eleven o'clock and made a list of stops I wanted to make while I was out, including the library, Piggly Wiggly (where I would buy nonperishable food items such as Little Debbie snack cakes and Spaghetti-Os to hide in my room), and Delilah's clothing store for some jeans, T-shirts, and sneakers.

It took me twenty minutes to convince my parents I'd be fine on my own. Mom passed over the keys to my Lexus, which she'd used to transport me from Atlanta to Sweet, and I headed out on my merry way.

While it looks like my parents' place is in the middle of nowhere, it's only ten minutes from town. The West Texas plains are flat and dry, and you can see Sweet from five miles away.

The first stop was the Sweet Library. I've always been drawn to the place, and I love the building. It's as old as the town, which was settled in the early nineteenth century, and it reminds me of the Coutances Cathedral in France, though the interior isn't as elaborate. There are huge spirals at the top and it sits in the center of the small town. The arched windows and gargoyles over the double doors make it look like something out of a Grimm's fairy tale.

Inside, its two stories had rows of books crammed into every available space. I had spent a good portion of my summers in the corners of this place. It was my sanctuary away from home—and it had air-conditioning, something my parents' trailer had lacked back in the day.

I stepped through the front door and took a deep breath. There's something about the smell of books—the leather and the paper, and the slight mustiness of the older books—that is comforting.

"Kira Smythe, it's about time you stopped by." Mrs. Canard, who had been the librarian for as long as I could remember, stood behind her desk. Her short gray curls wisped around her face.

Moving toward her, I smiled. "I've missed you." I meant the words. She'd taken me under her wing the first day I stumbled in here at the ripe old age of five. To me she was part librarian and part magician. She always seemed to know exactly what I needed. Through the years she had become family. I never knew my grandparents, but Mrs. Canard was a great substitute.

"You are as beautiful as ever, though a bit pale." She gave me the once-over. "Are you just going to stand there, or give me a hug?"

I moved closer and paused. "I have mono," I whispered.

She waved the comment away. "Germs don't bother me, dear. Come here."

Her chubby arms wrapped around me and the scent of her Estée Lauder Youth-Dew filled my senses. For the first time since I arrived in Sweet, I felt like I was really home. She held me for a moment then let go.

The library had always been a magical place for me. I lost myself in new worlds every single day. It was the one place in Sweet where I felt like I really belonged.

"I have the new Janet Evanovich and a great selection of mystery authors, and a paranormal by Nora Roberts I know you'll love. That woman can tell a story. I know how much you love the classics, so I'll throw some of those in too. Maybe a little Edith Wharton; she's a wonderful read in the winter." She took off, flitting around the library like a fairy on speed.

Before I could grasp what she was saying, she put a pile of books in front of me.

"I really just came by to see you. I don't know if I can read all of these before I leave next week." I laughed. It was colder closer to the desk, and I shivered. *She must be cutting back on the cost of heating.*

"Fiddlesticks. You need rest and the best way to do that is with a book. Keeps the mind busy and the body still. I have no doubt that you'll be back for more by Wednesday." Waving the books under a scanner, she placed them on the counter. "My guess is it's been some time since you've read something for pleasure."

Right, as always, but I wouldn't admit to her that the majority of my reading materials had to do with research for various contracts, law reviews, and journals. It would be good to sit around reading for a few days. Funny that it had been one of my greatest pleasures, and lately I'd found so little time for it. I'd found little time for anything *fun* the last few years.

I gave her another hug. "I love that you always know exactly what I need." From the corner of my eye I thought I saw a shadow, but when I turned to look I didn't see anything.

Must have been the trees outside . . . except there isn't any sunshine to make shadows.

When I faced Mrs. Canard again, she gave me a strange look. "I'm the librarian, Kira. It's my job to *know*." She gave me a tight squeeze, then pushed me toward the door. "Look at the time—didn't you say you had a doctor's appointment? When you feel better, come back and see me. We can catch up."

"Uh." No, I hadn't told her about the doc visit. At least, I didn't remember saying anything. I tried to turn around to look at her, but she kept pushing me. "Take care of yourself, Kira. You have an important job to do."

I shrugged. "Okay."

She was getting up there in age, but she'd always seemed together mentally. Now I wondered if Mrs. Canard might be heading toward senility. While she'd never said much about it, I knew she didn't think corporate law was the right occupation for me. I distinctly remembered her face when I told her I'd be studying law at Harvard. There was disappointment there along with wariness. I never realized she thought what I did at Zeb Corp. was *important*.

Of course, I didn't even remember telling her about my doctor's appointment, so I had no right to point fingers at her for acting a little strange.

As I stepped out of the library, I heard a voice before the doors closed. "She's not ready," a husky-voiced man said. Mrs. Canard answered back, "She will be, and you're lucky she didn't see you."

No one else had been in the library during our brief chat. I wondered who had been talking.

I arrived at the doc's right at eleven, signed the various forms, and handed over my insurance card. I sat in the waiting room. I hadn't been sick much as a child, and when I was, my mom used home remedies. Still, I'd been to see my old doctor, Dr. Levy, for sinus infections and various other ailments the herbs couldn't quite cure.

The waiting room hadn't changed. The white walls were covered with pictures of hunting dogs, and magazines from the nineties and some of the same worn children's books I'd read years ago graced a small wooden coffee table. There was a brown plaid couch and some chairs that matched.

I must have been the last appointment for the morning, because no one else was there.

Five minutes later, the nurse said, "The doctor will see you now."

She led me down the hallway to a small room. "Have a seat." Sticking a thermometer in my mouth, she grabbed my wrist. Once she had my pulse she wrote it down and told me I had a temp of one hundred.

I'd actually been feeling better until she said that.

"He'll be here in a minute."

About the time I wished I'd brought one of the library books with me, the door opened. I looked up and gasped. "Sam?"

The magnificent hunk of man smiled. "Yep."

"What are you doing here?" I hadn't seen him in years, not since he graduated from Harvard. He was going to medical school while I was studying law. We had met in a pub when we were both on horrible blind dates and become the best of friends. He's gorgeous, with dark wavy hair and a body most actors in Hollywood would pay big bucks for, but he's always been like a big brother to me. "I mean, I thought you were working in Chicago." I jumped off the table to give him a hug.

"I've been in Dallas the last few months. Dr. Levy's a friend of my dad's and had asked him if he knew anyone who could help while he takes care of his mom in Omaha. I needed a break, so here I am."

"Wow." I saw something in his eyes and realized there was more to the story. I'd been keeping up with him through the grapevine and I knew he was on his way to becoming one of the best neurosurgeons in the country. After his residency, every hospital in the country wanted him. I'd also heard his engagement had been called off at the last minute, but I never knew why. "It's . . . weird for you to end up here of all places, but it's really great to see you."

"So what is the woman who was set to take over corporate America doing back in Sweet?"

She had a mental and physical breakdown and needed her mommy. "This illness. My parents insisted I come home." I sat back on the table, and he moved closer. Putting his hands on my neck, he checked out my glands.

"Hmmm," he said. I hate when doctors do that.

"I can't stay much longer though, because I have to get back to work. But my brain feels like it's in some kind of weird fog. I can't concentrate, and I keep forgetting things."

Taking out his stethoscope, he listened to my breathing. When I took a deep breath, I coughed with a horrible hacking sound.

Sam clicked his tongue. He took some blood and finished his exam. "You really should be in bed," he chided as he wrote notes on my chart.

"Well, I didn't think you'd have time to make a house call." I smirked.

"I would for you," he said without looking up. "I'm afraid you are going to have to call the office and tell them you can't work for a while longer. You don't need the stress on your mind and body."

I wondered what he'd say if he knew I'd been talking to Justin daily and e-mailing paperwork back and forth. I did rest, but there was still so much work to do. I had to get back. It worried me more than anything that things had run so well without me.

"Sam, I can't just hand everything over. I'm in the middle of some huge contracts." The sound of paper tearing made me look down. My hands held two fists full of the paper that had lined the examining table.

Sam stared at my hands and then gave me a strange look. "You have to take some time off for your physical and mental health. If you can't take care of yourself, I'll haul your ass back into the hospital."

I clasped my hands in my lap, willing myself to stay calm. "Maybe I can rest the next few days."

I leaned back and stared up at the ceiling for a minute and then back at him. "Why can't I remember what happened on the roof? Am I going crazy?"

Reaching out, he squeezed my shoulder. "I've always thought you were a little soft in the head, but no, you aren't going crazy. Your mind isn't ready to deal with what happened to Melinda." I blanched. The mention of her name sent chills over my body.

Holding up the file, he said, "The doctors at the hospital faxed over your records. I'm sorry, really sorry, for everything you've gone through. Obviously very traumatic events have transpired, and your mind and body are defending you by shutting down. There's some healing that needs to take place first, which is why I want you to go home and rest."

I shrugged. "Okay, okay. I've already loaded up on books. I plan to stop at the Piggly Wiggly for supplies, and Lulu's for a real meal. My mother's been feeding me nothing but tofu and veggies. I'm craving beef."

He laughed. "That's actually your body trying to fight the infection. You do need more protein, of which tofu is an excellent source." He paused. "But I can't eat that crap either.

How about I buy you a hamburger at Lulu's for lunch? But then you have to promise to go home and go to bed."

I smiled. "That's the best offer I've had in weeks."

Lulu's has the best food on the planet. It's good Southern fare with a few surprises thrown in here and there. Seventy-year-old twins, Ms. Johnnie and Ms. Helen, who, according to the pictures on the wall, have lived a raucous life, own the café. There are photos of all kinds of famous people littering the walls of the cozy diner, including presidents, rock stars, and basketball teams, and the twins are in most of the pics.

Known for their colorful personalities, as well as their clothes, the twins never disappoint.

"Well, look at that. Kira's home and she already has the handsome Dr. Sam in hand." Ms. Johnnie winked at me.

"Kira?" Ms. Helen peered through the opening between the kitchen and the dining room. "I'll have you some lemon meringue out in just a sec."

Much like the library, Lulu's had been a sanctuary for me. My mother would never let me have sweets, or red meat for that matter. In high school, I would save birthday and Christmas money from relatives so I could buy hamburgers and pie. The twins even let me sweep the café for a free meal now and then. Sometimes I'd just come to visit, and they'd regale me with stories from the good old days while they piled plates of food in front of me. I loved them like family and felt guilty that I hadn't been back to visit in so long.

Over the last few years, time had slipped away and my life had become about whatever the next project might be.

Looking back I realized how much work had taken over my world.

"You both are as beautiful as always." I patted Ms. Johnnie's arm. Today she wore jeans with a bright red sweatshirt bearing a terrified looking turkey that read, "Thanksgiving, already?"

She seated us in a booth at the back of the café. "Special's chicken fried steak today." Her words made my mouth water. I'd been set on eating a hamburger, but I couldn't resist.

"Sounds good to me."

"Me too." Sam added.

She brought us out some iced tea and hot biscuits with butter. We were enjoying the carb-loaded delights when someone walked up to our booth, a handsome man with sandy blond hair. He wore low-riding jeans and a denim shirt, but it was his eyes that transfixed me. Deep lapis blue, almost black. Then he smiled and I suddenly found myself very interested in everything he had to say.

"Hey, Doc." He reached to shake hands with Sam.

"Caleb, good to see you. When did you get back in town?"

"A couple of days ago. I didn't mean to interrupt your lunch. I just wanted to say hi and thanks for that sinus medicine. Best stuff I've ever taken. I couldn't have made the trip without it." There was something about his scent, pine mixed with man. I had an urge to reach out and touch him. Which is weird, because it had been a while since I'd even been on a date. I hadn't met a man who had seemed worth the time.

"I've been rude. Caleb, this is my friend Kira." Sam waved a hand toward me.

Caleb tipped his head. "Nice to meet you." He looked

like he was going to say something else but stopped himself.

"Hi," I whispered, not really trusting my voice.

"Would you like to join us for lunch?" Sam offered.

"Tempting," he smiled down at me, "but I need to get back. Deliveries are coming in—new tile for the bathrooms and the wood floors for the rest of the house."

"Oh, are you remodeling your home?" My voice sounded a little throaty and I heard Sam snicker. I shot him a death stare.

"Not my place, just helping out a friend." Caleb turned to Sam. "I'll see you later, Doc. Nice to meet you." He waved good-bye to me.

"Now that was interesting." Sam laughed.

"Shut up."

Thankfully, Ms. Johnnie showed up with our food.

We'd been eating for a few minutes when Sam said, "I bet you haven't been on a date in months. I could set you up. He's a really interesting guy." He waggled his eyebrows.

I threw a green bean at him.

"Don't play with your food," he teased.

"Stop being annoying. And how would you know if I've been on a date? I haven't seen you in a long time."

His eyes zeroed in on me. "You're the same driven woman I knew in college, and you didn't date much then either. I'm just saying it wouldn't hurt for you to mingle with the human race now and then. I bet I can guess exactly what you've been doing every single day since I last saw you: work, work, work." The last words were said with a smirk.

Picking up another green bean, I made a threatening gesture. "I'm mingling with you. And you're the one who told me I needed to go home to bed. Besides, as soon as I'm better, I'm out of here and going back to the real world." I raised an eyebrow. "A place where my doctor doesn't try to fix me up with strangers off of the street."

"Ohhh. I think she liked him," he said in an annoying singsongy voice.

"You really need to stop. You never could sing."

He threw a hand against his chest. "I'm crushed. I can't believe you said that. Just because some guy's hot for you doesn't mean you have to take it out on me."

The lemon meringue showed up and it quite possibly saved Sam from living the rest of his life with a green bean sticking out of his forehead.

The truth hurt. I hadn't dated much, or had any fun for that matter. In fact, I didn't want to think about life back in Atlanta at all right now. It had been too long since I'd had a vacation. Though I did worry that maybe I should have Justin FedEx some of the contracts I'd been working on to the ashram. We'd been in the middle of two big deals, both of which depended on mergers coming off as planned. It was my job to make sure everything ran smoothly.

"It's going well," a voice said in my ear. I turned to see who it was. No one sat behind us. The lunch crowd had thinned out and the café only had a few customers. The only diners were up near the front of the café.

"Did you hear that?" I looked at Sam.

"What?" He dug into his pie with manly gusto.

"I thought I heard—nothing." *Great. I'm hearing voices. This mono thing is worse than I thought.*

He eyed me warily. "Maybe I should drive you home."

"I'm fine."

Sam shrugged.

Maybe I really was losing my mind.

Five Things I Like About Sweet

1. The library
2. Lulu's
3. Free coffee at the Piggly Wiggly
4. Wide open spaces
5. Caleb

Chapter 4

❧

I don't like work—no man does; but I like what is in the work, the chance to find yourself.

HEART OF DARKNESS
By Conrad, Joseph, 1857–1924
Call #: F-CON
Description: 146 p.; 22cm

For three days I did nothing but sleep, eat, and read, with the occasional walk to the vineyards. After so many years of ninety-hour weeks, I'd practically forgotten what it was like to relax. Okay, I did make a few calls to the office, but much to my chagrin Justin seemed to have everything under control.

It bothered me a little that the world of corporate law seemed to keep on turning even though I wasn't there. Irked me, really, but I had to concentrate on getting better so I could get back to it.

My body responded by healing faster than anyone expected.

Sam came out to check on me at my parents' place and deemed me fit for short excursions into town. "Nothing too taxing," he warned. Then he wrote me a prescription for chicken fried steak. This is why that man is my friend.

He also mentioned that a certain someone was curious about me. "I had a strange call the other day." Since he'd just stuck a thermometer in my mouth, I could only give him a perplexed eyebrow. "Seems Caleb needed refills on his sinus medication. At least that was his excuse for calling. Of course what he really wanted to know is if you and I are dating."

I snorted. Sam had never been anything more than a big brother to me. I don't know why, but we'd just never had that kind of chemistry.

"Yes, that's what I told him." Sam grabbed my wrist and took my pulse. "Looks like you may have an admirer."

My stomach did that flip-floppy thing that happens when a boy you think is cute likes you too. It's so high school but it's true. Though I didn't experience much of that in my teens. I certainly noticed boys, but I was the "smart girl" with frizzy hair who wore hippie clothes, and they paid me no attention.

I couldn't tell Sam that. He turned away to write something in the medical file he'd brought with him.

"He can be interested all he wants. A couple more days and I'm out of here." I tried to sound nonchalant, but I was just the tiniest bit excited. It'd been a really long time since a hot guy had shown any interest in me other than for my brains. I know, I shouldn't complain, but every once in a while it's nice to be thought of as something besides a "damn fine lawyer," as my boss always called me.

"I don't know about that." He waved the chart in front of my face. "You won't be ready to go home until well after Thanksgiving."

I leaned forward in the chair. We were in my room at my parents' place. "Oh, no. That won't do at all. I have two separate contracts that have to be written up by the end of the month."

"Kira, you aren't going to get well if you start back to work too soon. In fact, there's an eighty percent chance of relapse if you do. You can maybe handle a couple of hours in town, but that's it."

I waved him away. "But I feel so much better."

He stared at me for a moment. "It's up to me to write your release papers, and you're not going back to work until I feel like you are ready."

"Sam, I'm the one who should judge how I feel and—okay, okay." He was staring me down again. "Fine. I'll do some more resting if that's what you want."

I looked at the prescription he'd written. "I don't suppose you could add some pumpkin pie to this?" I held the white piece of paper where he'd written, "Chicken fried steak, twice weekly."

Taking it from me, he wrote, "And as much pie as she can down."

I stood and hugged him. "So are you heading to your parents' in Chicago for the holidays?"

"Nah. I'm on call here over at the nursing home and at the office." He loaded his instruments back into his brown leather doctor's bag. I'd never actually seen one before except in movies, and it was kind of cool.

"Why don't you come out here to celebrate? Mom and Dad would love it, and I want the company. Maybe you could stop by Lulu's and pick up one of their meals to go with turkey and all of the side dishes and pumpkin pie. In fact, I'll go order it tomorrow if you'll pick it up. Then my mom can't say anything."

He shook his head. "Why don't you just tell her the sight of Tofurky makes you ill?"

I made a funny face. "I don't want to upset her. Please, will you pick it up?"

Sam laughed. "Sure. I'm not that fond of Tofurky either. Um, I could ask Caleb to come along. I understand he's going to be alone for the holidays too."

My stomach did that weird thing again. "Uh. Sure. The more the merrier."

I wished I wasn't quite so excited about seeing Caleb again.

Mrs. Canard was right about me coming back to see her before the week was out. With my reduced work schedule, all I'd done was read the last few days. I'd already gone through the pile of books she'd given me.

After stopping at Lulu's to order a complete Thanksgiving dinner with all of the trimmings, and a short stay for Ms. Helen's chili and cornbread lunch, I headed to the library.

The temperature outside hung around forty, but inside the library it felt closer to thirty degrees. At almost four o'clock on a Wednesday the place was deserted. The whole town shuts down around six, so it wasn't that unusual. Only the local restaurants and Piggly Wiggly stayed open until nine.

As I made my way through the vestibule, I saw shadows that looked like people. Squeezing my eyes shut tight, I opened them again. The shadows were gone.

Maybe I need new glasses. I wore reading glasses sometimes, but that was only after a long day of viewing the tiny type on contracts.

I heard someone shelving books a few rows back and

found Mrs. Canard on a short stepladder in the biography and nonfiction section. Today she wore a soft baby blue sweater over navy pants.

"Mrs. Canard?" I whispered.

Startled, she almost toppled off the ladder. Grabbing the wooden shelf, she righted herself. "Dear me. I didn't hear you come in, Kira." She peered at me over her spectacles. "You have some pink in your cheeks and look much better than the other day."

I reached up to help her down the ladder. "I am better. Why don't you let me shelve those for you?" Before she could protest, as I knew she would, I added, "I could really use a cup of tea. It's kind of chilly in here."

She smiled at me, knowing full well what I was up to. "Yes, I have some new cinnamon spice tea, which is delightful." Her hand in mine, I helped guide her down. "I'll put the kettle on, and then we can have a nice long chat."

I shelved the remaining biographies, except for one on P. L. Travers that I wanted to check out for myself. I'd always loved Mary Poppins and was curious about the woman behind the wonderful books. I'd heard she was very eccentric, and those kinds of people always fascinate me.

By the time I finished I noticed Mrs. Canard had set the small break room table with a colorful china teapot and cups. Next to it was a plate of chocolate chip cookies, my favorite. I smiled and made my way through the doorway, but the librarian wasn't in there. "Mrs. Canard?"

"She ran upstairs for something, but she'll be right back," a man said from behind me. Swirling in a flurry, I searched for the owner of the voice. I made my way down the rows in the back of the library, but didn't see anyone. I walked quickly to the front. Empty. I stood by the front desk with my hands on my hips. A chill ran down my spine.

Had I really heard something? Or was my subconscious talking to me? *Yes, your subconscious is a deep male voice. That makes a lot of sense.*

Since the accident, I'd been hearing things and seeing shadows. Maybe it was the medication. *Or you're going crazy.* There was always that.

"Kira?" I heard Mrs. Canard calling for me.

"Be right there," I said with fake cheerfulness.

I made my way back to the tiny break room, where the librarian poured tea. "Did you hear someone when you came down?" I sat at the small table, across from her. An Irish lace tablecloth with delicate pink and white roses adorned it.

The room was a small box with a sink, cabinets, and counters along all the walls.

She smiled. "No, dear. Would you like some sugar? If I remember right, always two lumps."

It'd been years since I'd used real sugar in my tea. I usually used one of the chemical substitutes to save the calories. "Yes, thank you."

"So what does the handsome Dr. Sam say about your health? I understand he visited you yesterday." The implication in her voice was that we might be dating.

I laughed. "He is a very good friend and nothing else, and he says a few more weeks and I'll be good to go." I gave her a wink. "I need to get back to Atlanta, so I'm not sure I'll be able to take his advice. How did you know he'd been to see me?"

She put a cookie on a plate and handed it to me. "It's a

small town, Kira, I *know* everything. So you are determined to go back to being a lawyer?"

What an odd question. I frowned. "Of course. I mean, what else would I do? I would have gone right back to work after—um, after I got sick, but the doctors wouldn't let me," I covered. I'd almost said, "after the accident," which is stupid because it wasn't an accident at all. It was a tragedy. "I can't really imagine doing anything else."

"Oh, that's too bad, dear. I guess I had hopes that some-day you would come and take over the library for me." She patted my hand. "A silly old woman's wishful thinking."

I squeezed her fingers. "If I weren't a lawyer, I probably would be a librarian. You know how much I love doing research—almost as much as I adore books. I'm so glad you set me straight the other day and made me read something that didn't have to do with work. I'd forgotten the sheer joy that comes from books.

"And there is absolutely nothing old or silly about you." Though I had noticed that she seemed a bit more fragile this trip. I mean, she looked great for an eighty-year-old woman, but her skin appeared thinner and she stooped a little more than I'd remembered. Yet she still hopped around the library like a rabbit on speed. "How have you been feeling?"

She frowned for just a moment and her eyes looked misty.

I thought she might cry for a minute, and I worried maybe she was seriously ill. "Mrs. Canard?"

She sighed. "Oh, fiddle-faddle. I didn't ask you to tea to talk about my health. That's what old people do. I want to hear about your life in Atlanta."

I started to say something, but stopped when I saw the

look in her eyes. She was begging me to leave the subject alone. Next to my parents, I loved this woman more than anyone I'd ever known. She truly was my savior as a child. She had introduced me to the magical world of books, where I could lose myself in a new place every day. I had to find out what was wrong with her, but now was not the time.

"I love Atlanta and my job keeps me very busy." I told her about my friend Justin and my condo in one of the city's high-rises. But there wasn't much more to tell. My entire life had become about work. I had acquaintances at the office, but Justin was my only real friend there.

"I wanted to thank you for the books you recommended," I said as we finished our tea. I took the cups and saucers to the sink.

"I'll take care of those later. Don't worry about them." She tried to brush me out the door.

"No, you made my favorite cookies. The least I can do is clean up. Maybe you can find some books to get me through the holiday at my parents'. I'm going to need massive distractions to stay sane. My dad has been pestering me to take yoga classes and it seems like every five minutes Mom shoves another cup of some kind of herbal tea down me."

She laughed. "It's time you accepted those people for who they are, Kira." She touched my shoulder. "They love you very much and they are good souls who mean well."

I nodded. "I know. I'm trying to do that this trip and I am beginning to see them through different eyes. I never realized how talented they were. Mom's business is booming and Dad has become quite the artist."

She sighed. "I think it sometimes takes us many years to truly appreciate our parents." Then she was off, flitting around the library, gathering another pile of books for me.

I left the clean dishes and teapot on the drain board and wiped my hands on a tea towel. Even the break room with its gray walls and small wooden cabinets seemed special. I loved this library and I'd never felt more comfortable anywhere else. Not even in my apartment in Atlanta, which I'd decorated to suit me exactly.

I sighed. *When did I become so melancholy?*

At the checkout desk she had two piles of books ready for me. "I've put the new Jasper Fforde and Jim Butcher in for you. As well as that P. L. Travers biography." She pushed the stack of more than twenty books toward me. "There are also some of the classics you used to love." Charlotte Brontë's *Jane Eyre* and Jane Austen's *Emma* topped the pile. Back in the day Brontë had been very critical of Austen's work, but I loved them both.

Something occurred to me. "Are you going to Dallas to see your daughter for Thanksgiving?" I put the books in a large grocery bag she handed me to transport them to the car.

"No. The kids are in Vancouver at my son-in-law's parents'."

"Would you mind coming out to Mom and Dad's? We'd love to have you. Dr. Sam will be there and maybe a few others. Mom will cook her idea of Thanksgiving, but I've also ordered a complete dinner from Lulu's."

"That's very sweet of you. I'll certainly think about it, and if I do come, I'll bring some extra pies."

"Oh, you don't have to bring anything but your lovely

self." I reached across the desk and hugged her. "But I do hope you'll come."

On the way home I heard a strange ringing and realized it was my BlackBerry. It had been so long since anyone had called, I'd forgotten about it.

I pushed the speaker button on the Lexus. "Hello?"

"Is it there yet?" Justin sounded harried on the other end of the line.

"Is what here yet? What are you talking about?"

"The FedEx package. I just found out about ten minutes ago that the Official Asshole—you know, your boss—sent you a package, but it didn't come through me. I want to know what's in it," he demanded.

"Well, I'm in my car at the moment, but I'm pulling in the drive right now. I'll call you back when I get inside."

He sighed. "I don't think my heart can take it."

"Justin, what's going on? Why are you so upset?" He could be a bit of a drama queen, but this time he was tied in knots. "Take a deep breath and just tell me."

"You know how I get bad vibes about things . . . Well, that they didn't have me send the package to you makes me think there's something in there they didn't want me to see."

"Did you ever stop to think that it's probably just some confidentiality agreements for one of the contracts I'm working on? Stop being a goofy brat. The *boss* probably just needs me to look over something and had his assistant send it out."

There was silence on the other end.

"Is there something you aren't telling me?" Now he was making me nervous.

"I don't know. Just promise me you'll call as soon as you get the package," he pleaded.

"Okay, okay. I promise. But I bet a sushi dinner it's nothing but contracts. I'll talk to you in a bit." I pushed the button to turn off the phone and opened the car door.

As soon as I opened the door to my room, I saw the FedEx envelope on the bed, a very thin one. I dumped the books on the small bedside table and picked it up. It couldn't have been more than a page or two. For a second I was worried, and then I laughed. Justin was playing a practical joke. He was probably just messing with me.

I rolled my eyes and ripped open the package.

Two pieces of paper floated out to the bed.

The first was a letter with the header for Zeb Corporate and it said:

Dear Ms. Smythe,

We appreciate your many contributions to our organization. You are a sterling employee and your efforts have been duly noted.

Unfortunately, we regret to inform you that we must cut our department budgets by thirty-five percent. Beginning immediately, your employment here has been terminated. You will receive full medical coverage for as long as necessary as part of a generous severance package.

We wish you well in your future endeavors.

Martin Landover
Vice President, Corporate Affairs

The second piece of paper was a detailed outline of my severance package. It was a good one, excellent by most standards, but I still felt like someone had kicked me in the stomach.

Sucker punched.

Confused, I sat on the bed. He couldn't fire me while I was on medical leave; it was against the law.

I should be furious. I'd just read a letter telling me they didn't give a crap that I'd dedicated my life to that job, but . . . somehow, I didn't care.

That's not true. I did care. I was angry, but also relieved for some reason.

The cell phone rang again. "What the hell is going on? They're moving me to a new department," Justin yelled.

There was no getting around the truth. I took a deep breath. "I've been sacked."

"What?" He screamed so loud I had to hold the phone away from my ear.

"You heard me." I told him about the budget cuts.

"That's ridiculous, you made those bozos millions of dollars the last few years."

My hands were shaking. "Evidently it wasn't enough."

"You know why this is happening, and you know you can fight it," Justin urged. "They can't blame you for what happened to Melinda."

Oh, they can. I do. "Yes, but I don't want to fight anymore. I'm done with that." After the last few months I no longer had it in me.

It had taken me a few days here in Sweet to realize why I'd really come home. I, the ruthless Ice Princess, had been emotionally and physically devastated. Not just by Melinda's death, but by the events that had led up to it. I'd given up on everything, including myself.

That was about to change. I wouldn't fight the layoff, but I would do something about my life.

"It's time for me to move on." I stood and began pacing. "I need you to do me some favors. Do you still have the key to my condo?"

"Yes. And I'm not working at this place without you."

"Justin, I appreciate the loyalty, but you know how much you need that job." He was still paying off his college loans. "When you get off work, go to my condo and e-mail me a copy of my résumé from my desktop. Then call Cynthia Jordan, that headhunter who has been after me. Give her my number and tell her to call if she's interested. I'm going to get a new job," I said determinedly. "And as soon as I'm settled I'm bringing you on at twice your current salary. How does that sound?"

"Like the Kira Smythe I know. I'm with you all the way, girlfriend." I imagined his hand swinging back and forth in a sassy snap. "You haven't been yourself lately, and I, for one, am glad you are back."

I wasn't sure about being back, but the letter had been a good reality slap.

We hung up and I sat back on the bed.

It's a temporary detour. I can handle it. I'm Kira Smythe. I can do anything.

Five Bad Things That Are Worse Than Losing a Job

1. Dying
2. Going crazy
3. Losing a loved one
4. Being bedridden with some horrible disease
5. Being betrayed by someone you love

Chapter 5

'Tis misfortune that awakens ingenuity, or fortitude, or endurance, in hearts where these qualities had never come to life but for the circumstance which gave them being.

THE HISTORY OF HENRY ESMOND
By Thackeray, William Makepeace, 1811–1863
Call #: F-MAK
Description: 415 p.; 19cm

"Ms. Smythe, so happy to hear from you." I'd called Cynthia Jordan after she'd told Justin to have me contact her immediately.

"Thank you for taking my call. I realize it's the day before Thanksgiving." It hadn't occurred to me that she might be out of the office. "Are you on vacation?"

"I'm going through security as we speak on my way to Belize. Don't worry about it. I'll be here for at least another hour. Listen, Justin tells me you're ready to move on from Zeb bore, excuse me, Zeb Corp. Does it have anything to do with the jumper?"

I should have expected the question, but it startled me. The news reports had said I was on the roof with the police when Melinda jumped. Of course, I had no memory of it. No, that's not exactly true. I have a vision in my head of her on the ledge, but that's it. I wasn't sure I wanted to remember what happened. "Let's just say I'm ready to move on."

She clucked her tongue. "Of course. I know Bachman, Ride, and Yoren is looking for a new contract lawyer. And Telrine wants someone to lead up their legal affairs office. Both would be perfect for you. I'll call them to set up appointments for next week and get back to you with the details."

"Okay." I hadn't expected things to move quite so fast, but in a way it was good. I didn't want to sit around twiddling my thumbs for the next few months searching for a job.

We hung up and I downloaded my résumé onto my mom's office computer. Justin had e-mailed it and I always kept it up to date. It's something ingrained in me from my days at Harvard. "Always be prepared for all contingencies," my professors would say.

I filled out the form Cynthia had sent from her BlackBerry, and attached it and my résumé to an e-mail back to her.

My mother came in just as I was finishing up. "How are you feeling, honey?"

I smiled. "Good." Then I noticed the black cloth suitcase next to her. "Are you going somewhere?"

She pursed her lips and scrunched her face. "Your dad and I are needed in Laguna. Our manager out there, Sherry, is having her baby and her husband has just taken her to the hospital. She's almost a month early. They have a full house at the ashram, so your dad and I have to go take care of things."

Walking forward, she sat in the chair in front of her desk. "I want you to come with us. We have plenty of room in the Piper." My dad had learned how to fly a couple of years ago, and my parents' business had done so well they had their own plane. The craziness never stopped with these two. "I'm worried about you being here alone, and I can't stand that the first time you're home in two years we have to leave. And you've just been so sick."

I waved her away. "You guys go. As you can see, I'm fine. In fact, Sam is coming over tomorrow to hang out, so you don't have to worry. I'll have my personal physician on hand." She couldn't see it but inside I was jumping up and down screaming, "Woo hoo! No Tofurky! And I won't have to explain my atypical parents to hot guy Caleb." "I'll miss you guys, and thank you so much for taking care of me." I meant the words. Her homeopathic recipes, though not terribly delectable, had helped me heal faster.

I hugged her. "I have to head home on Saturday for some meetings on Monday." She started to argue, but I held up a hand. "Thanks to your great care, I'm feeling so much better. I'm going to leave my car here and fly back. I don't think I'm up for the fifteen-hour drive yet. But I'll come pick it up the first chance I get."

She sniffled. "Now I feel really horrible about leaving you for Thanksgiving. We probably won't see you again for a couple of years."

Hello, mothers' guilt. I shook my head. "I'm sorry, Mom. I haven't been around much, but you know I love you. And I promise I'll try to come back to visit sometime around the end of the year." *Depends on the new job.* "And I'll definitely have to get my car, so don't worry."

Dad walked in. He thumped himself on the head. "Oh, kiddo, I knew I forgot to tell someone. You were gone when the call came in this afternoon. Can you get packed fast? We need to go."

I grinned. "I'm not going, and don't worry about it, Daddy. I'm fine. Mom will tell you my plans. You two go on. Enjoy some of that California sunshine for me."

He hugged me and ruffled my hair like he did when I was a kid. "Everything okay in Atlanta? A package came for you today."

I cleared my throat, caught off guard. I shrugged. "Just work stuff. One of the reasons I need to get back soon."

I finally pushed them out the door an hour later, after receiving explicit instructions on how to lock the place up. Mr. Johnson would be responsible for the care of the vineyards and he'd check on the gardens. Mom and Dad would be back on Monday to usher in their new crew of Zen wannabes. So I pretty much had the place to myself.

I knew I should do some research on the Web about some of the companies the headhunter had mentioned, but I needed a break.

My dad's love for yoga had rubbed off. I'd taken a few classes and was hooked. I remembered enough of the poses to go through most of them, even without my dad. After an hour of meditating and doing deep breathing exercises in my room, I took my last cleansing breath.

"It's almost time." I heard a voice in the corner of the room. My mind snapped into gear. I stood up, trying to see who was there. I thought I saw an arm and part of a leg. I blinked and the images were gone.

"She doesn't know and I don't think she'll be ready," a woman said.

I jumped up. "Who's there?" The room had to be forty degrees and my teeth chattered. My hands shook and my voice trembled a little.

"Look. I know someone's here. I'm not crazy."

"Of course you aren't." It was a husky voice, slightly feminine, but deep.

I whipped around, but still couldn't see anyone. "Where are you?"

"Right here in the corner. Sorry. I don't think you can see us yet. That you can hear us is a very good sign. Some people don't think you're ready, but I know you are well on your way."

"My way to what? Being psychotic? I'm talking to air."

"Honey, don't get so upset. Just because you can't see someone doesn't mean they aren't there."

"No! Go away. I'm not crazy!" My hands squeezed my head.

"Whatever you say, hon." The voice faded away. I threw on my sweater and waved my hand across the access panel on the door.

I searched the house for the source of the voice. Some nasty person was playing tricks on me. By the time I made it to the kitchen I'd convinced myself I must have been dreaming. *Maybe it was that third eye Dad's always talking about.* I found the controller for the heat, and it was set at sixty-eight.

Splaying my hands on the cold granite countertop, I took a deep breath. "Well, that sure as hell was weird." I turned on the lights as I made my way back to my room. It was warm now. I checked my face in the bathroom mirror and cleaned up some mascara under my eyes with a tissue. I put on some lipstick and pulled my curls into a low ponytail.

"Much, much better."

But I didn't want to be there. Third eye or not, I was hearing strange things. *I am not going crazy.* I'd said that to myself so many times the last few days it was ridiculous. Feeling antsy, I grabbed my purse and keys.

Since it was the night before Thanksgiving, the town had rolled up the sidewalks even earlier than usual. The only light on in the square was Lulu's. When I got out of the car the smell of smoked meats drifted my way. My stomach growled.

"Thank goodness for Ms. Johnnie and Ms. Helen," I said aloud.

"I was thinking the same thing," a man said behind me.

I jumped and turned around. Caleb's handsome face smiled back at me. He was dressed in a cable-knit sweater under a dark jacket and he wore jeans and boots. My heart did a little happy dance at the sight of him.

"Hey." *Now there you go being profound, Kira.*

"It's good to see you." He held out his hand and I shook it. His hand was so much larger than mine, and very warm. He didn't let go. "I wanted to thank you for the invitation tomorrow."

I pulled my hand back, reluctantly. "Oh, I'm glad to have the company, and since Ms. Johnnie and Ms. Helen are providing the meal, it should be delicious."

"Are you headed in for dinner?"

I nodded.

"Those two do know how to cook. I highly recommend the special. Meatloaf with mashed potatoes, and cherry pie for dessert."

I have to admit I was extremely disappointed that he'd already eaten. He'd be at the house tomorrow, but the company tonight would have been nice. "Thanks. That does sound good."

We stared at each other for a few seconds, and I could feel a blush creeping up on my cheeks under his scrutiny. I gave a little wave. "Well, I guess I'll see you tomorrow around two. Have a nice evening."

He nodded and began to move away. "Um." He stopped. "I could use another cup of coffee, and come to think of it, I wouldn't mind another piece of that pie."

I couldn't keep from smiling. "You're welcome to join me."

Opening the door, he guided me in.

The smells when you walk into Lulu's are always pleasing, but the day before a holiday they are almost overwhelming. Turkey, sweet potatoes, pumpkin pie, all of it hits you head-on and it's a traffic jam of homey smells.

My favorite place in the café is the back booth; I like watching as people come in and out. When I was a kid I'd observe Ms. Johnnie and Ms. Helen interacting with the locals. As wild as the two women were, they garnered a certain amount of respect.

"Have you lived in Sweet most of your life?" Caleb's question pulled me out of my reverie. We'd sat down and I'd been staring at the menu for the last few minutes, lost in thought.

Hello, Kira? Hot guy sitting across from you. Maybe you should pay attention. "Yes, and no." I grinned. "We moved here from Laguna when I was about four. So yes, until I went away to college, this was home. I've been living in Atlanta the last few years."

"Sweet seems like a great town to grow up in. Nice people and no crime from what I've seen."

I shrugged. "It's quiet, but I honestly couldn't wait to get out of here."

"Big city calling your name?" He put two sugars in his coffee and added some cream. I did the same.

"I just never felt like I fit in here." *Geez, bring out the violins.* "I mean, well, my parents were, excuse me, *are* hippies. None of us are magic, and a lot of the people who live here are either witches or warlocks or different in some special way. But you're right. It was certainly a safe place to grow up. As soon I had the chance, though, I was out the door."

"Hippies? I thought that was back in the sixties." He laughed.

I smiled too. "Yes, well. My parents tried to bring the lifestyle back in the eighties and haven't noticed that it didn't catch on. So where did you grow up?"

"All over the place. Born in San Antonio, but I'm an army brat. My dad was in special ops and we moved every two years. They're still moving. In fact, they're in Korea now."

"Wow. That must have been cool and difficult at the same time, living in new places." I dug into the meatloaf Ms. Johnnie had put on the table with a wink at me. She hadn't even taken my order. She knew I loved her food; didn't matter what it was. I'd noticed her and Ms. Helen peeking over at our table more than once.

"I'm pretty adaptable and I never minded much. My mom liked living wherever Dad worked, so we could see him when he wasn't on assignment. Now I have friends all over the world, which is handy when I need a place to crash."

I thought it odd that a carpenter had the funds to travel the world, but didn't say it. I scooped up a forkful of mashed potatoes. The girls had added sour cream, and the spuds were super creamy. "How did you end up here?"

He rolled his eyes. "I'm looking after a friend's sister. She bought a house here and I've been helping her fix it up."

I wondered what he meant by the rolled eyes. "That's nice of you. Um, do you not like the sister?"

He sputtered his coffee and laughed. Mopping his lip with his napkin, he cleared his throat. "She has her moments. Her name's Bronwyn, have you met her?"

I shook my head. "No, but I haven't seen much of anyone since I've been home. I've been kind of sick."

He looked concerned. "Is it serious?"

This time it was my turn to laugh. "No. Just mono."

"The kissing disease? Hmmm. And here I was thinking you weren't that kind of girl."

I raised an eyebrow. "How could you know what kind of girl I am?"

He held up his hands in surrender. "Sorry."

I laughed. "Unfortunately, I don't think I caught mono from kissing. I've been working kind of hard the last few years and it all sort of caught up with me at once." I sighed. "But I'm much better. Actually, I'm heading home on Saturday."

He frowned. "Why so soon?"

Something in his eyes made me want to tell him everything. He cared what happened to me. I didn't know why, but he did. "It's work. Something's come up and I have to be in town to take care of it."

"That's too bad. I was kind of hoping you'd be around awhile."

I don't know what made me do it, but I reached out and put my hand on his. It was warm and strong. I just wanted to touch him. "I'll be back." The words came out in a whisper and sounded much sexier than I intended.

He cocked his head. "Good." He squeezed my fingers and lifted them to his mouth.

Every nerve in my body went on high alert. The warmth from his lips spread from my fingers all the way to my belly. I couldn't keep from smiling. I looked down at the table and took a deep breath. "I . . . things are kind of . . . well, complicated."

He stood and put some money on the table to pay for our meal. "Are you married?"

"No," I said as he reached out a hand and pulled me up beside him.

"Then there are no complications we can't handle," he whispered in my ear. Then he kissed my cheek.

"I'll see you tomorrow." He squeezed my hand one last time and walked away.

I couldn't move for a minute.

"I think that boy has a thing for you, girly." Ms. Johnnie was to my left and I hadn't even noticed.

God, I hope so. I most definitely had a *thing* for Caleb.

Cool Jobs For Which I Have No Qualifications

1. Opera singer
2. Oceanographer
3. Train conductor
4. Biophysicist
5. Architect
6. Astronaut
7. Librarian
8. Dance therapist
9. Museum curator
10. Gymnastics coach
11. Truck driver
12. Design magazine editor
13. Magician
14. Teacher
15. Artist

Chapter 6

For life be, after all, only a waitin' for somethin' else than what we're doin', and death be all that we can rightly depend on.

DRACULA
By Stoker, Bram, 1847–1912
Call #: F-STO
Description: vi, 326 p.; 21cm

I'm not sure what woke me at three a.m. I'd had a series of strange dreams. Funny, since I can't remember having a dream since I left Sweet for college.

It's unusual, but true. When I moved to Cambridge, Massachusetts, for school, I stopped dreaming. I was barely seventeen at the time. I think the pressure of trying to fit in and the hours of study kept me from any frivolous thinking. Or perhaps it was that I spent most of my waking hours in the Langdell Reading Room of the Harvard Law School Library, and by the time I made it back to my dorm all I could do was pass out from exhaustion.

For me dreaming was a luxury, and my first one back in Sweet had Caleb, dressed in a letterman's jacket and jeans, asking me to go steady. I wore a pink poodle skirt that was very itchy on the inside. He kept asking, and giving me this strange look, but I couldn't get my mouth to work. All I could think about was scratching.

The next dream was weirder. During a job interview I suddenly realized I didn't have on any clothes. I kept trying to hide my boobs and other parts with a carefully placed Marc Jacobs tote.

Then the dream shifted to the truly bizarre. I looked down to find myself on the stepladder at the library. I tried to shelve books, but I couldn't remember the alphabet. A fog had entered my brain and I could barely remember my name.

There were men and women standing all around me, whispering, but I didn't understand what they were saying. Then I saw Mrs. Canard in the biography and nonfiction section. "It will be okay, dear, you'll learn it all soon enough. I'll be here for you when I can."

Then I woke, sitting straight up in bed and gasping for air. Sweat dripped down my face and I was twisted in the sheets.

My cell rang in my bag across the room, and I jumped out of bed to grab it, stumbling on the sheets as I went.

"Hello?" I said as I tried to catch my breath.

"Kira, it's Sam." He sounded sad.

I looked at the clock. It was exactly three a.m., and nothing good ever happened this time of morning. "What's wrong?"

"It's Mrs. Canard; she's had a stroke."

Making my way back across the room, I sat on the bed. My brain wasn't fully functioning quite yet. "How bad is it?"

He cleared his throat. "I don't think she has long. It hit the brain stem. She has a DNR, so there's not a lot we can do."

"DNR?" I knew what the letters meant, but I couldn't believe it.

"Do not resuscitate. We're having trouble finding her family. I know how close you two are and I thought maybe you'd want to come down to the hospital."

"Of course. I'll be right there. And, um, she said something about the family being in Vancouver."

A sinking sadness overwhelmed me and the tears fell the minute I clicked the off button. I wouldn't let myself lose it. Mrs. Canard needed me. My hands shook as I threw on clothes and shoes. I pulled my hair into a ponytail, grabbed the keys, and took off.

Though it was only a ten-minute drive, it seemed to take forever. I pushed away tears the entire trip. She had believed in me and loved me at a time when I didn't think anyone else did. My heart ached. *She's going to be okay. You just saw her. She's going to be okay.*

Outside the emergency room I dug around for some tissues in the console of the car. Finding one, I cleaned my face, got out, and then headed inside.

No one sat behind the admitting desk, and the waiting room was empty. "Is anyone here? Hello?"

"Just a minute, please, I'll be right there," I heard a woman say.

I didn't have any patience. I wanted to get to Mrs. Canard as soon as possible. I pushed on the door separating the waiting room from the treatment area, but it was locked.

"Augh," I huffed.

"I'm sorry, I was with a patient. Can I help you?" a soft female voice said from behind the desk.

I moved so I could see her. She seemed familiar and then it dawned on me. "Margie?"

She smiled. "Kira?"

Reaching across the desk, she hugged me, and I squeezed her in return. Margie had been my one real friend in high school. The other kids weren't exactly mean to me; it was more like they ignored me. She always had my back and made me feel like I belonged. I tried to do the same for her, though I was painfully shy and could never come up with the sardonic remarks she managed.

"Are you okay?" She looked me up and down.

"What? Oh, yes. I'm here to see Mrs. Canard. Sam called."

She pushed a button behind the desk. "You're the friend." She smiled again. "I guess I was expecting someone a little older. Sam said someone was on the way. Come on back. We're getting ready to move her upstairs."

We stopped outside a blue curtain. "Is she awake?" I whispered.

"No. She's slipped into a coma. I don't think there's much hope for her coming out of it." Margie opened the curtain. Laying a hand on my shoulder, she whispered, "I'm sorry."

Fluffy pillows framed Mrs. Canard, and her short gray hair looked like a halo around her head. While she'd always been pale, now the blue veins were visible in her hands and on her face. She seemed even more fragile than she had this afternoon.

"I was with her earlier today. I don't understand. She seemed fine."

Margie checked the machine that was keeping a watch on Mrs. Canard's stats. "That's the horrible thing about strokes; one minute the person seems perfectly fine, the next they can't speak and they're paralyzed. It's terrible."

Two orderlies arrived with a bed and moved the older woman onto it so gently I barely saw her jostled. Sweet is a small town, but the hospital is state of the art. It isn't very large but there are four floors. I rode in the elevator as we made our way to room 411.

Sam was there and helped get her settled. "I'm sorry, Kira. I know how much you love her." I'd told him about her when we were in college and how she was the one who encouraged me to go after my dreams.

"Is there nothing you can do to make her better?" It was more of a plea than anything.

"We can try to make her as comfortable as possible, but there's just been too much damage to the brain stem." He hugged me.

"It isn't fair. There isn't a kinder woman on the planet." I choked up, trying hard not to sob.

"I know. So let's make her last few hours as peaceful as possible. We can play her favorite music, and it's important for you to talk with her. Do you know what she loved most?"

That was an easy one. "Books." I pulled away from him. "I have a paperback she gave me earlier in my purse."

"That would be great, and I'll go downstairs to see if I can find a CD player or radio. Music is always good." He paused at the door.

I stared at Mrs. Canard. She already seemed so peaceful, her mouth curved in a gentle smile, her skin smooth of tension. "She loved music too. Whatever you find will be fine."

He smiled. "You keep talking to her. We still haven't found her family, but we're working on it."

Sam left and I moved a chair closer to the bed. I took her hand in mine. It was a little cool, and I rubbed her fingers.

"I want you to know how much you are loved, not just by me, but by this whole town." I sniffled. "You taught half of Sweet how to read and encouraged the rest of them to love books as much as you do. When I was a kid I wanted to be you. I thought librarians were the coolest people in the world.

"Well, until I saw that episode of *The Practice* and decided I wanted to be a lawyer." I laughed softly. "I remember the look on your face when I told you I wanted to study law. You were so surprised, and then you went and found some college textbooks on corporate law for me. What they were doing in the library, I have no idea. I thought they were boring at first, but you told me everything must be looked at in context. You were right. Years later, when I could compare those cases to others, I was absolutely fascinated."

I sighed. "You did that for everyone you met. Helped them along with their dreams." I scooted my chair closer.

"Okay, enough with the mushy stuff. You know how much I love you." I cleared my throat. "I happen to have a copy of *Emma* in my bag. I know what an Austen fan you are." I read to her about Emma Woodhouse and her misguided schemes until my voice was a hoarse whisper. When I could read no more, I rested my head on my arm and dozed for a few minutes at a time.

Around five in the morning, a hand rubbed the middle of my back. Thinking Sam or Margie had come in to check on her, I turned with sleepy eyes to see Mrs. Canard standing beside me.

I closed my eyes and opened them again. She was still there. Then I looked down at the bed, where she lay looking even paler than before.

I'm dreaming.

"Kira, I'm sorry. I don't want to frighten you but it's time for me to go." She patted my shoulder.

I shook my head, not really understanding.

She smiled. "I must pass to the other side. I've foisted a huge responsibility onto your shoulders and I want you to know that no matter what you choose to do, I will always love you. You can walk away from it all, and I will never think less of you. But know you are special and your talent can help so many. It will be difficult at first, but you'll come to love it as much as I did. If you give it a chance." Mrs. Canard turned her head as if listening for something.

"I'm confused. What responsibility? If you need me to take care of the arrangements I will. Money is not a problem."

"Oh, no. All of that was taken care of months ago. I really must go, dear, but I'll be back to help you along when I can. These things take time. Remember, you are special. No matter what, never forget it."

She faded and an alarm started beeping. Sam and the nurses rushed in and stood beside the bed.

We all watched as her struggling breaths slowed and then stopped.

"We've lost her," Margie whispered as she checked the machine.

Sam looked at me, and then at the clock on the wall. "Time of death, five after five."

Chapter 7

Indeed, when I am in really great trouble, as any one who knows me intimately will tell you, I refuse everything except food and drink.

THE IMPORTANCE OF BEING EARNEST
By Wilde, Oscar, 1854–1900
Call #: F-WIL
Description: 154 p.; 23cm

I'm not sure how I made it back to the house, but I did. I couldn't stop the tears and my chest felt hollow as I fell back into bed in a fitful sleep. Mrs. Canard's words about responsibility weighed heavily on me, and I wished I knew what she meant.

Around two in the afternoon someone buzzed the front door. At first I tried to ignore it, but they wouldn't go away. I'd never bothered to change, so I stumbled to the door in my wrinkled jeans and sweatshirt.

Sam and Caleb stood on the other side of the door.

Sam pushed his way in. "I know you're upset and you don't feel like eating, but you're going to anyway."

Caleb looked at me and shrugged. "Happy Thanksgiving."

Thanksgiving? I'd forgotten all about it.

"Hi," I croaked, suddenly very aware I had morning breath at two in the afternoon, my throat still sore from reading for so long.

"Hey." Caleb touched my arm. "I'm sorry about Mrs. Canard. She was one nice lady."

"Thanks." Sam had taken off toward the kitchen. "Well, I guess since Mr. Bossy Man has taken over, we might as well put the meal together."

"Might as well," Caleb answered as he closed the door behind him. "Everything has already been heated, we just need to open the packages and dig in."

I hadn't had anything to eat since dinner with Caleb the night before and my stomach growled. I showed him to the kitchen, and we pulled out the plates and platters.

"Do you guys mind if I run and freshen up a bit?"

"Brush your teeth while you're at it," Sam quipped.

"Oh, nice one." I stuck my tongue out him.

Caleb laughed.

"I probably look like crap." I grimaced.

"I don't think so," Caleb said softly.

Sam snickered. "Well, hurry up. Once we get this food on the plates I'm not waiting."

When he was in bossy mode, there was no getting around it. I ran back to my room and jumped in the shower. Eight minutes later I was ready to go. No makeup—since Caleb had already seen me at my worst, I didn't see any reason to waste the time.

Rather than setting one of the tables in the dining room, they put everything on the end of the large granite breakfast bar. They were talking about football teams when I walked in.

"Okay. Let's eat." Sam sat down on one of the bar stools. Caleb waited for me to sit, and then he did. It was very gentlemanly.

"Kira, it's your house, so you say the blessing." Sam bowed his head.

I panicked. I'd never been to church much, and though I believed in God, I wasn't really up on the latest prayers. "I, uh . . ."

Caleb put a hand on my arm. "You're probably still tired. Would you like me to say grace?"

What I wanted to do in that moment was kiss him. My head bobbed up and down.

"Dear Lord, thank you for this food. Please be with our family and friends who could not join us today. And Lord, we ask that you look after our dear friends who have come to join you in heaven. Bless this food to our use. Amen."

I choked up at the sentiment. "Amen," Sam and I both whispered.

I was saved from making much dinner conversation as we were in rapture from the meal Ms. Johnnie and Ms. Helen had prepared. The silence wasn't weird, just peaceful.

After a few minutes Sam finally broke the silence. "Are you still going back to Atlanta this week?"

I hadn't really discussed my plans with anyone. Though I didn't know Caleb well, I felt like I could trust him. "I have some interviews with various firms and companies beginning Monday. So I have to get back."

"Interviews?" Caleb put down his fork. "I thought Sam said you worked for Zeb Corp."

I cleared my throat. "I did until this last week. Seems

there were some budgetary concerns and there have been layoffs."

Caleb looked perplexed. "They showed a thirty percent gain last year. That's insane."

It seemed odd a carpenter would know Zeb Corp.'s profits for the year before, but he was right. Almost 20 percent of that was due to deals I brokered. "You must have stock with the company."

Caleb sat back and gave Sam a strange look. "Not exactly, but I do keep up with the financials of the top one hundred companies."

I waved a hand. "Well to be honest, I'm glad to get out of there. It's time for a change and this situation forced the issue." I meant what I said. For the first time in a long time I felt like I could breathe. There wasn't a heavy weight resting on my chest. "I'm kind of looking forward to seeing what's out there. Who knows? Maybe I'll even move out of Atlanta."

The idea hadn't even come to me until then. I was free. I could live anywhere in the country I wanted. As upset as I'd been over being let go, they had set me free.

Sam scooped the last of the potatoes onto his fork. "After we clean up, would it be okay if we toured the vineyards? I've been meaning to get out here to check them out, but I never seem to have the time."

"Sure." So full I could barely breathe, I picked up my plate and reached for Caleb's.

He moved it out of reach. "I'll get my own. If we all pitch in we'll finish faster."

I smiled and nodded. I really did like this guy.

Opening one of the two dishwashers, I began loading in the silverware.

Sam stopped me. "I'm all for convenience, but why don't we do this the old-fashioned way. That way you won't have to worry about the dishes later on."

He pushed me out of the way and began washing the dishes by hand. Caleb dried them and I put everything away.

We worked for several minutes, each of us busy with our chores. "Any word yet from Mrs. Canard's family?" I finally ventured.

"Her daughter called this morning. She's in Vancouver, but she's heading this way tomorrow. She'd already been on the phone with Tate's." That was the funeral home in Sweet. "There won't be a funeral, but they do plan a memorial for a week from Friday. That's what Mrs. Canard wanted."

I turned away. Looking out of the window onto the stark but beautiful West Texas plains, I had to crinkle my nose to keep from tearing up. "This place won't be the same without her." My voice was a little froggy sounding.

Caleb put a hand on my shoulder. "You're right. We're all going to miss her. I'd visited the library to do some research on architecture a few weeks ago and the books she came up with were amazing. It was if she always knew exactly what you needed."

I smiled at him and nodded. Turning again to face Sam, I told him, "I don't know when all of my meetings are scheduled, but I'll be back on Friday for the service no matter what." I'd said my good-byes to her at the hospital, but now I would pay my respects.

I'd convinced myself the dream involving Mrs. Canard had been my way of dealing with the greatest of tragedies.

But I wondered what my subconscious was trying to tell me when Mrs. Canard mentioned the responsibilities. Maybe she meant moving on with my life. Or maybe that's what I was trying to tell myself; that it was up to me to make new choices and to be smart about them.

The guys were talking as we finished up, and I realized I'd zoned out.

"I think that's the last of it." Caleb handed me the platter that had held the turkey.

"You guys make sure you take the leftovers. I'm leaving tomorrow and I don't want Mom and Dad coming home to a fridge full of meat and sweet potatoes with marshmallows. My mom will have a cow"—I laughed—"or at least a soy bean if she sees that crap in her house."

"We'll take care of the leftovers," Sam promised.

I went in search of a jacket. I didn't really have one that was appropriate for the thirty-degree temperatures outside. In my mom and dad's room I found a parka I thought would work. It belonged to my dad and was about four sizes too big. I looked like a big green apple when I put it on. I grabbed a knit cap and made my way to the back of the house.

Caleb and Sam were already outside looking at the sculptures. "These are incredibly cool," I heard Caleb say as he stared at a huge funnel-like creation made out of rusted metal. "Who did them?"

In that moment I was really very proud of my dad and his "yard art." "My dad." I pulled the cap down over my ears and stuck my freezing hands in my pockets.

"Has he had any showings?" Caleb was a man full of surprises. He had an interest in art and seemed to know what was going on in the business world.

"I honestly don't know. I haven't been home much the last few years since I moved to Atlanta." I moved past them. "I don't think there's much to see because most of the plants are dormant this time of year, but the vineyards are this way."

They followed me up the hill. It was around four in the afternoon and the sun had dipped pretty low, and so had the temperatures. I shivered even with the big jacket on.

The vineyards were on various levels of the hills, almost like they'd been carved out of them. There were acres of vines draped on wooden posts and wire.

"I hadn't realized they'd done so much this last year." Sam climbed to the top and looked down. "He's got pinot noir and chardonnay. Do you know who is buying his harvest?"

Again, I didn't have any answers. I'd so disengaged myself from my parents that I didn't know anything about their lives now. It was sad. "No."

"Well, find out for us. I'd love to come back in May and taste some of the grapes." Sam walked back down, Caleb right behind him.

"Your parents must be cool people." Caleb pulled on his gloves.

I shrugged. "When they're your parents, you really don't see them that way. I guess they kind of are, except for their unreasonable worship of bean curd."

Both men laughed.

Back at the house, Sam checked his watch. "I'd better get to the hospital for evening rounds." He headed for the fridge. "I put a couple of slices of turkey and some sweet potatoes in a plastic bag for you, just in case you get hungry tonight."

After everything we'd eaten, I was pretty sure it would be a couple of days before I could stomach anything else.

He gave me a stern look. "You have to take better care of yourself. Eat three meals a day and preferably something that doesn't come in a bag. Get sleep and take a vacation now and then." I followed him to the front door, his arms loaded with leftovers.

Sam was one to talk, given his hours. Between his practice and the nursing home I'd bet he didn't have much more free time than I did. "Yes, Doctor."

He leaned in and kissed my cheek. "I'll see you next Friday, and if you don't look any better I'm putting you in the hospital and hog-tying you to the bed."

I did a fake gasp and put a hand to my chest. "Why, Sam, I never knew you were so kinky."

He gave a stern look and then laughed. "Just be careful this week. Your temperature barely broke and your defenses are down. Your immune system is a walking sponge for germs."

The visual on that was nothing short of gross. "Okay, okay." I waved him out the door.

Caleb had been watching the whole exchange with great interest. He held a couple of grocery bags filled with the leftovers Sam hadn't been able to carry.

"This was fun." He lifted a bag. "What time are you leaving in the morning?"

"Around ten. My flight isn't until four tomorrow. I figure with the three-hour drive to the airport that should be just about right."

He nodded. "I could fly you into Dallas if that would help."

"Wow. Thanks. That's incredibly generous, but I'm going

to leave my car there so I can get back for the memorial service on Friday."

He shrugged. "I can come get you then, if you'd like, and bring you back. Hell, I can fly to Atlanta and pick you up."

Warning lights went off in my head. Too much, too fast. Did the guy have any idea of the price of fuel these days? I couldn't figure out why he was being so nice, and I wasn't sure what to say.

I must have looked startled, because he laughed. "Whoa. Sorry. I just wanted to spend a little time with you before you left, and I'm sure that came off sounding crazy."

I shook my head. "Oh, no."

His right eyebrow lifted into a look that made me laugh. "Okay, maybe a little." I paused. "You want to spend time with me?"

"Yes. You are incredibly beautiful and I happen to like the way your mind works. I enjoyed our dinner the other night."

I smiled. "Me too."

"How about we set a real date for a week from Saturday? I'll pick you up here around seven."

I should have said no. The last thing I needed right now was a date. But my mouth spoke of its own volition. "Sure." The truth is, it was just a date. Caleb was hot and he thought I was beautiful. So what if we lived fifteen hours away from one another?

Before he stepped through the door, he kissed me full on the mouth. Cupping one hand behind my neck, he pulled me to him, and electricity zinged when our lips met. My eyes shut and I saw those little sparkly things floating by as my body filled with heat. His lips were soft and he tasted like gravy.

When he pulled away I stopped myself from groaning with disappointment.

"I have mono." I spurted out the words.

He chuckled. "I know, but I couldn't wait. Besides I've already had it a couple of times, so you can't really give it to me again."

Stepping over the threshold, he stopped. "I don't want to scare you, but I think that might have been the best kiss of my life." Then he walked out.

His comment took my breath away. All I could do was wave as he backed his truck out of the drive.

I had no idea what was going on, but I was pretty sure I'd just kissed the man of my dreams.

I shut the door and headed for the office. It took me a minute, as I sat down at the desk, to recognize the strange feeling that had come over me.

I was happy. For the first time in years I had a real smile on my face and my heart was doing a little dance.

"Geez, Kira. It was only a kiss. Get a grip." I rolled my eyes, but I was still smiling when I logged on to my e-mail.

Thanksgiving Food I Like Best

1. Pumpkin pie
2. Yams with mini-marshmallows
3. Cheesy green beans
4. Soft buttered rolls
5. Turkey soaked in gravy

Chapter 8

There are two tragedies in life. One is not to get your heart's desire. The other is to get it.

MAN AND SUPERMAN
By Shaw, George Bernard, 1856–1950
Call #: F-SHA
Description: 120 p.; 20cm

"Ladies and gentlemen, we are making our final descent into Atlanta. Please make sure all tray tables are secure and seatbacks are . . ."

I woke to the flight attendant's instructions. We'd been flying for about three hours and it was dark now. I'd managed to get a seat in first class, but it was by a window. Normally I can't handle the claustrophobic feeling of being trapped on a plane like that, but with holiday travel over Thanksgiving weekend, I was lucky to even have a seat.

I popped my neck and rolled my shoulders. The woman next to me was reading a book and we'd barely acknowledged each other. It's funny how that works sometimes. She was dressed casually, in James jeans and a soft sweater. I'd worn the Armani suit Justin had packed for me weeks ago and the Jimmy Choos. I was overdressed for Saturday travel, but it was that or the sweatshirt and jeans I'd bought in Sweet. I decided that since I was returning to my hometown on Friday I wouldn't bother with luggage.

As I passed by baggage claim, it dawned on me that I'd have to get a taxi. That's when I heard, "Kira!"

Justin hopped up and down, waving. His curly hair had been spiked and he was wearing low-riders with a long-sleeved black T-shirt. Every time he raised his arm he showed a corner of his perfectly tanned and well-honed abs. I'd missed the boy.

Pushing through the swarm of travelers, I nearly ran into his arms.

"I missed you," I warbled against his chest.

He squeezed me tight. "I missed you too. I brought someone to see you."

Behind Justin was Rob, his lover of three months. The longest relationship he'd ever had. A little older than Justin, Rob was in his early thirties. "Hey, doll." Rob reached to hug me.

"Oh, you guys are so sweet to come and get me. I was just wondering how I would get home."

Justin looked puzzled. "As if we'd let you take a taxi. Please. Besides, we want to help you put together your interview suits."

Rob smiled. "Justin wanted to help you. I'm going to make you dinner."

I smiled at them. "I love you guys."

An hour later we were in my condo, with half of my closet on the bed. I'd given up trying to have any say in my wardrobe for the week, as Justin considered himself my personal stylist.

Rob was in the kitchen making California and spicy tuna rolls. I wasn't sure Justin had any idea how much that man adored him, but I hoped he figured it out soon. If Rob were straight, I'd snatch him up in a second.

"For Bianco, Kant, and Reeves, you should do the black Armani Collezioni wool suit with the pants. They are a little more progressive than some of the other firms, but you definitely want the sophisticated hot look.

"Now for Kelo Corp. I'd go with the St. John space-dyed suit in gray. You look good in that one, and they are a little bit more uptight."

I sat on the chaise at the end of the bed and listened.

"Now for shoes. The Prada square heels will be great for the Armani, but you need something sassy with St. John. Hmmm." He tapped his forefinger against his chin. "I think these Versace quilted pumps will be perfect." He sighed. "That will get you through Monday."

I didn't have the heart to tell him that the interviews were an hour and a half apart and there wouldn't be time to change. I'd most likely wear the Armani because it was safe, but I did love the Versace pumps, so I might do those instead of the Choos I'd normally wear.

"Sushi is ready," Rob called from the kitchen.

He'd set my dining room table with candles and long, rectangular plates with sushi lined up like little soldiers on each one. Black plastic chopsticks angled across the geometric dinnerware, and he'd even done an arrangement of white roses in a low fishbowl.

"This is wonderful." I walked around to hug him.

He shrugged. "Justin told me how sick you were when you left and we've decided to make you take better care of yourself. That means at least one real meal a day with plates and everything."

"You guys are the best."

"So . . . you haven't talked much about your trip home." Justin picked up a California roll. "How did it go?"

I looked down at the table. "Well, there were some good things and some bad things. Remember me telling you about Mrs. Canard, and how she kind of helped me through my formative years?"

"Yes," Justin answered.

"She . . . she passed away on Thursday." I couldn't talk about it. The hurt was still very close to my heart.

Justin jumped up and hugged me. "Oh, honey, I'm so sorry. I know how much you loved her."

I managed to keep the tears from overflowing. "I'm going back on Friday for her memorial service. I was with her when she died. It was . . . tough."

He nodded.

Rob reached across the table and squeezed my hand. "Wow, you really have been through it."

I took a deep, steadying breath.

I grabbed a roll and dipped it in the soy and wasabi I'd mixed together. "I also sort of met a guy."

Justin, who had sat back down, nearly choked. "What did you say?"

"Don't freak out. He's just a guy I met back home." I smiled. "Who, oh my God, is hotter than any man has a right to be."

The men laughed.

"He must be something for your cheeks to go all pink like that." Rob gestured at my face.

I put my hands on my cheeks. "He does get the blood flowing." I sighed. "But he's a thousand miles away and I'm"—I waved a hand around—"here. We have a date next Saturday."

Justin laughed out loud. "You know, a long-distance relationship might work for you. He wouldn't care that you spend eighteen hours a day at the office."

I'd been thinking about that, though I wasn't exactly ready to articulate it. I didn't want to ever make my life all about work again. In a way I felt betrayed. I had thought if I worked hard and dedicated myself to the job it would pay off.

And it did in a way. I had more money than I'd ever imagined possible, but when it came down to it, the company had tossed me aside as if I were nothing. They didn't care about the thousands of hours I'd given them. I wouldn't do that again. I was young, and I'd been hiding behind my job.

"So how are things at the office?" I ventured. I didn't want this to be a weird thing between Justin and myself. He'd avoided talking about the office all night, and I knew it was on purpose.

"Same old crap." He stared down at his plate.

"Who did they stick you with?"

He shrugged. "The Bitch."

I gasped. The Bitch was Nancy Tucker, a senior vice president who was known for cutting off heads with a single command of her voice.

"I'm so sorry." My heart went out to him. The guy talked a good game, but he was a tender soul.

Justin leaned back in his chair. "It's not as bad as you might think."

"You don't have to pretend with me. I've worked with her on a couple of deals; I know how she treats her employees."

He suddenly looked guilty. "No, I mean after what happened with Melinda and then you, she's sort of taken me under her wing. Oh sure, she rants, but at everyone around me. She's so nice to me it's creepy. The third day I was there I found an error in one of the legal briefs one of the other lawyers had given her, and she gave me a pay bump. I'd been so afraid to tell her, but she liked that I spoke up. She says everyone else kisses her ass because she's a bitch, and she liked me because I didn't do it."

"Wow! Well, I guess that's good, right?"

"It's not the same as when you were there. The fun has gone out of the job, but it's okay while I'm looking for something else."

I nodded. "You tamed the wild beast. I'm so impressed."

"Well, after putting up with your persnickety self the last two years, I've learned a few things about dealing with tough women."

I threw my napkin at him. "That you have, my friend. Let me know if you need reference letters. I'm also happy to call in a few favors."

"We'll see how things pan out over the next few weeks. Our favorite headhunter, Cynthia, is doing some work for me too."

"Excellent." I yawned. Glancing at my watch, I noticed it was barely ten. "Man, I'm getting old."

"You need your rest." Rob stacked the plates on the table. "Let's get things cleaned up, Justin."

"No. You guys took care of me, and I'll get the dishes. Don't worry about it."

"I won't hear of it," Rob said. "You go take a nice hot bath.

By the time you're finished we'll have things cleaned up and we'll be out of here."

I kissed them both on the top of their heads. "You really are wonderful."

I whispered to Justin, "Hold on to this one." My friend hadn't had much more luck with men than I had in the last few years . . . though he'd certainly dated more.

Justin grinned and kissed my cheek when I bent down for a hug.

"Are you sure you don't mind about the dishes?" I asked one more time.

Rob gave me a mean look. I held up my hands and ran for the bathroom.

When I bought the condo I had paid special attention to the renovations in the bathroom. The large round tub had jets that beat the tension out of a body, as did the multi-jet shower.

I poured vanilla bath oil into the hot water as it filled the tub. I knew I should feel guilty about leaving guests to clean up, but it was Rob and Justin. They were more like family.

A half hour later I was a prune. I wrapped up in my favorite robe and peeked out of the bedroom. The guys were gone. I walked to the windows looking out onto the city of Atlanta.

Even after the long soak, I felt antsy. I chalked it up to the interviews the next morning, but there was one thing that always soothed my nerves.

I sat down at my small baby grand. It was another of my impulse buys, but I used it all the time. One thing we always had around our trailer was music. My parents were passionate about it. My dad had an electronic keyboard, and by the time I was six I could play piano concertos from the adult lesson books I borrowed from the library.

As my fingers slid across the keys my thoughts drifted back to earlier in the evening. Even though I'd lost my job, I still had everything I'd ever wanted—the cars, the beautifully decorated home, and *money*. I'd made so much money the last few years with my investments I didn't have to go back to work at all if I didn't want to. Ever. I had choices.

I looked around at my living area. The perfect couch in soft blue faced the bank of windows. The chocolate walls were warm with the silver mirrors and picture frames. The modern art I'd acquired over the last two years was hung perfectly.

None of it made me happy. Not in a jaded, I-have-everything-I-want way. I took stock of what I'd thought I'd wanted all these years and realized it was crap. These were just things, and while I liked having them around, they didn't make me happy.

I could walk away from it tomorrow, all of these things I thought so important, and I wouldn't care. My problem was I didn't understand why I felt this way all of a sudden.

Maybe it was time to make the move to New York. I'd talked about it since my first year at Zeb Corp. For the first time in my life there wasn't a five-year plan, and I didn't like it.

I didn't feel comfortable in my own skin.

The temperature dropped in the apartment. Pulling the robe tighter around me, I went to check the thermostat. Everything was fine.

I'm just tired. It's been a long day and I'll feel better when I wake up in the morning. Please, God. I need to feel better.

Reasons I Hate Job Interviews

1. Snap judgments
2. Inane questions
3. Self-important interviewers
4. Small talk
5. Sickening nerves

Chapter 9

You can hire logic, in the shape of a lawyer, to prove anything that you want to prove.

THE AUTOCRAT OF THE BREAKFAST TABLE
By Holmes, Oliver Wendell, 1809–1894
Call #: F-HOL
Description: 300 p.

My first meeting was at nine thirty. I still had that feeling of not caring about anything. I simply didn't want to be in Atlanta, and I really didn't want to go on job interviews.

I had a horrible urge to call and cancel the entire week, but I forced myself to walk out the door.

That's probably why the meetings were so successful.

Five months ago I would have been a barracuda going into those interviews. I would have said, "This is what I can do for you," and set out spreadsheets. I would have laughed at their jokes and made intelligent small talk.

On this particular day I felt like they were lucky I showed up at all. I answered questions and I was professional, but I was far from the barracuda.

These guys were used to people kissing up in a major

way. I wasn't in the mood. Over the past two years I'd put together contracts for my company that made them billions of dollars. They either wanted me or they didn't.

They'd done their homework. They knew about what happened with Melinda Jackson and my involvement in her case. They knew why Zeb Corp. had let me go, and yet they still wanted me.

Greed. There is no other reason. There were offers that came with large sums of money and even relocation to New York City.

I told them all the same thing: "I'll take the offer under consideration and let you know in a few weeks." I didn't know what I wanted to do. I had no plan, and I wasn't about to make any decisions without a solid one.

The interviewers must have thought their offers weren't good enough.

"Kira, I hope you understand that this is only a preliminary offer. We want to make sure you're happy," said Mr. Grayson at the first firm.

"Oh, it's more than generous." I smiled. "I just need some time to make certain I do what's best. I'm sure you understand." I stood and reached out my hand. He shook it, his mouth agape. "Thank you again for meeting with me this morning." I picked up my briefcase and left Mr. Grayson stuttering behind me.

"But surely we can come to some kind of terms?"

I shook my head. "I'll let you know."

After I did the same thing at the next meeting I knew something was wrong with me. I called Sam. It took a few minutes for him to get to the phone.

"Hello?" He sounded rushed.

"Sam, I'm losing my mind," I whispered into the phone. I was walking down Peachtree Street to my next appointment a few buildings over. The weather had turned chilly and my breath made wafting clouds.

"Kira?" He paused. "Tell me what's wrong."

"I'm having this weird feeling. Really it's no feeling. All of a sudden I don't care about anything." I caught myself waving my hand in the air as I passed a window and stopped. "I was offered the job of a lifetime. The job I've dreamed about since I entered law school, and I told them I'd *think* about it. What's wrong with me?"

He cleared his throat. "First, take a deep breath and let it out."

I did what he asked.

"Hold on one sec so I can make it back to my office. I'm in the reception area." He put me on hold and I waited.

I glanced at my watch. I only had another twenty minutes before my next appointment.

"So the job interviews are going well?" He came back on the line.

"Exceptionally well. But last night . . . I don't know. I was in my apartment. It's a place I've loved and I just didn't want to be there. I don't want to be here—in Atlanta." I could hear hysteria creeping into my voice.

"Look, you've been through so much the last few weeks. It's not unusual to feel some aftereffects. Though you can't remember what happened with your friend, you did see what happened. And it happened to you there in Atlanta, which may be why you feel panicked. We can't know how that affected you mentally. It shut you down physically with the mono. You were smart to follow your instincts and tell them you'd consider the offer. I suggest you do the same for the rest, until you can talk to someone.

"I'm not a psychologist, but it sounds like post-traumatic stress disorder, and you really don't want to make any major decisions right now."

I stopped to wait for the light to change. "What? That's what soldiers get. I mean, what happened was bad, but nothing like what those men and women in Iraq have gone through."

"There are different levels of stress," Sam added. "What you saw was no less traumatic than what happens in war. And then Mrs. Canard died, and the mono kicked your butt, and you aren't completely recovered from it. Well, anyone would be uneasy."

I sighed. "I have this terrible feeling. Like I just can't do the attorney thing anymore." My eyes began to water and I sniffed. "This is my life. This is my dream."

I was so involved in the conversation that it took me a minute to realize the guy walking next to me was giving me a strange look. I stared back at him and he moved on.

"Kira, stop it. No matter what happens, you can do whatever you put your mind to. You know that as well as anyone. What's going on with you right now—think of it as an illness that's making you feel this way. Depression can make you think things you wouldn't normally. That's a big part of what makes post-traumatic stress disorder so dangerous. Does that make sense?"

"I don't know. I guess." That's when I realized where I was. "Oh, no." I hadn't intended to walk this way. I staggered back against the windows of the Zeb Corp. lobby.

"What's wrong?"

I ignored Sam.

The pavement had been scrubbed clean where she had landed on the sidewalk. It was as if the horrible events of Melinda's death had never taken place. Looking up toward the roof of the building made me dizzy and queasy.

The image of her flashed in my brain. Her hair flew out around her and then—darkness. I couldn't remember anything after that. I squeezed my eyes shut to stop the tears.

"Kira? Damn cell phones. Can you hear me?"

"Sam, I have to go. My next meeting is in a few minutes and I've got to try and get myself together." I turned and walked back the way I had come. It meant going two blocks out of my way, but I couldn't go past that spot.

"Do me a favor and give yourself a break. Listen to what these guys have to say and just don't make any commitments right now. You weren't wrong about needing time to consider. You have to heal your body and your mind."

"Okay, Doc. Thanks. I know you were probably with patients."

"Don't worry about it. If you want I can get you some referrals for some great counselors there in Atlanta, or there's actually a terrific one here in town you might want to talk to. I'll see you on Friday. Don't hesitate to call if you need me again."

"Okay."

We hung up. As I turned the corner I saw the reflection of the same guy who had been looking at me so strangely. He wore a ball cap pulled low over his eyes and a camouflage jacket with jeans.

Why is he following me? Stop being paranoid. There are tons of weird people in downtown Atlanta. You know this.

I took a deep breath and increased my speed. I was only a half block from my destination and I power-walked into the lobby, heading straight for the security desk.

"Hi," I said to the guard. "I have an appointment on the eighth floor. You might think I'm crazy, but I think that guy out there"—I pointed to the man in the jacket—"is following me."

The guard looked from me to the man outside. "Guys like that are always following pretty women and scaring them," the guard grumbled. He grabbed his nightstick. "I'll take care of it. You go on up." Handing me a visitor's pass, he moved from behind the desk. He turned back at the door. "You make sure you call down for a taxi when you leave, and we'll escort you out."

"Thanks," I said, but he had already gone out the revolving door. I didn't stick around to see what happened. My hands shook, and a quick stop in the lobby bathroom showed I was even paler than normal. *I can't think about this. You can have your nervous breakdown later. Get it together.*

The weird thing was, the idea of going back to Sweet made me happy. It's the only thing that got me through the rest of the day. Maybe it was Caleb, or maybe it was something else. I wanted to go home, and that was no longer Atlanta.

One thing was for certain, I was screwed up in a big way and I had to get my head together.

"Kira, it's Cynthia Jordan from the agency." The headhunter called and left a message on my voice mail. "Mr. Grayson told me what happened and says he'd like to sweeten the deal with a sign-on bonus of a hundred thousand dollars."

I was back in my apartment drinking a bottle of water and I almost choked.

"He also said you have your choice of offices here, New York, Chicago, or L.A., and he's willing to wait."

Let me explain something important. These guys don't wait for anything or anyone. They are power brokers of the highest degree. Mr. Grayson's investment firm pulled in billions last year, and I'm small potatoes in the grand scheme of things.

All of the meetings for the day had gone well. Some better than others, but Mr. Grayson had made the best offer by far. I didn't understand why he wanted me so bad. I could make him more money, but so could any other decent lawyer worth anything.

My BlackBerry rang again. Expecting Justin, I picked up.

"This is Kira."

"Hey, it's Caleb."

"Oh, hi." I smiled even though he couldn't see me.

"How's Atlanta?" His voice was deep and sexy, and did strange things to parts of my body.

Other than a psychotic meltdown, everything's great. "The interviews are going well. Lots of choices, which is a good thing."

"Absolutely." He cleared his throat. "Listen, I have to go out of town for a job, and I wanted to let you know."

My smile faded and the deep, dark depression made a fast return. He was breaking our date.

I felt like a dork for being so excited about it in the first place. I should have known.

"Okay. Well, I appreciate you calling and letting me know you won't be able to make it Saturday."

"What? No, that's not why I was calling. I'll definitely be there Saturday. Sorry. I was trying to say that I'm not certain I can make it back for the memorial service. I'll do my best. I know how much Mrs. Canard meant to you and I wanted to be there for you."

"That's so kind of you." *Thank you, Jesus and Buddha.* My parents were Buddhist and I was open-minded when it came to religion. "I understand. No one would expect you to be there. You barely knew her."

"I know. I just wanted to be there for you. It's going to be a rough day. I'm looking forward to Saturday, though."

"Yeah, me too." I suddenly felt shy. This guy was so totally awesome. My phone clicked with another call.

"Well it sounds like someone's trying to get through; I'll let you go. I'll see you this weekend. And if I can make it back by Friday I will."

"Okay."

He hung up and the next call rang through.

"Hey, I just got your message that you wanted to cancel dinner." I'd called Justin on the way home from the last interview. Even though the day had gone well, all I wanted to do was put on my pj's and hang out at home. But Caleb's call had changed that. I suddenly felt energized and excited.

"Um, is it okay if I change my mind again? I've decided I really am hungry for the Spaghetti Feast."

"Now that's the Kira I know. Sure. After Rob gets off work at seven, we'll stop by and pick you up on the way to Alfred's. Our reservations are at eight," Justin informed me.

I noticed the stacks of mail. There weren't many bills.

Most of those came to my e-mail and I paid everything online.

"Okay, I'll be ready."

Putting down the phone, I flipped through the envelopes and ads. "Ninety-eight percent of this is junk." I tossed catalogs and direct mail ads into the trash by the front table. Then I came across a letter that had been addressed in pen.

Huh? I didn't know anyone who still wrote letters. There was no return address. I opened it and pulled out a single sheet. It had one sentence that read:

"You're responsible and you'll pay."

I let the letter float to the floor. Who would send me something like that? Were they talking about Melinda? My hands shook, but I stooped down to pick it up, reading it over and over again.

My stomach churned and I was afraid I might be sick any moment.

You'll pay.

Did that mean whoever wrote the letter wanted to hurt me? I turned to double check the lock on the front door. Taking the letter, I stuffed it back in the envelope and put it in one of the drawers.

I remembered the guy in the cap. I hadn't recognized him, but what if someone really wanted to hurt me? Still shaking, I sat on the couch. My mind whirled, emotions just on the edge, the tears threatening to spill over.

"*No!*" I said the word out loud. I wouldn't let myself fall off the edge of the precarious cliff on which I'd found myself. *It's probably some jerk's idea of a prank, a horrible, nasty, mean-spirited joke.*

Taking deep breaths, I willed myself to calm down.

I thought about calling the police, but it seemed an overreaction. I didn't have any enemies, and I didn't feel like dealing with the police department right then. Besides, the letter and the guy following me probably weren't even connected. It was my overactive imagination hard at work. The letter writer had obviously mixed me up with someone else. There was no reason for anyone to be after me.

Think about something else.

It would be hours before Justin and Rob showed up. I looked up and saw the CNN logo on the television. Christiane Amanpour, one of the most respected journalists I know of, was giving a report about refugees.

My phone rang again, and I jumped.

"Geez. Chill," I said out loud. I reached over to the coffee table and picked up the cell.

I didn't recognize the number but answered anyway. Any distraction was good right now.

"This is Kira."

"Ms. Smythe?" an elderly sounding gentleman asked.

"Yes."

"This is Mr. Pierce. I'm the executor of Mrs. Mabel Canard's will. I wondered if I might have a moment."

I sat up. "Yes."

"Mrs. Canard left specific instructions for me to speak with you about her will. She's left you something and asked that we chat face to face. Is there a chance you'll be in Sweet anytime soon?"

Mrs. Canard had left me something? I guessed it would probably be some books, something special she thought I might want. My eyes watered, and I had to clear my throat before speaking. "I'll be in town on Thursday, in time for the memorial service on Friday."

He sighed. "That's wonderful. I thought I might have to make a trip to Atlanta and these bones aren't what they used to be. Would it be possible for you to meet me at the office at nine on Friday morning?"

"Certainly."

"That is good news. My office is upstairs from where the old hardware store used to be. It's a women's clothing store now."

Delilah's—it's where I'd picked up the jeans and sweat-shirt I'd worn in Sweet. "Yes, I know where that is. I'll see you on Friday morning."

After I'd been gone for so long Mrs. Canard still thought about me. It was beyond sweet. The tears rolled down my face in big fat drops, and I let them fall. Mrs. Canard was a wonderful woman and she deserved every tear I shed.

I didn't know what she'd left me, but I would treasure it for the rest of my life.

My curiosity was almost enough to take my mind off the horrid letter I'd opened earlier. Almost.

Chapter 10

❧

It is curious to look back and realize upon what trivial and apparently coincidental circumstances great events frequently turn as easily and naturally as a door on its hinges.

KING SOLOMON'S MINES
By Haggard, H. Rider, 1856–1925
Call #: F-HAG
Description: xxx, 240 p.; 21 cm

It was odd to come back to Sweet so soon after my last visit. I flew into Dallas early Thursday and made the three-hour drive west. I stopped by Lulu's to grab a quick lunch of roast, mashed potatoes, and green beans.

Then I visited Sam, who had given me orders to stop by his office when I arrived in town.

It was almost two and I wasn't sure he'd returned from lunch, but when I walked into the reception area he yelled, "Be with you in a minute."

I heard some footsteps and he looked through the reception window and waved at me. "Hey, you. Come on back. Let's have a look at you." I hugged him and then followed him to one of the exam rooms.

"I thought the office would be full." I sat down on the

table. He stuck a thermometer in my ear and then wrapped the blood pressure cuff around my arm.

"We're trying to take a half day off on Thursday afternoon. It gives me a little more time at the hospital and nursing home and for the hospice visits. This small-town doctor business is busier than I'd imagined."

"Hmmm. Temp's still ninety-nine point five. Have you been resting?"

I crossed my arms, as his office was slightly chilly. "Yes. I had several meetings but the rest of the time I laid around on the couch or in bed. I promise. I mean, it's down from the other day, so obviously I've been doing something right. And I don't feel as tired, though I could use a nap right now."

He used the stethoscope to listen to my breathing and I stopped talking.

"Sounds much better. I want you to keep taking the antibiotics and antivirals."

I nodded. "This all sounds vaguely familiar. I promise, I'm fine. I feel so much better than I did a few weeks ago."

He smiled. "I know, but you're my friend and I get to worry if I want. Just take care of yourself. I'll see you at the service tomorrow. Do you want to catch some lunch after?"

"Sure. I don't know what kind of company I'll be."

"You can sit and stare at the wall. I don't care. You know that." Sam put my chart into a file cabinet and I followed him out to the reception area.

I shook my head. "Every time I think about it I get teary. At least I have some emotions. I was beginning to think I'd turned into a robot. What happened in Atlanta was weird. I couldn't get out of that place fast enough, and it's been my home for two years."

"Let's get you through the next couple of days, and then I'd like you to talk to a friend of mine here in town. He's a good guy, and you'll like him."

I didn't know about that. Unlike a lot of the women I know, I don't talk about my feelings much. Well, until I realized I didn't have any.

"We'll see. Can I go home now?"

He gave me a sad look. "Things are rough right now, but it's going to get better."

I laughed, and sniffled a little. "You know, it's strange, but now that I'm here, I feel better. I'm sad, and I'm not looking forward to tomorrow at all, but I don't feel as restless."

He squeezed me a little tighter. "Do you think that might have something to do with your date?"

"What? Oh, geez. I have a date on Saturday night." I slapped a hand against my head. "I can't believe it's only two days away."

Sam chuckled. "I told Caleb he'd better have you home by midnight, and if you looked too flushed or pale to bring you home immediately."

"Thanks. But I have a dad. And he's just as big a worry-wart as you." I shoved a finger at his chest.

Sam laughed.

I left his office in a very good mood but a little scared at the same time. Here's the truth: I've had dates in the past two years. Well, two dates. One was with an accountant who was part of a merger team. Technically, it was more of a business meeting, but we did have a few drinks and talked about things other than the job.

The other one was with a guy . . . whose name I can't even remember. Justin fixed us up for New Year's. We arrived at the party and the guy's ex-girlfriend was wrapped around another man. He freaked out and confronted her, and I didn't see either of them the rest of the evening. Justin kissed me on the cheek at midnight to celebrate the New Year. Sad, but true.

I've been married to my job. Or, at least, I had been. It shocked me when I thought about what I'd done to my life in the last few years.

I wasn't going to let that happen again.

By the time I made it to Mom and Dad's it was almost four. I said hello to both of them and made sure I was staying in the same room.

My mom patted my back when she hugged me. "That's your room, Kira. It always has been. We never give it to guests. We have a full house, though, so there will be visitors around."

"Not a problem." I started to walk out. "Mom?"

"Yes, honey?" she said distractedly.

I pursed my lips together. "I'm really proud of what you and Dad have done here. I walked the vineyards the other day and—I'm just proud of you."

My mom had been searching through some papers on her desk. She looked up, her eyes wet with unshed tears. "So your hippie parents aren't an embarrassment after all?"

I walked around so I could hug her again. "Oh, no, you still embarrass the hell out of me, and you eat crazy crap. But I love you and I'm proud of you."

She laughed. "I'll take what I can get." She leaned back and looked at my face. "You look a little pale. Go get some rest, and I'll have dinner ready for you when you get up."

I paused on my way out the door.

She cleared her throat. "I had Dad pick you up some turkey, provolone, and even some eggs. But I refuse to have beef or pork in my kitchen. I'll make you a turkey sandwich. Sam called and said you need your protein and he thinks you might be allergic to soy. So no tofu for you."

It was all I could do not to laugh. God bless Sam. I owed him big for this one.

"That'll be great, Mom."

I dumped my bag in my room, but I was more restless than tired. I put on my yoga pants and shirt and did a few postures in my room. It felt good to relax the muscles and I stretched out onto the rug on the floor. As I moved through each pose I could feel the tension leave my body.

Afterward I showered and found the turkey sandwich my mom had left for me in the fridge. I could hear everyone in the conference room toward the back of the complex. My dad was giving a speech about herbs and their healing powers. I stood there listening for a long time. He was a good speaker, erudite and even funny.

I laughed softly as I made my way back to my room. For the first time since I left for college, it felt good to be home.

I wasn't sure what to wear. The day of the memorial service I had to dress quickly in order to make my meeting at the lawyer's office. I couldn't choose between navy and black but decided to go with the black Carolina Herrera suit. It was appropriate without being stuffy or harsh.

An elderly woman who looked like someone's great-grandmother greeted me in the reception area of Mr. Pierce's office. Turned out she was Mrs. Pierce. She handed me a cup of tea and seated me in a small conference room. "He'll be right with you, dear," she informed me.

A few minutes later Mr. Pierce came in. He was a small, wiry man, slightly stooped, with gray hair that tumbled onto his forehead. He shook my hand and then sat across the table from me.

"First, let me say how sorry I am about Mrs. Canard. She was a dear woman and one of the finest librarians I've ever known." He opened a file folder.

"She left a good portion of her savings to her family, along with many of her antiques and belongings. But her most prized possession she left to you. She wanted you to read this before I explain everything."

He pushed a sealed envelope toward me. I hadn't known what to expect. I thought maybe she'd given me a first edition book or one of her art collections.

The seal was a red wax stamp with a C. I opened the envelope and pulled out two sheets of typewritten paper. It was a letter.

Dear Kira,

You are a special young woman and it's important you understand that. I've known that fact since you first walked into my library. You were a messy five-year-old missing her front teeth and I fell in love with you on that day. You might as well have been my own child. The love ran that deep.

You may not realize it, but you have a passion for books that rivals my own, and I tried to feed that as much as I could. I worried sometimes that helping you escape what you thought were difficult times might have been a mistake.

I know growing up in this town was hard for you, that you felt like you never fit in, but I beg you to look around. It's a town of oddballs. None of us really fit anywhere but here in Sweet. For all of its faults, this is a place of peace and of love. There are people who care about you here, and as you move forward in the world, I want you to remember that.

At the beginning of this letter I mentioned that you are special, and you are, more so than you might have ever believed. There are people like you and I who see things that others don't. I know you've probably heard the voices. It usually happens not long after you turn twenty-five.

No, you aren't going crazy. They are real. They are dead, but they are real. It will take you a long time to get used to what is happening, but you will make it through. I'd hoped to prepare you more. To help you understand that this is a gift that only a few of us truly share. It is a glorious and wonderful thing and will allow you to do great good in our world and others.

It is because of this that I have bequeathed my most prized possession to you: the library. Few people in Sweet know the truth, but I own the building, the books, and everything within its walls. It is a privately owned collection that I have shared with the town for more than thirty years.

Before I took ownership, Mary Elizabeth Barnes was the proprietor and she bequeathed it to me. Yes, she was "special" too. The library is something beyond what most people see, and you'll soon understand. I couldn't possibly explain it all in this letter, but there are books in the library to help along the way. That is, should you choose to follow this course and follow the conditions Mr. Pierce will explain to you.

Kira, it's so important that you understand this is your choice. Do not take on this opportunity out of guilt or for any other reason. You must follow your heart and your dreams, and if they aren't in Sweet, then that's the way it is meant to be. It's a calling, and if you don't feel the pull, then it isn't the right choice for you.

I love you, dear girl, and will always be with you.

Mabel Canard

The tears had puddled around my chin. Mr. Pierce handed me a tissue. I dabbed and tried to catch my breath between sobs.

"She left me the library?" I looked up at the kindly old man.

"Yes." He pushed the file toward me. "Should you choose to accept her offer, the library and its contents become yours. There are some provisions. Only you can run the library. If you choose not to become the new librarian, the building and the contents will be sold at auction and the proceeds donated to charity."

I pushed my hair behind my ear. "Wait. If I don't open the library, then the town must go without? That's crazy. She wouldn't want Sweet to be without a library."

I thumbed through the papers.

"That is the way she has the will worded and she was very precise."

Sitting back in my chair, I read the words. He was right, but it didn't make sense.

"She loved this town and the books. I—why would she do this?" It was a rhetorical question and Mr. Pierce didn't bother answering.

"I didn't notice any time limit. How long do I have to decide?"

He slid another file across the table. "You have one month. She wanted, if possible, for you to live the life of a librarian, and to understand the responsibilities the position holds. If after that month you choose not to stay with the job, then we'll proceed with the sale."

I crossed my arms. It was too much to take in. I remembered the voices in my room, and the feeling that I was being watched the last few weeks.

Could it be real? The dead aren't so dead? What, and now all of a sudden I'm psychic?

When things got out of hand at the office, I shut down and focused on whatever was in front of me at the time. Hence my ice princess persona. But my mind was in this weird fog, as if there were thoughts just out of reach that would clear this craziness up. Nothing made sense anymore.

There was a knock on the door. "I'm sorry to interrupt, dear, but you're needed on the phone."

Mr. Pierce nodded at his wife. "If you'll excuse me, I'll be right back."

Leaning forward I put my head in my hands.

Mabel Canard, what have you done?

Chapter 11

❧

We surely know by some nameless instinct more about our futures than we think we know.

THE STARK MUNRO LETTERS
By Doyle, Arthur Conan, Sir, 1859–1930
Call #: F-DOY
Description: xxxvi, 500 p.; 24cm

The memorial service passed by in a blur, and there were so many people in attendance that it was standing room only in the Methodist church. I'd sat outside in my car for almost twenty minutes trying to pull myself together before going in.

The wind howled, making the thirty-degree temperature feel much colder. The Canard family was in the narthex leading into the sanctuary. I made my way through the throng to pay my respects. Cheryl, Mrs. Canard's daughter, was a younger version of her mother. It was easy to pick her out of the crowd. I introduced myself and she hugged me tight. "She talked about you like you were family. She loved you so much."

I gave her a wavering smile. "She was like family to

me—and I loved her." The last few words came out a hoarse whisper.

Cheryl nodded and her eyes watered. I bit my lip on the inside to keep from sobbing. I can't stand seeing other people cry and I was on the edge already. I hugged her again and went to find a seat.

Mom, Dad, Sam, and Caleb had gathered in a pew near the back. Caleb wore a dark blue suit with a crisp white shirt and a tie, and I was happy to see him there. The Levi's-wearing carpenter I'd met a few weeks ago looked like he'd just stepped off of Wall Street. The suit he wore certainly hadn't come off of any rack.

I felt so guilty because I couldn't stop looking at him, and at the same time I wanted to know how he afforded such luxurious clothing on a carpenter's salary.

After saying a quiet hello to everyone, I sat between Caleb and Sam. Their body warmth helped to take some of the chill from my bones. At one point, Reverend James talked lovingly about the many people who spoke to him about Mrs. Canard and how she was the one who had taught them to read. The sadness ate away at me until I felt raw and uneasy.

Caleb handed me a hankie and I gave him a watery smile. His deep blue eyes stared back at me, but he looked worried. He reached down and grabbed my hand, and the heat from his grasp gave me strength.

I needed it. His presence made everything a little easier and he was the perfect gentleman.

I, on the other hand, was a big mess. My mind kept going back to why she would do something so crazy. Mrs. Canard knew how much I loved law and that it was my future. I mean, I adored books, and had a great respect for the occupation, but a librarian's life was not for me.

Mr. Pierce had given me the key to the library. It was one of those old-fashioned brass keys, which opened the large wooden doors. It burned in my pocket against my leg.

After the ceremony the attendees made their way to the Family Life Center for lunch and to visit with the Canard family. People in Sweet like to eat. For both happy and sad occasions, food is always at the ready. The very idea made me queasy, and the church had been so crowded that I craved air.

As soon as I could, I slipped out and hurried to my car. A few minutes later I sat in front of the library. The key still felt hot against my leg.

"Go in, girl. You won't know unless you try," a voice whispered behind me.

I yelped and jumped, looking around. No one was there. The message in the letter came back to me. *They are dead, but they are real.* Mrs. Canard might be right about the dead, but that wasn't something I could deal with at the moment. I mean, how much is one person supposed to take? If dead people could come back and visit, then there was life after death . . . and I wasn't in the mood to change my entire philosophy about life and death in that moment.

One step at a time, Kira.

Someone knocked against the car window and I jumped again. I saw Caleb peeking in. I pushed the button to roll down the window, my heart thumping so loudly I could hear it.

"Are you okay?" He stared behind me, probably to see what I'd been trying to look at in the backseat.

"I'm fine." I cleared my throat. "You startled me."

His eyes returned to my face. "Sorry. I saw you leave the church and you seemed upset. I just wanted to check on you."

I nodded, not really sure what to say.

"Sam wanted to know if you were ready for lunch. He's over at Lulu's holding a table."

I pushed open the door and he moved back. Rolling up the window, I had the sense to reach over and pull the keys out of the ignition. I grabbed my purse and I locked the door. "I forgot about lunch. I need to check on something in the library. Could you tell Sam I'll take a rain check?"

I headed up the stone steps, stopping for a moment to take in the gargoyles hanging over the door. "The watch guards of the beauty inside," Mrs. Canard used to say. When I was a kid I named them Jones and Pete.

I could have sworn Pete gave me a wink as I stood there. *Maybe I need to rest after all.*

"Are you sure I can't help?"

I turned to see Caleb standing behind me with his cell phone in his hand.

Shrugging, I turned back to the library. "No, but thanks." I moved forward and put the key in the door. The brass made a large scraping sound and then a loud pop. I pulled down on the handle and the heavy door opened.

"Sam, Kira has something to do at the library. You want to pick up some burgers and meet us over here?" I heard Caleb but my attention was already captured by the darkness within. It was almost as if I could hear the voices. "Come in, Kira. Come in."

I knew stepping over that threshold meant something, I just wasn't sure what.

Turning so I could see Caleb, I told him, "I need to be alone for a little while." He tried to interrupt but I held up a hand. "This is important to me. Tell Sam I'll catch up with you guys later this afternoon."

He had a hurt look on his face, as if I'd snubbed him. At first I didn't think he'd taken me seriously, but then he backed down a step. "Okay, but I'm calling to check on you in an hour or so," he said quietly.

"What?" All I could think about was getting inside. Out of the bone-chilling cold and into—I wasn't sure what.

"You're pale and your hands are shaking. I'm worried about you."

It was sweet. It had been a long time since any man, besides Justin, Sam, and Dad, had cared anything about me.

I reached out and touched his arm. "I'm fine. I'm just cold."

He looked at my hand and then patted it with his own. "Just the same, I'll be calling to make sure."

"I'm not going to wig out on our date. I promise."

He sighed, the cold air curling around his head. "I'm not worried about the *damn* date. I just want to make sure you don't pass out or something."

Geez, who knew he was so bossy?

I waved a hand. "Sorry, I'm a little distracted today. Sure. I'll talk to you later." I paused. "It meant a lot to me that you were there today. We haven't known each other very long, but I appreciate that you care enough to look after me. I just need to do this on my own right now."

He nodded, and then watched me walk in. I shut the heavy door behind me and locked it.

There was a small vestibule with a scrolled-iron hat and coat rack and an umbrella stand on one side. Shelving with various flyers for Texas tourism and classes varying from art to rock climbing, and other advertising brochures, lined the other wall.

The floors, even in the entry, were a deep mahogany wood.

The large arched entryway led to the main library hall. I paused for a moment and watched as the only light in the room filtered through the high windows. Shadows from the trees outside danced along the marbled front desk and wooden tables in the front of the room.

Moving to the right, I found the long row of light switches and flipped each one on.

"She's here. She's here," I heard, but chose to ignore the whispers around me. It was easier for now.

My breath made puffy clouds. The next mission was to find out how to turn on the heat. My best guess was a large panel I'd seen in the break room in the back. I walked among the tables, gazing at the long rows of books.

It was a two-story room with the second-story books on shelves along the wall. There were staircases leading up to those rows on both sides of the main floor. The balcony area extended about eight feet along the back and sides of the room, so that most of the main floor was open to the second story.

I took a moment to turn in a circle, looking at the entire building as if I were seeing it for the first time. I love books. I have since I was a child.

"Kira, you are one of the few people who truly understands the real joy of books," I heard Mrs. Canard's voice whisper. Only this time it wasn't one of the voices surrounding me, it was a memory.

Staring at the hardbacks and paperbacks I finally realized what she had given me—her heart. These books spoke to her, were a part of her being. No one loved them as much as she did. She took the "knowledge is power" phrase to the nth degree.

This place was hallowed ground for her. The place where gods were born and angels sang. Where a prince could sit next to a pauper and a fairy next to a gremlin. As I passed the front desk I noticed some photos. There were a few framed ones of her family—her daughter and grandchildren, all of whom had been at the service a few moments ago. By the computer I saw something that surprised me. A picture of a towheaded child missing a front tooth, thoroughly involved in whatever book she was reading. A smile of complete and utter joy lit her face. It was me. I didn't remember the photo being taken, but I couldn't have been more than five. I was so happy, and I didn't even remember ever being that happy as a child.

The cold air whipped around my shoulders, and I pulled my black coat tighter around my body.

It's definitely time to find the heat.

As I made my way back to the break room, the air grew colder. "Brrrr." I stuck my hands in my pockets.

I flipped the switch in the darkened room and found the thermostat on the wall. It was set on sixty-eight, but I swore the building was at least twenty degrees cooler. I turned it up to seventy-two and made myself a mental note to turn it back down when I left. There was no telling how much it cost to heat this place, and for now I had a feeling those bills would be my responsibility.

Curiosity soon turned my attention from the temperature. I'd never ventured past the break room, where I had shared more than one cup of tea and a number of cookies with Mrs. Canard.

There were two doors, one on the back wall, the other to the left of the sink. I opened the back door and was surprised to find a large storeroom of boxes.

There had to be a least fifty of the cardboard containers filed against the walls. A few had the tops open, and I could see they were full of books. "She can't have meant these to be shelved." I ventured in a few steps farther and pulled back the flaps of a couple. Some were research volumes—something you might see in a university biology department. Another box was filled with children's books for elementary-aged kids.

I'd never known there was so much space back there and couldn't imagine how Mrs. Canard could afford such a large inventory. I didn't have time to search all the boxes, as I wanted to investigate the other door leading off the break room.

The door by the sink opened outward and led to a stairwell. It took me a minute to find the light switch in the small, dark hall. The stairs were wooden and narrow, and curved to the right. Making my way up, I expected more storage and was thrilled to find a real treasure.

Over the storage area downstairs was a huge loft apartment. It had to be at least a thousand square feet. Here the light was abundant, as the back wall facing the west was a bank of floor-to-ceiling windows. The view of the rough hills was breathtaking.

The small kitchen, painted a soft yellow with red accents, had a dishwasher, an oven, a gas stovetop, and a fridge, all stainless steel. A short, curved wall that didn't go to the ceiling set apart the dining room. And the back part of the room had a glass block wall where a bedroom had been fashioned.

The living area, in front of the bank of windows, had a small chenille couch and several cushy chairs. A few antique tables were scattered about. While it wasn't exactly a room one might find in *Elle Decor*, it had a homey, comfortable feel.

I made my way to the sofa and sat down. I had no idea this space even existed. It explained why it seemed as though Mrs. Canard lived at the library.

Amused and pleased, I was also frightened. Scared out of my wits really. All of this was mine.

Ten Things Every Home Should Have

1. Love
2. Happiness
3. A forty-inch plasma
4. Snacks for every occasion
5. One bathroom for each person living there
6. The perfect bed
7. Room-sized clothes closets/tons o' storage
8. Books
9. A space for dancing/yoga/Pilates
10. A computer with Internet

Chapter 12

❧❧

Oh, child, men's men: gentle or simple, they're much of a muchness.

DANIEL DERONDA
By Eliot, George, 1819–1880
Call #: F-ELI
Description: xx, 220 p.; 21cm

I watched the low clouds roll by for several minutes. Slipping off my Prada ankle boots, I pulled a patchwork quilt off the back of the couch and wrapped myself in it. It was strange to sit in a living room that smelled of Mrs. Canard—a mixture of spicy tea and baby powder—and to know that this place was mine, at least for now.

Breathe. I had to remind myself to take long, calming breaths. So much had happened the last few days since the librarian's death. The job offers. The weird letter in Atlanta. The will. It was too much to process, and I decided to give myself a little while to figure things out.

I needed a plan. I would eventually sit down with the pros and cons of each situation and make a decision. But I didn't have to do it right now. That thought helped me relax. My shoulders dropped and I leaned back against the sofa pillows.

As I drifted, I thought I heard someone say, "Everything will be all right."

"I hope so," I whispered.

A half hour later I sat up with a start. I'd drifted off, and it took me a second to realize it was my cell phone ringing that had brought me back to consciousness. I'd left my purse on the table in the downstairs break room. No use running after it; by the time I reached it, whoever it was would have hung up.

I'd only rested for a few minutes, but I felt better than I had in days. I pulled on my boots and folded the quilt. After looking around the room one last time, I made my way back downstairs.

My Prada tote sat on the table where I'd left it and I dug through the bag to find my cell. The red light blinked and I had two missed calls and voice mails. I hit redial, and it didn't even ring before I heard, "Kira, are you okay?"

Caleb was on the other end and it sounded like he was running.

"I'm fine, why?" I picked up my bag and began making my way to the front door of the library.

"I called twice and you didn't answer. I was worried," he huffed.

"Sorry, I didn't hear the phone. Are you jogging?"

There was a knock and I walked quickly to the door. "When you didn't answer I ran over from The Bakery to check on you."

I laughed. "So you would be the man behind the door?"

He coughed. "Yes. A very cold man."

I found him on the steps, still in his suit, wearing a long black wool coat that looked as though it had been tailor-made for him. The man had excellent taste when it came to clothes. His chiseled cheeks were pink, and his eyes a little watery from the wind outside but filled with concern for me.

I laughed as I pulled him in. "Where did you say you were?"

He shrugged. "The Bakery, but it's in the teens out there and with the wind . . . I was grabbing a cup of coffee and it dawned on me that you probably haven't eaten much today. After seeing how pale you were, I worried you might have fainted. By the way, are you supposed to be here? I know you have the key, but since Mrs. Canard . . . Well, I wouldn't want you to get in any trouble." His eyes scanned my face.

It was sweet of him to be so worried about me. "Everything is fine and I promise to explain later." The cup of coffee sounded like heaven. I hadn't eaten anything since early morning. "Would you mind braving the cold again? We can take my car."

"Sure. Where do you want to go?" He buttoned his coat around him.

"To The Bakery. You mentioned coffee and I could certainly use some." I dug for the keys and flipped off the lights.

"She'll be back. I know she will," I heard a woman say. I sighed as I turned the lock in the door. That was one part of this weird situation I didn't want to deal with—yet.

I pushed the button to remotely start the car. One of the things I loved about the Lexus was by the time I had backed away from the library, the warm air already flowed from the vents.

Caleb adjusted the seat on the passenger side so his knees

were no longer in his chest. The drive to The Bakery took all of a minute. It was only a block off the main square. Like the rest of the town, the outside of the store was dressed in a gothic design. Displayed in the large arched window sat a wedding cake with amazing details. Flowers trailed from the top down to the bottom layer.

Mr. Owen, the shop owner, usually closed at three each day, but for the past few months he'd been staying open until seven on Friday and Saturday nights. He offered a variety of flavored coffees and teas and an incredible array of baked goods.

The pastries at The Bakery were melt-in-your-mouth delicious and calorie-laden. My mouth watered at the very thought of one of his cream puffs.

Caleb stood at my car door ready to open it before I even realized I'd parked. I'd been in the middle of my pastry reverie.

Reaching out his hand, he helped me out, and I think I fell hard for him in that moment. Part of it was the heat from his hand on mine. A surge of energy ran through me at the point of contact.

It was also such a gentlemanly act, but it meant more because I could tell it was a part of his nature. He'd been raised this way. I love Southern men. Then it dawned on me: I didn't even really know if he was from the South. He'd said earlier that he'd lived all over the world, but I didn't know much about him at all.

He put his hand on my back and guided me into the store.

Mr. Owen had moved to Sweet from South Africa more than twenty years ago. I'd always been fascinated by his heavy accent and his deep chocolate skin. He was also tall, and when I was ten I'd imagined he came from someplace where giants grew. He had to be at least six foot seven, but his soft voice made him more like a large teddy bear.

Today he was behind the counter, tossing powdered sugar on some kind of cookie bars. The three small tables, all the bakery could accommodate, were full.

Mr. O looked up when he saw me and wiped his hands on the front of his pristine white apron. "The little Kira has grown into a beautiful woman." He reached over the glass shelf showcasing his wares and took my hand in both of his. "It is good you are home."

I smiled. "Hi, Mr. Owen. It smells wonderful in here."

After giving my hand a squeeze, he moved to the sink to wash his. "I have something special for you." He moved through the archway and into the kitchen.

"You two must be old friends." Caleb stood beside me.

"Oh, yes. He looked out for me when I was a kid. My mom would never let me have sugar. Between Mr. Owen and the gang at Lulu's, I developed a strong love for the stuff. In fact, I'm in love with his— Oh, wow!"

Mr. Owen had walked out with some of his cream puffs. They were so big only four would fit in a bakery box.

"I love these. I can't believe you remembered."

The baker's smile increased. "Would you like some coffee?"

I rolled my eyes. "Of course." Turning to Caleb I confessed. "It was Mr. Owen who served me my first cup, and I've been hooked ever since. He was the one who helped me stay awake for all of those AP tests in high school."

The baker waved a hand. "I take no responsibility. You begged and begged. I only gave it to you to shush you. I worried it might stunt your growth." He poured the golden brown liquid into two large to-go cups.

For the record, I'm a healthy five foot eight, but I knew that was relatively small to him.

"She wouldn't listen. Smart, this one," he said as he put the plastic lids on the cups. "From the time she was eleven she could argue almost anyone and win. Of course, she barely took her nose out of the books to see the world around her. But if she wanted something, she would do whatever it took to get it." His eyes moved from the cups to me. "I hear the reading paid off. You are a big attorney in Atlanta."

Was. I nodded. There was no way I could tell him the truth. Not yet. Lifting the lid off my coffee, I poured in three packets of sugar. I noticed he had some sandwiches in the case. "Can I have two of those tomato and mozzarella sandwiches?" I pointed.

Mr. Owen reached in and pulled them out. "And for you, sir?"

Caleb shrugged. "I'll take the turkey pesto."

Putting the sandwiches in a large white bag, he handed them to Caleb, who took out his money clip.

"Hey, I'm going to pay." I reached for my wallet. "I invited you."

"Yes, you did, but I'll get it this time. Thanks just the same." Caleb gave me the tone. It's a thing Southern guys do. They never let you pay for anything, which is incredibly sweet and annoying at the same time. Maybe he really was from the South or had lived here long enough to learn the ways of the true gentleman.

I started to argue, but I looked at Mr. Owen's face. He was expecting a good row.

I laughed. "Fine. *This time.*"

Since the tables were full and it was freezing outside, I

headed for the car, not really sure what to do next. I turned on the heat again, along with the seat warmers, and Caleb climbed into the passenger side.

"Um, it's kind of crowded in there. I can take you to your car if you want." I wasn't sure what to say.

"Oh," he looked disappointed. "I thought maybe we could hang out. Unless you have plans."

Officially we weren't supposed to have a "date" until tomorrow and I hadn't really readied myself. Still, I didn't want to be alone.

"I'm good with that. Any ideas on where we could go?"

He looked out the window. "I'd invite you to my place, but it doesn't seem appropriate. Besides, I'm renting one of the cabins on Lake Calabas and it's pretty stark. I don't have much furniture." That made sense. He was a carpenter here to do a job for a friend, and he was probably trying to save cash.

My parents' compound was full of people, as was Lulu's, and I didn't feel like grabbing the attention of the town gossips. Besides, as much as Ms. Johnnie and Ms. Helen loved Mr. Owen, they didn't appreciate anyone bringing in food from the outside.

Then it dawned on me. "I have an idea." I put the car in reverse.

Caleb looked surprised.

"There's something I want to show you," I added.

This time he almost choked on his coffee. "Kira Smythe, are you asking me to your place?"

I rolled my eyes, but smiled. "Not exactly."

"I'm intrigued," he whispered.

Me too.

Favorite Pastries

1. Cream puffs
2. Chocolate éclairs
3. Chocolate-filled croissants
4. Chocolate-filled doughnuts
5. Boston cream kolaches
6. Cherry turnovers
7. Blueberry turnovers
8. Apple turnovers
9. Cinnamon twists
10. Chocolate macadamia coconut tarts

Chapter 13

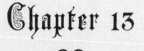

The sound of a kiss is not so loud as that of a cannon, but its echo lasts a deal longer.

THE PROFESSOR AT THE BREAKFAST TABLE
By Holmes, Oliver Wendell, 1809–1894
Call #: F-HOL
Description: xxxviii, 457 p.; 24cm

As we made our way up the stairs from the break room at the library, I shivered, more out of nervousness than anything. I'd just invited a man up to *my place*—at least my *temporary* place—and I worried what he might think.

When we made it to the top of the stairs, I flipped on the switch and the room was flooded with light.

"Wow. This is cool," Caleb said behind me. "I bet the view during the day is amazing."

I nodded. "I just discovered it today. All the years I spent here, and I never knew this loft existed." The last part came out as a whisper. I still couldn't believe I'd found this lovely little haven.

Caleb put the packages on the table. "So how did you end up with a key to the library?"

I stared at him for a few seconds, judging what I should

say, and decided to tell him the truth. "It was willed to me."
I paused. "The key, the library, the books, and all of this."
Oh, and the dead people. I wasn't going to share that bit of in-
formation until I'd explored it further.

He sat down and pulled one of the sandwiches out of the
bag. "But doesn't the library belong to the town?"

I handed him a white china plate I'd found in the cabinet
near the sink. "That's what I thought. Turns out Mrs. Canard owned everything, including the building. It's a privately owned collection she shared with the town."

He sat back in his chair. "I've never heard of such a
thing." He shook his head. "I mean there are many privately
owned libraries, but few are shared with the public like this
one. That's incredible. I mean, every book I ever asked for
she was able to provide. If she didn't have it that day, she'd
have it the next. I thought she was tied in to the state net-
work."

I handed him a paper towel and took one for myself to use
as a napkin. I'd seen linen napkins in another drawer, but I
didn't want to dirty them. I still felt like an intruder. "Me
too. Trust me, no one was more surprised than me when Mr.
Pierce showed me the will. I loved her. She was like family to
me, but I never thought . . ."

He glanced up and gave me a look. "What? There's more,
right?"

He was too intuitive for his own good.

I bit my lip. "If I don't take over the library, the whole
thing is going to be sold at auction. Can you imagine? Leaving the town without a library?"

"Huh."

"I know, right? It's crazy. I mean, I have—well, had—a

successful job in Atlanta. She knew that. I just can't understand why she would do this."

"Did she leave you some kind of note?"

I didn't want to lie, but I also didn't want to disclose the contents. "Yes. She told me it was my decision and that she knew it was a difficult one." I looked down at my food, not wanting to meet his eyes. I couldn't tell him about the being *special* part of the document.

"Damn, that's quite a load to put on someone, especially since you don't even live here anymore. So when will you put it up for auction?"

I took a bite of sandwich so I didn't have to answer right away. I shrugged my shoulders.

We ate in silence for a few minutes, both of us lost in thought.

"Could you hire someone to run it for you? Keep ownership of the place, but just have someone to help out?"

I shook my head. "She says I have to run the library. There are provisions for volunteers, but not an employee." I waved a hand. "I honestly don't have a plan yet. I have some time to make a decision, and I'm going to take that time. I never like to rush into anything."

Something crossed Caleb's face and I couldn't tell if it was disappointment or amusement. Taking a sip of coffee, I tried to make myself relax.

"Have you always been a carpenter?"

He looked up. "I've always worked with my hands. It's my way of getting rid of stress."

"Oh. And you said you were working on a friend's house?"

"Yeah. Bronwyn. Her brother, Brett, is my best friend. She bought a house here earlier in the month and I've been helping her get it fixed up. The place wasn't in such bad shape. Needs a bit of work here and there, but the conservatory where she's planting her herbs and stuff is a mess. We've had to replace the majority of the glass and find some way to get ventilation in there to protect the plants against the heat this summer. Bronwyn's had some great ideas. I think she'd been planning this garden room for a long time. She's lived all over the place but this is the first time she's really settled somewhere."

I wondered if there might be more to their relationship. Though he acted like she was a kid sister, I could see a certain fondness in his eyes when he spoke about her. Caleb didn't seem like the kind of guy who would ask a girl out while he was dating another, but I couldn't be sure. I could count the dates I'd had in the last five years on one hand. First there had been school, and then work. There had never been time.

"It's nice of you to help her out."

"I'm . . . between jobs right now, so it's good to have something to keep me busy." He frowned for a moment, and then I saw him force a smile, as if he were trying to push bad memories away. "Who knows, I may look for more work around here. I kind of like the town, and the company."

I smiled back at him, wishing I could wipe away the sadness that touched the corners of his eyes. My imagination went crazy and I thought perhaps he'd just come out of a bad relationship. Or maybe someone close to him had died.

Picking up my plate, I moved to the sink. "Have you ever had one of Mr. Owen's cream puffs?" After washing the dish, I put it in the rack and reached for his.

"I had a blueberry muffin that shamed all the others I'd

ever had before." He took the cream puff. "I'm almost afraid to eat it. What if all the other cream puffs after this pale in comparison? I could be setting myself up for a lifetime of disappointment."

I giggled. I couldn't help it. Getting hold of myself, I told him, "It doesn't matter to me. If you don't eat it, then more for me."

He pretended shock and took a healthy bite. Closing his eyes, he gave a soft moan, "Mmmmm."

"You are now officially ruined for life." I took a bite of mine and did the same thing he did. "Thankfully you forget after a few years just how magnificent the things really are. I think he uses some kind of magic."

"Well, it's that kind of town. Protected by a coven of witches—you never know who or what you are talking to. But I like it. The people are friendly and the food is the best I've ever eaten. And I've been around." He took another bite.

"Do you have a home base somewhere?"

"Yeah. I work out of Dallas. I have a condo I've renovated downtown. That's the place I call home, but I travel a lot with the job."

I thought most carpenters worked with contractors and stayed pretty close to home. There was something odd in the way he said "job."

"Caleb, what do you really do for a living?"

"For a living?" He finished off the cream puff. "I'm a writer. At least that's what's been paying the bills for the last few years."

"Seriously?"

He chuckled.

I don't know why, but I always think of writers as being bookish types—skinny, pale men and women with big, dark glasses. Caleb wasn't anything like that. He was strong and muscular, and so damn sexy it was ridiculous.

I cleared my throat. "I thought you were a carpenter. What do you write?"

"Features for magazines." He looked at his watch. "I do a lot of renovations for friends. I like to keep busy in between assignments." He stood up. "Do you know if the television works? I wanted to catch the world news if that's all right with you."

"Oh, sure. I mean, I don't know if it works, but go ahead." I cleaned up the rest of the dishes and put all the trash in one bag to carry out when I left.

He fiddled with the satellite box for the television and then settled in on the couch to watch Charlie Gibson run down the list of things that were wrong with the world.

Nervous, I wasn't sure where to sit and I landed on the opposite end of the couch. I tried to focus but my mind wandered over the day. It seemed surreal to be sitting in this room with a handsome man, watching the news.

I hadn't met that many writers before and I wanted to ask Caleb more about his job. I wondered why he didn't talk about it. If I hadn't asked, I didn't think he would have ever told me what he did. My cell phone rang and I jumped up to get it.

"Hello?"

"Kira, where are you?" It was my mom. I moved back toward the bedroom so I wouldn't disturb Caleb. I didn't feel like explaining about the library. "I'm having dinner with a friend."

"Oh." She paused. "Well, you ran out after the service rather quickly and I wanted to make sure you were okay. Any idea when you might be home?"

"No. Don't worry, I'm fine. I'll see you guys later." I sounded snappy, but I didn't mean to. I'd been out on my own for years and it was weird for my mom to check up on me.

"I didn't mean to make you angry, dear." Mom's tone was patronizing and I knew I'd hurt her feelings.

I sighed. "Mom, it's been a long day. I'm sorry if I sound curt, but I'm fine, really. I'll talk to you later."

I hung up. I know it was rude, but I didn't feel like playing twenty questions with her.

Peeking around the curvy glass wall, I took in the bedroom. There was a full-sized, cherry wood sleigh bed and a dresser that matched. A beautiful ring quilt spread across the bed. The baby powder and cinnamon tea smell was strong here.

There was so much I didn't know about Mrs. Canard. She obviously had wonderful taste when it came to antiques. And she had a sense of humor. There were whimsical touches throughout the loft, a painting of fairies here or a modern sculpture of the goddess Hera there. Odd little pieces that all seemed to fit together in this eclectic space.

"Are you okay?" Caleb was right behind me.

I jerked back into the wall of his hard chest.

He steadied me with his hands. "I bet I've asked you that thirty times today."

"Twenty-seven." I laughed. "I keep finding things here"— I pointed to the painting of the fairies over the bed—"that surprise me."

Turning me in his arms to face him, he held me there for a moment. I thought he might kiss me, and then he pulled me tight and held me. A hug so wonderful and giving, and exactly what I needed in that moment. Everywhere his body touched mine, I warmed instantly, and I wrapped my arms around him. We stood there for a full minute, not moving. Then he kissed the top of my head.

"I don't know what it is about you, but I've wanted to do that since the first day I met you," he said against my hair.

"You should have done it sooner." I backed out of his arms and my hand flew to my mouth.

He laughed.

My cheeks burned. "I have no idea where that came from."

He grabbed my hand as I passed by. Then he pulled me to him again, and this time his mouth captured mine. I couldn't think, only feel. His lips were soft and his tongue pushed through my teeth, gently exploring. My arms curved around his neck and I held on, my body thrumming.

Now he was the one to back away, but he held my hands. "I'm sorry. I've wanted to do that again since Thanksgiving." He laughed. "Maybe I should go. You've been through a lot today and I seem to be having a difficult time keeping my hands off of you."

He let go, and I wanted to say, "Stop! Come back and make love to me, you walking Adonis." But my common sense kicked in as the hormones fled.

Instead I picked up the bag of trash and said, "I'll follow you out." As I locked up the library for the second time that day I heard someone say, "Is she crazy?"

Yes. I am.

Caleb led me to my car. He started to walk away and paused. "I'll pick you up at seven tomorrow night."

I stared at him blankly.

"For our date?"

I nodded, like of course I knew what he was talking about.

"Will you be here or out at your parents'?"

I thought about trying to explain Caleb to my mom and dad.

"Um, meet me here. Bye." I waved and he did the same.

I heard giggling in my backseat. I didn't bother to turn around. Once I was on the main highway, I glanced in the rearview mirror.

"I don't know who you are, but I'm not ready to deal with you. So can it."

Someone snickered.

"I'm not joking. Leave me alone," I growled. Silence followed.

I don't know when my life took a turn toward crazy, but I wanted it back on track.

Pros and Cons of Dating Caleb

PROS
1. He's gorgeous
2. He's sweet
3. He's smart
4. He thinks I'm pretty
5. He makes me feel very warm inside

CONS
1. The last thing I need is a man in my life
2. He lives a thousand miles away
3. He's mysterious
4. He's hiding something
5. He's a man, and I can't trust him

Chapter 14

Nothing contributes so much to tranquilize the mind as a steady purpose.

FRANKENSTEIN
By Shelley, Mary Wollstonecraft, 1791–1851
Call #: F-SHE
Description: 238 p.: ill; 21cm

The next morning I woke with a case of severe determination. I'm not the kind of woman who is wishy-washy about any part of my life. Most people at work, and even my friends, describe me as the calm, intelligent, confident one. I'd been none of those things for weeks.

Part of it was the illness, and I'm certain much of it had to do with the rather emotional events I'd experienced. If I was going to move forward with my life and decide what was going to come next, I had to let go of all of that.

I'm also known for having great instincts, and it was time for me to apply that talent to my life.

The first order of business was to get to the library. Loopholes existed in every contract. Though I'd been through the will a half dozen times, I knew there would be some kind of answers either at Mrs. Canard's loft or in the library. I just had to find them.

I threw on a pair of True Religion jeans and my favorite black cashmere sweater to wear with my boots. I also grabbed a pair of slacks and a jacket for later. I didn't know how casual my date with Caleb would be. I assumed we'd probably go to Lulu's, in which case the jeans would work fine. If he had something fancier in mind, I could make a quick change into the suit.

My parents were near the entry and I felt like I had to give them some kind of explanation as to where I was going. I told them about the will and that I wasn't sure what to do. They took it in their usual laid-back fashion.

"I can't believe she thought I'd drop everything to become a librarian," I said at the end of my long diatribe.

My parents looked at one another and then at me. "She obviously saw something special in you, Kira," Mom said. "Something that made her think you would be an excellent person for the job."

"Your mother is right. We are behind you and believe in you. You'll make the right decision." My dad patted my head. "You always do."

Mom handed me a parka. "The weather's too cold for that wool coat of yours. Wear this." It was puffy and white, but I put it on anyway. I was grateful for it once I stepped outside.

"Be careful, and don't stress yourself too much," Mom added. "When the time is right, you'll know what to do." Holding on to both of my arms, she leaned in to give me a kiss on the cheek. "There are times when we must think with more than our heads. Be open and perhaps the answers will come to you." She shut the door.

I loved that they had this unfailing belief in me. I wished I felt the same way.

After a quick stop for coffee and an egg sandwich from Lulu's, I made my way to the library. The wind, which was coming out of the north with a mighty blast, made it difficult for me to shut the door. I locked it and flipped on the lights.

"She's back." I saw something out of the corner of my eye by the computer. It was more of a shadow than anything.

"Yes, I'm back and I need to do some work. So leave me alone," I said to no one in particular. All I heard in reply was the hum of the fluorescents and the sound of the heat as it kicked on.

After reading Mrs. Canard's letter, I knew the voices were probably real, but that didn't necessarily mean I was ready to accept that fact.

Depositing my bag under the large front desk, I looked for the switches for the computer and monitor. The machine came to life and I clicked her desktop icon to view her files.

Before I could open a document titled "The Librarian's Duties," there was a knock on the door. I tried to ignore it.

Then I heard a young girl's voice, actually several young girls' voices. "Hello? Please, is anyone in there?"

I grabbed the key and unlocked the door. Four young girls, who looked like high school freshmen, stood on the steps.

"Oh, yay," the small brunette in front said. She was wearing a thick jacket and pink stocking cap, her hands wrapped in matching gloves. The girls behind her hopped from foot to foot, trying to stay warm.

"Can I help you?"

They all nodded.

"Are you the new librarian?" the one in front asked.

"Not exactly."

Their faces fell.

"Crap," the girl's hand flew to her mouth. "Sorry. It's just—we have a report due on Monday, and with what happened with Mrs. Canard and the library being closed, we couldn't get the books for our research."

"Oh. Don't they have the books at your school library?" I knew I should be more helpful, but I was busy with my own research.

The girls snorted. Then I remembered our high school library. It was the size of three telephone booths stuck together. I knew they had expanded it a few years ago, but it wouldn't have as much research material as what was inside this building.

I pursed my lips. "Why don't you come on in, and we'll see what we can do."

The girl reached out and touched my arm with her gloved hand. "Thank you," she said dramatically. "You've totally saved us."

After ushering them in, it seemed weird to lock the big wooden door with the kids there, so I left it unlocked.

"What's your paper about?"

"We're studying *King Lear*. I mean, like how crazy was that guy?" A petite redhead took off her hat, and her bouncy curls fell around her shoulders. "Anyway, Mrs. Canard promised to get us some"—she turned to the tallest of the four girls—"what kind of books were they, Tanny?"

"Literary criticism," the girl answered softly.

"Right," the redhead continued. "So we have to do our own criticism and then compare it to some of the books written by others."

Now this kind of research I could handle. "Did you try the Internet?" I moved to stand behind the computer.

"Yeah, but we're only allowed to use it for one source, and we have to have five," groaned the girl who had spoken for the group outside.

I wondered if they had Mrs. Chapin for English. She was a tough one, but also a great teacher. Her lessons made you think and you had to study to get a passing grade in her class. Getting an A had taken up any extra time I might have had back then.

I clicked on the electronic catalog to bring up the books. "Looks like you guys are in luck." I pointed them in the right direction. When I looked back down, I saw a notice flashing. It was sticky note on the electronic calendar. "*King Lear*, Box A-12."

I drummed my fingers beside the keyboard. Everything in the library was organized by rows labeled according to the Dewey decimal system and none of them were marked A-12. I wondered if maybe the note meant some of the boxes in the back room.

"I'm going to check something, I'll be right back," I told the girls. Unlocking the storage room door, I clicked on the lights. Each set of boxes had a letter and a number, and then double letters like AA, BB, CC. Hmmmm.

I went to the boxes under A and looked for one marked with the number twelve. It didn't take long. It was the second box in the stack. I moved off the top one, which was heavy with books, and opened the second one. There on the top was a sticky note that read, "For Tanny and her class-mates." Three books had been tied up in a string. As I picked them up to take them up front, I saw another sticky note: "Maggie Charns's cookbook request." Under that was another stack tied in string for someone named "Bronwyn." Those were for Caleb's friend, and the bundle held books about magic.

I closed up the box and put the other one back on top of it. Mrs. Canard must have had the books on order and been waiting for library patrons to come in.

"Hello?" I heard one of the girls nearing the break room.

"I'll be right there." I flipped off the lights, vowing to check the rest of the boxes later on.

I helped the girls for more than two hours, researching King Lear and his daughters. I love research. It's one of the things I adore most about law. You dig and find case studies to support your cause, and really it's the same thing with freshman pre-AP English. By the time the girls left at two, they had a solid thesis and more than enough material to be-gin backing it up.

My stomach grumbled, and I needed a quick snack. I put on the big fluffy coat and grabbed the stocking cap my mom had stuffed in the pocket. The lunch crowd was gone at Lulu's, and Ms. Johnnie had retired to the back room to take her afternoon nap.

Ms. Helen greeted me with a hug. "I saw you this mornin', but things were a-crackin' and I didn't have a chance to say hello."

I squeezed her back. "It's good to see you. I'm starving.

Do you have any leftovers from lunch? Something light, I have a d—" I paused. I hadn't meant to blab about the date.

"Oh, I know all about your date. That young man was in here trying to find out something about you. Nosy fella, but a handsome devil. Asked about some of your favorite foods and wanted to see what we had planned tonight. I told him a couple of things, but said he needed to ask you the rest."

I smiled, pleased that Caleb wanted to make things special for tonight. I'm sure a nice shade of pink spread across my cheeks, because I could feel the heat.

"Do you want to eat here?"

I thought about the work at the library. "I'd better get it to go. Maybe just a sandwich and a cup of coffee."

"Comin' up." I watched as she put roast beef, provolone, tomatoes, and pickles between two slices of rye. My mouth watered just looking at it. I loved that she remembered I only liked lettuce in my salad, never on my sandwich.

She packed everything up and poured coffee into a large paper cup and put a lid on it. "Okay, you're all set." I handed her the money and then leaned over and kissed her cheek. "You're the best."

"Aw, now. You go on and git." But she laughed when she said it.

On the way back across the street I had a moment of inspiration. If I could find out more about the woman who owned the library before Mrs. Canard, I might have a clue as to how I ended up the sole owner of one of Sweet's most prized possessions.

I gulped down my sandwich and headed to the microfiche vault. I searched for copies of the town newspaper from more than thirty years ago. That's when Mrs. Canard had moved to Sweet.

It took almost four hours, but I found something I thought might be helpful. It was an article about Mrs. Canard taking over the library from Mary Elizabeth Barnes, who had died three days before.

NEW LIBRARIAN
TAKES CHARGE

Mrs. Mabel Canard is the new proprietor of the Sweet Library, which was bequeathed to her by the late Mrs. Mary Elizabeth Barnes.

"Mrs. Barnes was my mentor and a dear friend. I feel she has given me the greatest gift, one that I shall always cherish."

The article went on to talk about how Mrs. Canard planned to institute after-school and adult literacy reading programs, and how she would add several book clubs and allow organizations to use the reading room for meetings after hours.

Hmmm. Interesting, but not exactly what I wanted.

Dogs barked—a little yippy one, and then another with a deep scary tone, and it was if they were two feet away. But there were no dogs anywhere near me.

Someone knocked on the door, and I glanced down at my watch. It was six fifty-two. *Crap.* I'd lost track of time.

I ran for the door and pulled it open. Caleb stood there in a leather jacket and a cable-knit sweater with jeans, looking fresh and as gorgeous as ever.

"Hi." He smiled.

"Hey, come on in." I opened the door and stared past him. "Did you happen to see some dogs?"

Caleb gave me a strange look. "No."

"Huh. I'm running a little behind. Can you give me five minutes to freshen up?"

He followed me up the stairs to the loft. "Sure, I'm early anyway."

Washing my hands in the bathroom, I reapplied lipstick and freshened my powder and eye shadow. Adding a little more mascara for glamour, I worried what to do with the hair I'd piled on my head hours ago. I pulled out the silver clamp and for once it behaved, falling in loose waves around my shoulders.

Not bad. I ran my fingers through it for a quick fluff, washed my hands, and decided that since he was casual, my cashmere sweater and jeans would be fine. A quick dab of Angel on my wrists and I was set.

He glanced at his watch. "That was fast. You look beautiful, by the way."

I looked down at the floor, embarrassed and incredibly pleased at the same time.

"So where are we off to?"

"That's a surprise."

I bit my lip. "Well, because I'm worried she'll say something, I have to admit Ms. Helen told me you'd been asking about me."

He laughed. "That woman can't keep a secret to save her life. Did she tell you everything?"

"No." I smiled. "Just that you'd been asking about me."

"Well, good." As we were heading downstairs, he stopped

and turned to face me where we stood on the landing. "I'm kind of known for being frank and saying what I mean."

His serious expression worried me. "Okay." *Where's he going with this?*

"I've been on a lot of dates, but none that made me as nervous as this one." He reached out and took my hand. "There's something about you. I don't know. Anyway, if I make a fool of myself, that's why."

I giggled like one of the teens who had been in the library earlier in the afternoon. I don't know what made me do it, but I couldn't stop. "I'm with you on the being nervous. Let's just go have some fun. I could use a little."

At the front door, I heard an elderly man whisper, "That boy's in trouble."

Why First Dates Are Usually Horrible

1. You know nothing about the other person
2. Nerves
3. Queasy stomach
4. You're trying so hard to find something to say that you don't hear the other person
5. That awkward moment at the end where you know you'll never see the guy again. Or he's way more into you than you are him.

Chapter 15

❧

Men always want to be a woman's first love. That's their clumsy vanity. We women have a more subtle instinct about things. What we like is to be a man's last romance.

A WOMAN OF NO IMPORTANCE
By Wilde, Oscar, 1854–1900
Call #: F-WIL
Description: iv, 216 p., 23cm

Dating in a small town is tricky at best. There's not much privacy, and by the time the night is over, everyone knows your business.

I knew this before we ever set foot in Lulu's. When we entered the diner there was a momentary hush, and then everyone started talking again.

Caleb didn't lead me to the only empty booth in the full diner. Instead he picked up a picnic basket at the register.

Picnics are at the top of the romance meter, but has he realized that it's twenty degrees with a wind chill of zero outside?

He handed over the cash for the meal, and I didn't bother to dig for my wallet. From our recent encounter, I knew he'd have none of that. Even though we'd spent the previous evening together, this was our first "official" date.

As we left, I noticed Margie at one of the tables by the

window. She was out of her nurse's scrubs. Across from her, a cute dark-haired guy had stashed his cowboy hat on the back of the chair.

I gave her a quick wave and she winked at me. *I need to call her for lunch soon.*

In that moment, I decided to just go with the flow. My whole life I'd felt like I didn't really fit in here, so I didn't understand why I was so worried about what everyone thought.

I laughed.

"Hey, what's the joke?" Caleb turned on the ignition of his huge truck. It was much more luxurious inside than I'd imagined. The beige leather interior was accented with touches of black. He had an MP3 player belting out Tim McGraw. I don't know that much about country music, but I'd grown to like it while living in Atlanta. Justin loved going to gay cowboy bars, at least he did before he met Rob. I enjoy all kinds of music, though my first love will always be classical. Give me Igor Stravinsky's Symphony in C and I'm a happy woman.

"This town. For a moment back there I was worried about all the gossip. By nine o'clock tonight everyone will know that we were on a date."

He chuckled. "Oh yeah. We'll be the talk of the town, until someone else catches their attention." He glanced over at me. "Are you worried about the gossip?"

I sighed. "No. It's a date. I just never like being the center of—" I stared out the window. "Hey, where are we going?"

He laughed again. "It's a surprise."

I didn't want to be a spoilsport, but I'd had enough surprises over the last few weeks. About a mile east of town he pulled up in front of Young's Bar, a large lodgelike structure with neon lights. The only watering hole for miles around, it had an eclectic clientele. Or at least that's what I'd heard. I'd never been inside, but judging from the parking lot's mix of pickups, BMWs, Mercedes, and Buicks, the rumors looked to be true.

I've been in many bars over the years, usually meeting clients, sometimes to hang out with Justin or acquaintances, but I'd never actually been in a real Texas honky-tonk.

Go with the flow, Kira.

"Here we are." Caleb pulled his truck into a space on the right side of the building. He glanced at his watch. "We better hurry or we'll miss the opening."

Huh?

I followed him into the bar. The loud music and smoke-filled room I'd expected didn't exist. There were chairs lined up in front of a huge screen that was unrolling from the ceiling. I followed Caleb to a couple of seats in the back.

The rest of the seats were filled with an array of people eagerly awaiting whatever was on the big projector at the back of the room.

"What is this?" I whispered in his ear, taking in his piney scent as I did.

"Dinner"—he raised the basket—"and a movie." About that time the room darkened and the projector clicked on. I couldn't help but smile when the title screen read *The Philadelphia Story*. Cary Grant, Katharine Hepburn, and James Stewart—it's my all-time favorite movie. I love the dialogue, the actors, the sets—well, everything about the film.

I couldn't believe how lucky I was to be in a bar in West Texas watching this film on our first date. I didn't know how he'd managed it, but it brought Caleb to the top of the Cool Guy list.

A half hour into the film, around the third time C. K. Dexter Haven, played by Cary, raises his eyebrow in sheer mirth, Caleb handed me a bottle of Coke and an Italian sub from Lulu's. I'd forgotten he was there. I nodded my thanks and dug in. I know it's terrible, and that I probably should have been paying more attention to my date, but I was totally absorbed in the movie.

I did happen to take notice of his arm wrapping around my shoulders after he'd finished his meal. It felt good to be close to him, and he seemed to enjoy the film. At least he laughed in all the right places.

When it ended, I let out a happy sigh. "I don't know how you made it happen, but you couldn't have picked a better movie. How did you know that's my favorite one? I doubt even the gang at Lulu's could get that one right. Did you talk to Sam?"

He shrugged. "A man has to have his secrets."

I shook my head. "Doesn't matter. It's been a wonderful night." Everyone around us moved their chairs off the dance floor and back to the tables. Caleb and I did the same.

"Night's not over yet." He tossed our trash from dinner into the can beside the bar.

"It's not?"

He gave me a quizzical look. "It's only nine o'clock. We still have the dancing portion of the evening, which will commence at nine thirty when the band hits the stage."

"Oh, that's so—um, I don't know how to dance to country

music," I confessed. The words flew off my tongue before I could stop them.

He motioned a waitress to our table. "I don't think you need to worry about it. I'm not that great, so we should be a good match."

A woman in a short T-shirt, tight Wranglers, and cowboy boots made her way to our table. Her breasts were spilling out of her scoop-necked shirt, but Caleb didn't seem to take any notice.

He grabbed my hand across the table. "What would you like, Kira?"

I started to order a cabernet, but it really wasn't that kind of place. "What are you having?"

"A Bud," he answered, watching me carefully.

I'm not a big fan of beer, but I had spent many a study group in brew houses in Boston. Being from Texas, I always felt a loyalty to the beers from here. "Do you have Shiner Bock?"

She nodded.

"I'll take one."

Turning away from me, she gave Caleb a wink and pursed her ruby lips. "I'll be right back."

He gave her a short smile and turned his attention to me. *Score one for Kira.* I know it's petty, but I liked that he didn't even really notice her.

"So, back to the dancing. I can teach you the two-step. I've got that one down pretty good. I'm wobbly with the waltz." He squeezed my hand in his and my stomach did a weird tumble.

"As long as you don't sue for any broken toes, I'll give it a try," I joked.

His face turned serious. "You can step on my toes any time you want. I just want you close to me."

My heart went *ba-bump* and I nearly fell out of my chair. His hand was so warm in mine, and I didn't want to let go.

Once our beers arrived, we took a few sips and then Caleb led me out to the dance floor. The woman on stage sang about having had too much tequila the night before. I definitely related to the song. I'd done that in law school a few times after some tough finals, and had a hard time remembering what had transpired during my tequila haze.

Taking my hand, he rested it on his hip. Then he took my other hand in his. "You might want to hold on to my belt loop at first," he suggested.

I wound my finger into it and held on.

"Now, you just do the reverse of whatever I do. We're going to take two quick steps, then a slow third, a pause, and then we'll do it again."

The first time he stepped, I moved the wrong foot and almost slipped on the sawdust-covered floor.

He smiled. "I told you that belt loop would come in handy."

I know my cheeks were pink with embarrassment.

We tried again, a little slower, and by the time we made the corner turn I had the basics down.

"Stop looking at your feet and don't pick them up so much, it's more of a slide."

I did what he instructed.

"I knew you could do it." His fingers wrapped around my waist and tapped to the music. Even though the dance floor was crowded with couples, I noticed no one but him.

The next song was a little slower, and this time he pulled

me tight against him with his hand at the small of my back. I'm not sure I've ever felt so intimate with someone in front of so many other people.

With my breasts tight against his chest and my head wedged at the crook of his neck, it was almost too much. He smelled so good, and I wanted to let my lips loose on the sensitive skin where his shirt opened.

"This just feels right," Caleb whispered, splaying his hand on the small of my back.

I gave a happy sigh.

We stayed like that for hours, and only stopped when the band took a break.

The band quit at one, and we headed for Caleb's truck. After the warmth of the bar, the frigid air seemed startling at first.

As he drove back to town we were both quiet. Not the strained kind, but comfortable. It was one of the best dates I'd ever been on, and I didn't want it to stop.

I considered asking him to come back to the library with me, but I don't sleep with guys on a first date.

And since I'd usually only had first dates . . .

Before I knew it we were in front of the library and my heart fell.

"Listen," he turned to look at me, "I have to take care of some business out of town and I won't be back for a while."

I tried not to show my disappointment. "Okay."

"Trust me, if I didn't have to go, I wouldn't." He took both of my hands in his. "I have no idea what's going on between you and me, but I can barely stand to be away from you. Which honestly scares the hell out of me. And we've only had one date."

My spirits picked up instantly. "Really?"

He nodded. "I don't know if you're heading back to Atlanta, or wherever, but I want you to call me. Any time." He handed me a small business card with his name and cell. "I'll find you, wherever you are, when I get back."

I smiled.

"At the most I'll be gone two weeks." He paused. "I kind of hope it doesn't take that long. What I'm trying to tell you is . . . I had one of the best times of my life tonight, and I know you may be two thousand miles away before I can make it back here. I sound like an idiot."

I grabbed his lapel and pulled him to me. "No, you don't. I feel it too." Then I reached up and kissed him. I meant for it to be a quick peck, but his arms circled me and pulled me tight into him.

We kissed for a full two minutes before he lifted his head away from mine. "You're making it tougher to leave."

I smiled. "Good."

"I know it's a lot to ask"—he looked down at our intertwined hands—"but could you maybe not two-step with anyone else until I get back?"

I bit my lip to keep from giggling with joy, and nodded. I liked that he was a little possessive.

He kissed me again and I realized I could totally lose myself in this man.

An hour later he bundled me into the Lexus and insisted on following me out to my parents' place. Once we arrived I waved him off, and he flashed his headlights.

I sat at the end of the drive for a few minutes, not really wanting to go inside. I love my parents, but I knew they'd ask about where I'd been. I wasn't ready to talk about it yet.

My head filled with questions. I hadn't had much experience with men, but I was certain I'd just fallen in love with Caleb on our first date. Maybe it was lust, but it didn't feel like it. I did know I'd never felt like this before and it was damn scary.

Five Reasons I Wouldn't Want to Be a Movie Star

1. Paparazzi
2. Air kisses
3. The phrase, "Let's do lunch"
4. Hair extensions
5. Botoxed expressions: How do you know what anyone is really feeling?

Chapter 16

✢

Honest people don't hide their deeds.

WUTHERING HEIGHTS
By Brontë, Emily, 1818–1848
Call #: F-BRO
Description: 492 p.; 24 cm

The next day, thanks to my somewhat devious nature, I was able to sneak out of the house before my parents came back from their morning hike.

Deciding the library was the best place to hide out, I stopped by The Bakery for a warm croissant, coffee, and a sandwich for later. A light snow fell and it was cold enough that it stuck to the ground. Soon Sweet would be a winter wonderland.

I gobbled down the pastry and went in search of the file on the computer about the librarian's duties. While I really had no intention of becoming a librarian, I would try to keep things running. That is, while I searched for a loophole in the will.

When I opened the document, I saw that it was long—almost twenty pages. I sighed. I knew being a librarian was harder than it looked, but there was everything from emptying the return boxes to shelving books to developing community programs to consider.

"I had no idea," I whispered to no one in particular and was surprised when, for once, no one answered back. Maybe the dead people were taking a break, but I didn't think I could be that lucky.

One of the main databases Mrs. Canard used to look up research was LexisNexis. I booted up the homepage and tried to think of something to search. I typed in Caleb Price, just for fun, as he was still very much on my mind.

Thirteen hundred sources came up, including several for AP photos.

Wow. There must be a lot of Caleb Prices around.

I clicked on the first link, to a Dallas business journal. There was Caleb's picture alongside his article about insider trading and how his investigation broke the story.

It was well written and decisive. The article noted his life had been threatened more than once for messing with some high-powered people. He'd led the police in the right direction and all of the criminals were in jail.

I spent the next three hours reading articles that covered everything from wars around the world to starving children to corrupt businessmen.

Caleb was a brilliant writer, and I knew nothing about him. I'd spent the last few days with the man and he was a complete enigma. Carpenter, schmarpenter. He was a highly respected journalist.

I picked up the phone and called Sam.

He didn't answer his cell, so I left him a message to call me.

Each link I clicked on frightened me a little more. The man I'd fallen for constantly put his life in danger in the pursuit of the truth.

Then there was the glamorous side of his life. Not only was he deemed the hottest bachelor in Dallas, he was named one of the top ten in the country.

I put my chin in my hands. What did he see in me, a boring lawyer?

There were pictures of him with supermodels on his arm and in the company of a bevy of actresses and heiresses. He smiled, and he was gorgeous, but in the photos the grin never quite reached his eyes.

Now I knew why even when he was laughing, there was an aura of sadness about him. He'd seen things most of us only read about in newspapers or magazines.

Caleb Price was a complicated package, and for the life of me, I didn't understand why he was hanging out in Sweet helping a friend's sister.

Maybe she's more than a friend.

I sighed. He'd been spending most of his time with me, but she'd been out of town.

My cell rang.

"Kira, what's up?" Sam was on the line.

"Why didn't you tell me?" I whined, though I didn't mean for it to come out that way.

"About?"

"Caleb?" I added.

"Um, you're going to have to bring me up to speed on the conversation. I'm lost."

"You didn't tell me he's some big-time investigative

reporter or that he's man of the year. The man dates super-models, for God's sake."

Sam laughed and it made me angry.

"I'm serious."

"I can hear that. Listen, I didn't think about it. I just met the guy. I knew he wrote for a living, but I really don't know that much about him. He's nice, seems to adore you. I think he's in Sweet to kind of get away from that celebrity hype. The guy's been in Kuwait, Iraq, Bosnia, the Sudan, and everywhere else in the world where there's been a war. He likes it here because it's quiet. What's the big deal?"

Men.

"The big deal is—what is *wrong* with him? Why the heck is a guy that perfect hanging out with me?"

"Hey, he's a nice guy, Kira. Just because he likes you doesn't mean there's something wrong with him." He paused. "Well . . ."

"Don't go there," I snarled.

"I'm just saying . . ." He had the nerve to laugh.

"I'm done with you. Go take care of your sick people."

"Man, touchy. Listen, if you want, I'll check around town and see what people have to say about him. Have you seen that witch he's helping? Geez, she's hot. Maybe you guys could set us up on a date."

"I'm hanging up now before I say something very nasty." I pressed the off button.

If I was in love, I had to make myself fall out of it before Caleb came back. Simple. It probably wasn't love at all. I mean, who falls in love on a first date? The whole idea was insane.

No more Caleb. My focus needed to be on the library and

figuring out what to do about that will. I didn't have time for some relationship that probably didn't even really exist. I was some port in the storm for the guy, an interesting sidebar during his stay in Sweet.

I felt foolish. *Time to get to work, Kira.* I sat and made a list of everything I needed to do at the library.

I'd do whatever it took to push that man out of my brain.

Cool Guys to Obsess Over Instead of Caleb

1. Jude Law
2. Cary Grant (dead, but cute)
3. Paul Newman (old, but cute)
4. Paul Walker
5. Hugh Jackman
6. Matthew Fox
7. Steve Carell
8. Paul Blackthorne
9. Hugh Grant
10. Hugh Laurie
11. Hugh Dancy (I seem to have a thing for Hughs)

Chapter 17

She did her work with the thoroughness of a mind which reveres
details and never quite understands them.

BABBITT
By Lewis, Sinclair, 1885–1951
Call #: F-LEW
Description: 392 p.; 22cm

I've always had the greatest respect for Mrs. Canard, but
it doubled over the last week. The woman must have
worked nonstop for the last thirty years. Being a librarian is
way tougher than I ever imagined.

In addition to answering questions over the phone and in
person, most of which people could have used Google for,
there was an extraordinarily long list of tasks that must be
performed each day. From cataloguing and reviewing titles
to researching and managing receipts of purchased items.
Then there are adult and children's programs, and maintain-
ing the collections. This is a private library and she had several collections from the literary and art worlds.

Overwhelming, to say the least.

I hit the floor running every morning and fell into bed
every night since opening the library on Monday. I don't

know what made me do it. After the girls from the high school had come in, it felt ridiculous to keep the library from the town residents just because I couldn't make up my mind.

And I needed to stay busy.

The headhunter, Cynthia Jordan, called daily and finally I told her I wouldn't be making any decisions until the end of the month. Once I said the words, I felt better. I told her that someone close to me had died and I needed to take care of family business before I took on a new position. Besides, no one starts a new job three weeks before Christmas. She wasn't happy with the news, but I was firm in my determination.

Over the last few days I'd helped kids with homework, taught adults learning to read, and tried very hard not to notice the strange things that were happening around me, including hearing a yippy little invisible dog and his huge wolf-sounding pal.

A couple of times I swore I saw Mr. Greenblatt, who had been my imaginary friend when I was a kid. He'd been the pharmacist in town and always snuck me a sucker at the drugstore when my mom wasn't looking. When he died, I didn't really understand what had happened and my imagination had turned him into a friend.

But twenty-five-year-olds don't have imaginary friends.

Monday, when I walked in, I saw several shadows in the shapes of people. Though I wanted to scream—out of frustration, not fright—I didn't. I closed my eyes and wished them away. When I opened my eyes again, they were gone.

Sort of gone, that is. One day at lunch, I thought I saw a hand around the teapot. I blinked and it was gone.

Then there were the books. If I couldn't find something that was listed as checked in, it would suddenly appear on the desk. I'd turn to look at the computer to make sure I was right, and when I'd glance back at the desk, there would lie the book I'd been looking for. More than a little freaky, but I've done my best to pretend I don't notice these things.

On Wednesday I found several boxes of Christmas decorations and wondered if I could force myself into the same giddiness that seemed to have overtaken the entire town. There were garlands and lights strung in every window and on the lampposts. Festively dressed trees with lights sparkling, and plastic snowmen, Santas, and candy canes were everywhere.

Mr. McGregory and his Beautify the Town team put up a large wreath between the gargoyles over the front door of the library and strung garlands down the long columns.

"We take care of the outside, you do the inside," the elderly man informed me.

I never did holiday decorating for my apartment in Atlanta, but when the kids came for the Homework Help session Wednesday afternoon and asked when I was putting up the tree, I hunted down the boxes.

After they read and finished their homework, they helped me decorate. I baked cookies and we broke the number-one library rule of silence and played Christmas carols on the small CD player I'd brought down from the loft.

I laughed so hard my stomach hurt as the kids danced around with the garlands and made earrings out of ornaments. Even the three teens who had been studying for midterms were into it. They helped me string the lights and hang the ornaments on the higher branches of the tree.

"My mom always has to do everything herself," complained Tanny. She was a bright girl who'd spent many afternoons here studying for her classes since she'd come with her friends that one Saturday. "I never seem to be able to do anything right when she's around."

She reminded me a lot of myself at her age, all gangly arms and legs, and hair so wild nothing could tame it. If we became better friends, I'd someday share my secrets of the gel-mousse combo to de-frizz. I squeezed her shoulders. "Well, you must have been watching her carefully all these years, because you are doing a great job."

Nathan Marks, who always sat at Tanny's table, but seldom did his homework, held up a shiny gold star. "Can I put this on the top?"

"Sure."

He jumped up onto the front counter and placed it gently on top of the tree.

Tanny ran around and flipped the switch and all of the lights came on. Everyone clapped.

I sighed. "It is pretty." We'd set up the nine-foot tree by the entry, next to the large counter. It meant I'd have to walk around the right side for the next few weeks, but it was worth it.

"It feels like Christmas now," Tanny whispered.

Holding my hands behind my back, I agreed.

We finished hanging the garlands in front of the counters and the smaller children completed their paper snowflakes for the tree.

At six the parents arrived to pick up the kids and suddenly

it all seemed very quiet. I'd just turned off the music and the lights when I heard whispering.

"Who's there?" I flipped the switch again.

"We were just saying everything looks beautiful. You did a wonderful job," the same husky voice I'd heard at the ashram said.

"Where are you?" The disembodied voices still freaked me out, but not to the point where I wanted to wet myself every time I heard them.

He chuckled. "Right in front of you. Don't worry, you'll be able to see me soon. This thing happens in stages. You'll be able to see a few of us now and then, or bits of us. Before you know it, you won't be able to tell the living from the dead."

I cringed. I'd been seeing shadows the last few days, usually out of the corners of my eyes. "I'm going upstairs. You guys stay down here. I don't care if this happens in stages or not, I'm not ready."

I heard several people laughing as I ran up the steps, and I let the break room door slam. I don't know why I thought it was a good idea to stay upstairs when I knew about all the strangeness below. Honestly, it was the only place I had any real privacy. My parents' business was thriving and if I left my room at their house I'd bump into strangers. At least here I could run around in my pajama bottoms and a T-shirt and not worry about it.

Most nights I was so tired, I fell asleep instantly. I could only hope tonight was one of those nights.

I'd just settled into my favorite fluffy reading chair with Jodi Thomas's latest. I'm not a big fan of historical romance, but she writes about Texas and has characters that grab me by the heart and don't let go. Soon after page five, I heard whimpering.

"What in the world?"

The sound grew louder as I neared the landing. Down at the bottom of the stairs was a huge dog, more of a horse really.

He pawed the first step and let out a low howl.

"How did you get in here? I think I would have noticed a dog the size of a small horse entering the library." I didn't know what to do. "Are you okay?" *Like he can answer, Kira.* "Um, are you hungry?" He pawed the step again. "I don't have much experience with animals. You aren't lunging for my throat or trying to kill me, so you're probably just hungry. You want to come up?"

The dog yelped and bounded up the stairs. He circled the large rug in front of the couch twice and plopped down with a happy sigh.

"Well, okay." I reached down and patted his shaggy head. The gray hair was much softer than it looked. I thought about calling animal control, but they would have been closed. The dog seemed perfectly happy to sleep on my rug. I couldn't shove it back outside, where the temperature was below freezing.

I put water and some leftover stew in bowls on the floor just in case the horse was hungry.

I sat back in my chair and watched the massive ball of fur sleep.

Where did you come from and how did you get in here? It snored and I laughed.

I picked up my book and lost myself in the story about a rugged Texas Ranger and the woman he wanted.

Several chapters later I looked up and the dog had moved.

"Where did you go?" I searched the apartment and then the library downstairs. The animal was nowhere to be found.

Great, now I'm seeing ghost dogs. I need serious help.

Favorite Dog Names

1. Nike
2. Spike
3. Noodles
4. Zorro
5. Scooby Doo
6. Tipper
7. Bobo
8. Max
9. Jetson
10. Dixie

Chapter 18

Life isn't long enough for love and art.

THE MOON AND SIXPENCE
By Maugham, Somerset (William Somerset),
1874–1965
Call #: F-MAU
Description: xi, 220 p.; 22cm

I was at the front desk, searching for what year the Beatles' *White Album* was released, when a vase of deep red roses came into my peripheral vision.

Looking up, I saw a hand holding a Waterford crystal vase with at least a dozen of the beautiful flowers. My eyes trailed up the arm to Caleb's gorgeous face.

I'm mad at him, I reminded myself. *He can't just woo me with a bunch of flowers.* I held up a finger and whispered, "One minute."

He nodded.

"Sir, the album was released in 1968," I said to the guy on the phone.

"Aha! 1968! Sucka," he yelled to someone on the other end of the line. "Give me my twenty bucks." And he hung up.

Turning to Caleb again, I bit the inside of my lip. I was confused. More than that, I was a little hurt that he couldn't share one of the biggest parts of his life with me—his job.

We hadn't known each other that long, but that didn't give him an excuse to hide something so significant.

He leaned in to kiss me, but I pulled back.

Frowning, he pushed the flowers to the side. "What's wrong?"

Just then the door banged open and a group of kids from the junior high wandered in.

"Library closes in ten," I reminded them.

"Yes, ma'am, Ms. Smythe," said Jason, a twelve-year-old dark-haired boy who had been spending a great deal of time in the arts section.

I heard the boys snickering.

"Kira, tell me what's wrong." Caleb put his palm down on the desk.

This time I frowned and put a finger to my lips, shushing him. "Later." I pointed to the back, where the children had gone.

Caleb didn't look happy, but he walked off toward the break room.

Two minutes later Jason had made his selection and brought it to the desk. It was a book about Rubens and featured his baroque paintings of women and angels.

"Excellent choice. I had no idea you loved art so much. I'm especially fond of some of his nudes," I said nonchalantly.

At this Jason and the other three boys gasped.

"Painting the human body can be difficult, and Rubens

made figures seem so lush and romantic," I continued seriously. "And the detail, the colors. Well, their beauty is beyond words."

They all looked down at the ground as if their shoelaces were doing a fantastical dance.

"Uh, I didn't know there was *naked* pictures in there," Jason said with his Southern twang. "If I get somethin' like that my momma's gonna be mad." Then he lifted his head. "Maybe you shouldn't have them kind of books in a library. I mean there's kids and stuff around."

I gave him my best serious look. "Yes, but we can't censor art. It's one of our greatest treasures." Free access to information was the librarians' creed. I'd learned that in the list of duties. I looked at my watch. "You boys better go home. I would imagine your parents are worrying. It's almost five."

"Yes, ma'am," they said in unison as they scurried out.

Trying not to laugh, I followed them and locked the door behind them.

Caleb clapped behind me. "I'd say you have the makings of one hell of a librarian."

I turned and leaned back against the door. "I've learned a lot in the last week."

"Want to tell me why you're mad at me?"

Picking up the book from the counter, I moved to the arts section to shelve it. "No."

He followed me. "What happened? A few days ago . . . Do you feel differently?"

I couldn't look at him. I was mad, but still very in love and I wouldn't lie. "A few days ago I didn't know you were a highly respected investigative reporter. You lied to me, and I can't deal with that kind of thing."

"I didn't lie, I just didn't throw everything at you at once."

Walking around the back of the bookcase I moved to the front to turn off the lights. "You let me think you were a carpenter who wrote a few articles to pay the bills." It sounded so stupid when I said it.

"You'd rather I were a carpenter than a writer?"

"It doesn't matter to me what you do for a living, I just want to know the truth. I can't stand people who lie."

He moved in front of me. "How can you say that? You're a lawyer."

I glared at him. "I'm really not in the mood for bad lawyer jokes."

"I don't know what to say, except I'm sorry. I don't run around telling everyone what I do. It's part of my nature to keep things close to the vest. If you'd asked me about the writing I would have told you, but I was more than happy for you to think it was something I did on the side."

Moving into the break room, I rinsed out the coffeepot. "It's not just that. This, whatever it is." I waved a hand. "We had one date. I don't know where I'm going to be in two weeks. You're here. Or in Dallas. It seems silly to get into something that can't possibly work. I don't want to do this. It's not a good time for me to be involved with anyone. I'm a wreck, really. A total mess. And if I told you half the stuff that's going on with me, you'd never be-lieve me."

"You're right." He leaned back against the door frame.

I almost dropped the pot. "Um, good. I'm glad you see

reason." I dried it off with a dish towel and set it down on the counter.

"We should definitely go on a second date."

I swung around. "What? No, you didn't hear me right. I can't date you."

"Yep. Tonight." He ignored me. "I think we should go to dinner and see if maybe that first date was a fluke. That's what has you freaked out. No one ever has a first date that perfect. They're supposed to be awkward and awful and then if you have the courage, you try it again. That's how you find out if someone is worth the second date, if you're willing to suffer through it all again."

I squinted. "I don't think I'm following you."

"I'm asking you on a second date."

"I get that part, but I don't get the reason why. I just told you this is fruitless. There's no reason for us to go out again." Even as I said the words I regretted them. There was nothing I wanted to do more than kiss him.

"We're going out on a second date, because that's when people get to know each other. Then they go on a third date and learn even more. Hell, by the third date we might absolutely hate each other."

I took a deep breath. "I really like you, Caleb. You're a nice guy, but let's just part as friends. Please. My life has more complications than I can deal with at the moment, and I don't have room for more."

His face fell.

Be strong, Kira.

"If that's the way you want it." He pushed off the wall and moved into the darkened library. Then he turned back. "Did you tell me everything?"

"Uh."

"Did you? You want full disclosure, but you didn't happen to mention what happened to you that made you so sick you were knocked out for almost a month. Or why you are really staying in a town that you ran away from years ago to keep this place open."

The picture of Melinda flashed through my mind. "Th-that's not the same." I stuttered a bit, and I never do that.

"It's exactly the same." He stared at me. "Do you care about me?"

"Yes." I couldn't lie.

"I'm going to scare the hell out of you now." Moving closer, he put his hands on my arms. "One date, and I think I'm in love with you."

I focused on his chest, unable to meet his eyes. There was no way this man could be in love with me. I mean, I'd fallen for him fast, but this wasn't possible.

"I know it's crazy. I don't fall in love. I've never fallen in love. But while I was gone all I could think about was you. Nearly got myself killed because of it. I wanted to kiss you again and to hold you against me."

My hands clenched by my sides, nerves so raw I was afraid to speak. It couldn't be true. He was crazy.

"Look at me." He lifted my chin. "Tell me you didn't think about me. That once I left, you didn't dream about our night together on that dance floor."

"I don't dream much." It was a lie. I had dreams all the time now, many of them featuring Caleb as the leading man. I tried to pull my chin out of his hand, but he wouldn't let me. I cut my eyes to the right. "Maybe I thought about it some."

"You're honest to a fault," he whispered. "You can't lie. You won't." Leaning down, he kissed me. "Tell me you want me to leave, Kira," he said against my lips.

"Where were you?"

"Just outside of Iraq."

I sighed. "What were you doing there?"

"Working on a story."

"About?"

He sighed. "I can't tell you that until it breaks, but it has to do with arms dealers."

"You almost died?"

He sat back on the edge of the table and pulled me with him. "Yes. We were on our way to an interview and I wasn't paying attention and almost ran the Humvee off the road. I was thinking about a pretty, if stubborn, blonde in Sweet."

"You should pay more attention to the road," I grumped.

"Okay." He tried hard not to smile, but I saw his grin.

"I would have been really angry if you'd died."

He held up his hand in a scout's-honor pose. "I promise to do better next time."

I wasn't sure I could handle a next time. His job was dangerous and would always be so. Loving him meant signing up for that.

"I don't like that your job is so full of secrets. It scares me."

"One thing I've learned is that we all have secrets. There's no getting around it. I know you have yours. I can see the sadness when it rolls over your face at odd times. And I hope someday you'll be able to share that with me.

"I'll tell you anything you want to know if I can. I won't lie to you, but I may not be able to tell you everything when it comes to the job."

I moved my arms up to encircle his neck. "I saw pictures of you. You were Dallas's sexiest bachelor. There are tons of photos of you with different women there and in New York City."

He sighed again. "If you're asking if I have a past, then the answer is yes. It's only our second date, but if you want to know how many women I've slept with I'll tell you." His brow furrowed. "What I can remember, anyway."

I groaned. The very idea of him in another woman's arms was torture. "That's terrible. And no, I don't want to know. I just want to know why me, and why now?"

"You're smart, beautiful, and a mystery. Every time I see you I feel like I discover something new, and you always manage to surprise me. I'm beginning to believe that cliché that you can't choose who you love, it just happens."

I laughed. I'm more reserved than most people I know, but I never thought of myself as mysterious. I liked that he saw me that way.

"Love? Are you sure it isn't lust?"

He smirked. "I won't lie. I want you in the worst way, but it's more than that. Something more to do with this." He pointed at my heart.

I wanted him in the worst way too. "So this second date, is it going to take a lot of effort? It's been a really long day."

"Hold on just a minute." He walked into the library and came back with the roses, some grocery bags, and a tote full of items. "I was going to cook you dinner. Either here, or out at your parents' house."

I pursed my lips. "You can cook?"

"Yep."

"What did you bring?"

He looked in the bag. "Fresh pasta and stuff to make my own marinara, and meatballs. Caesar salad, and some fudge brownie cheesecake from Mr. Owen."

"Huh. Well, I'd hate for all that food to go to waste." I sighed. "I kind of like spaghetti and meatballs."

Setting everything on the counter, he reached for me and kissed me hard until I was breathless.

I opened my eyes to see him staring at me again, as if he were trying to read my mind.

"Yes." I cleared my throat. "I'm definitely hungry."

A slow smile slipped over his face. "I think I can do something about that."

Chapter 19

❧❧

I don't want to repeat my innocence. I want the pleasure of losing it again.

THIS SIDE OF PARADISE
By Fitzgerald, F. Scott (Francis Scott), 1896–1940
Call #: F-FIT
Description: 243 p.; 24cm

Dinner was amazing. Caleb's meatballs were delicious. (Yes, I know that sounds disgusting.) In his tote bag he had candlesticks with tapers and a beautiful creamy lace tablecloth from Ireland.

It was romantic and sexy, and I couldn't wait to see how the night developed.

He helped wash up the dishes, and while I dried them he popped a movie into the DVD player. This one was *Bringing Up Baby*, another of my Cary Grant and Katharine Hepburn favorites. He had thought of everything.

As I dried the final plate and put it back in the cabinet, I made up my mind. I'd follow this thing between us through and see where it went. My life was in such chaos, what was one more thing?

Determined, I made my way to the couch and found Caleb sound asleep.

The man can't handle his carbs. Poor guy probably needed a short nap after his travels. I slid off his shoes and pulled his legs up on the couch so he could stretch out. Grabbing the quilt from the back of the sofa, I pulled it over him.

I turned on the DVD and made sure the volume was low so it wouldn't wake him. I sat down in the cushy recliner. Lost in the antics of Hepburn and Grant, I forgot about Caleb until the ending credits came up.

When I glanced over, he was still sound asleep. I laughed. Okay. Well, this was one exciting second date.

Getting up, I turned off the television and went in search of a book to read. I'd brought a few up from the library and stored them in the bookcases. In the mood for something light and funny, I picked *Gil's All Fright Diner* by A. Lee Martinez. I'd read the first couple of chapters a few nights before and he made me laugh with his story of vampires, werewolves, zombie cows, and a teen witch.

I took the knitted dark green afghan off the bed and sat on the recliner. Caleb snored softly, and I settled down to read.

The next thing I knew someone tickled my ear.

I squinted one eye open. Caleb was lightly brushing my earlobe with his finger.

I smiled. "So you woke up."

He laughed. "I'm so sorry. I was in such a rush to get here I didn't sleep for two days."

That he couldn't wait to see me made his falling asleep worthwhile. "Don't worry about it. What time is it?"

"About midnight. I feel terrible; I ruined our date."

"Seriously, don't even think about it. You made me a great meal, and *I* had fun watching the movie."

He sighed. "I can't believe I fell asleep. I'm such an idiot. I was so mortified I almost snuck out while you rested, but I didn't want to leave without telling you good-bye. I know you have to work tomorrow."

I didn't want him to go. "We never had the cheesecake."

His eyebrows went up.

"You can't leave without having dessert." I jumped up and headed for the kitchen. Before he could refuse, I placed a couple of pieces on some plates. "What would you like to drink?"

"Do you have any milk?"

"Sure." I pulled it out of the fridge and poured us each a healthy glass.

"Wow! You drink the real stuff."

"Oh, yeah. Whole milk, there's no other way to go. Who needs that watered down stuff?"

"You are a girl after my own heart." He clinked his glass against mine. "Sláinte."

The dessert was delicious. Trying not to lick off Caleb's milk moustache was tough.

"That should be against the law," I said as I finished the final bite.

"Pretty darn good. I'm going to warn Mr. Owen that he needs to keep a few of those on hand at all times. He said it was a new recipe he was trying out, and he seemed pleased that I wanted to try it."

We both stood for a moment staring at each other, and for the first time things were awkward. I didn't want him to leave, but I didn't know how to tell him to stay.

"Thanks for tonight." My words came out as a whisper.

"No, *thank you*." He smiled. "I really am sorry for falling asleep. It was a dumb thing to do."

"Nah. I kind of liked watching you. Oh, and did you know you snore?"

"Do not," he grumbled.

"Oh, it's not bad, but you definitely do. I thought it was sexy, in a manly kind of way."

He snorted. "If you say so."

Another moment passed.

Reaching, he took my hand. "Come here."

His lips met mine in a soft embrace that grew steadily stronger. So much so that it was making me dizzy. I backed away and took his hand, leading him to the couch.

I sat down, and he did the same. We stared at each other again and then I leaned into him. That's all it took.

Crushing me against him, he kissed me senseless. I wanted him in the worst way.

"Kira." He was short of breath and his cheeks were flushed. He ran his hands through my hair. "God, you're beautiful."

This time I kissed him, sending everything I felt for him into it.

"I want you." He whispered the words. His hands squeezed my butt tighter to him and I could feel his hardness. It excited me and scared the hell out of me.

It was like a splash of cold water, pulling me out of the heat of him.

"I can't." I sat up.

He blinked. "What?"

"I can't, um, do this."

He blinked again. "Oh."

I climbed off of him and stood. "I'm an awful person. I'm sorry. I didn't meant to . . ." *Lead you on.* Was it leading him on when I wanted him so bad it hurt?

He waved a hand. "No, no. It's my fault. I shouldn't have let things get out of hand. I'm sorry, Kira. You know I want you, and I don't want to push you or move too fast."

My laugh held a tinge of hysteria. Nerves. "Please don't apologize. I think it's more than evident that I wanted you too."

My stomach queasy, I wrapped my hands around my waist. "It's just—I have no idea how to tell you this." It was something I'd never shared with anyone. Not even Justin knew, and he was someone who was aware of my dating secrets. He'd been my best *girlfriend* for the last few years, and in drunken stupors we'd often shared entirely too much information, but only my GYN and I knew this particular bit.

He frowned. "What? We established earlier that you could tell me anything."

I backed away. I needed some space. *If he doesn't take the information well, then this isn't meant to be.* "Okay." I cleared my throat. "In the interest of full disclosure, there's something I have to tell you."

"Are you married?" His voice held a tinge of worry.

"God, no. What kind of woman do you think I am?" I stopped my pacing.

"A beautiful one. Apologies, it was the first thing that came to mind. Just tell me. Whatever it is, it will be okay."

I put a hand to my forehead, pushing my hair out of my face.

"Truth is, Caleb . . . I'm . . . a virgin."

Five Ways to Tell a Man You're a Virgin

1. Hi, my name is Kira, and I'm a virgin.
2. Oh, that old thing? It's just a hymen.
3. Have I got a big surprise for you!
4. Do you like cherries with that?
5. Yeah, I'm a virgin. Now what are you going to do about it?

Chapter 20

Let men tremble to win the hand of woman, unless they win along with it the utmost passion of her heart.

THE SCARLET LETTER
By Hawthorne, Nathaniel, 1804–1864
Call #: F-HAW
Description: vi, 169 p.; 23cm

There was silence, except for the wind whipping the trees against the windows.

Then he put a hand against his chest. "I think I almost had a heart attack."

"Why, because I'm a virgin? I know we're rare . . ."

"No, no. I just thought you were going to say something like you'd decided to be a nun or that you had some incurable disease. I think my heart stopped." He laughed. "Sorry, sorry. I'm being an insensitive jerk." Standing, he grabbed me and hugged me hard. "God. You really scared me."

I put my arms around him. "I didn't mean to lead you on like that. I mean I wasn't. I wanted it. Really wanted it."

"It's okay, baby." He kissed my hair. "Trust me, I want you just as bad. But let's take this slow."

I pushed against the hard wall of his chest. "See, I don't

want to. I kind of want to get it over with." I held up a hand in a stop motion. "That didn't come out quite the way I mean." I took a long breath. "There are parts of me that feel like they might explode if I don't—"

He chuckled. "Get it over with?"

"Yes."

"Do you want me to make love to you right now?"

"Yes."

"Are you on the pill?"

"Um, no. I didn't really have any cause until tonight." I flipped a hand toward him in a flapping motion. "Don't you have a condom in your wallet or something?"

He laughed again and then coughed a little. "No. But I'm embarrassed to say, I probably have some in the glove compartment of the truck."

"Then go get them," I ordered.

"No." He put his hands on his hips.

"No? What, you've decided you no longer want to get in my pants?"

He frowned. "No. I want to make love to you, Kira, until you can't think of anything but me. But I'm not going to do it tonight."

"Why?"

"Because you are a virgin for one, and I'm not going to take something so special away from you without knowing the reason why."

"Huh?"

"How did a woman who looks like you manage chastity all these years?"

I sat down in the recliner again and pulled my knees to me. "Oh. It's not as difficult as you seem to think. Not everyone sees me the way you do. To be honest, for years my life has been about school, work, and work. Not much time for dating. I don't believe in one-night stands. Maybe I'm naïve, but I think there should be at least some emotional connection between two people before they have sex. I'm not saying love and marriage, but a connection."

"I know from talking to Sam that you dated in college."

"Oh, I've had dates, but I never met a guy who made me feel like you do. Someone who makes me burn inside. And I do burn Caleb, but only for you."

I'm not sure what it was I said, but the next thing I knew he'd scooped me out of the chair and kissed me hard. "You're going to kill me, woman," he said as he put me down on the ground.

I smiled. "What a way to go."

He laughed. "I don't have the willpower to say no to you again, Kira. If you want me, I'm yours."

Mine. "Go get the condoms, Caleb, and bring more than one."

He was out the door in less than two seconds. I heard him running down the steps. A few minutes later he raced back up.

"Did you lock the front door?" I asked as he paused on the second floor landing to catch his breath.

Panting, he pulled something out of his pocket and nodded. Six condoms in red Trojan wrappers rolled down.

I smiled. "Six? You must be better at this than I ever imagined."

"You have no idea."

Minutes later we were under the large quilt in the bedroom, naked and staring at one another. I'd made him turn around while I took off my clothes and slipped under the covers.

"I'm a little scared," I admitted. I was feeling exposed even though my naked body was covered. I'd also seen parts of him that suddenly seemed very large and overwhelming.

The back of his hand rubbed the side of my cheek. "This is how we are going to do this: If at any time you want to stop, we will. No matter what. I mean it. We won't do anything you don't want to tonight."

I nodded.

This time when he kissed me it was tender and soft. He moved his mouth down my neck, and when he used his tongue to make tiny circles around each breast, my nipples stood at attention and something burned at my core.

As he teased and taunted my breasts, his hand slid down my stomach, and when he touched the slick heat below, I gasped.

He stopped and looked up. "Are you okay, baby?"

"Yes. Don't stop."

His tongue went back to work, as did his fingers.

My breathing quickened and I lost myself in the passion. All I could feel or think about was him. Everything blurred and spun out of control. When I screamed, it surprised me so much that I stilled in the middle of the most incredible experience I'd ever had.

"Breathe, Kira," Caleb whispered in my ear. He nibbled my earlobe and sucked in tiny bits of it. The tension built again and my body exploded.

"Please," I begged him.

"What?"

"Make love to me, Caleb."

"I am, baby."

"No." I reached down and took the hardness I'd felt against my thigh. I slowly rubbed my thumb over him.

This time he was the one who gasped.

"I'm barely holding on, Kira. Don't do that too much."

I smiled. The power of his desire made me feel strong.

"I need you." I slid my hand down and touched him again.

"Okay, okay. Let go, or I'm going to ruin this for both of us." He chuckled, but it was a husky, sexy sound.

I let go, and he moved over me. Pausing only to slip on the condom, he kissed me and wrapped my legs around him. "God, you are amazing."

He slid inside me a tiny bit. I could feel the stretching and I knew the pain was to come, but I didn't care. My body wanted him badly.

I squeezed his butt with my legs and shoved him inside me. As he pushed through a tight barrier, the intense pain passed quickly.

"Kira!" He stopped. "No, baby."

"It's okay." A tear slid down my cheek.

He started to pull out. "No!"

"It's good. It's really good." I shoved my hips against his. "Please."

We found a rhythm. It started slow and built into a beautiful crescendo of passion. Just when I didn't think I could take any more, my body a mass of overstimulated nerve endings, he drove me over the edge one more time. My breath came out in gasps, as if I'd been running a marathon, and then he came over the cliff with me.

He kissed me over and over again, whispering his love.

My body shook with emotion. I had to hold back the tears I knew would worry him.

"God, why did I wait so long?" I whispered.

"You were waiting for me." He slid out of me gently.

"Yes. Yes I was."

He moved to rest beside me and pushed the dampened hair away from my face. "You are the most beautiful woman I've ever met."

I remembered the pictures of him with the elegantly dressed women. *Why do I have to think about that now?* I must have frowned, because he leaned down and kissed me.

"Stop. Whatever it is you're thinking, Kira, just stop. You are *it* for me."

He knew me too well already.

I sighed. "I wanted to know, um, when could we do it again? According to all the books and magazine articles I've read, and there've been a lot of them, it takes at least forty-five minutes."

"Oh, really." He laughed. "Well, not everything you read is true." He kissed the side of my neck. "One look at you with that satisfied smile, and all I can think about is making it happen again. And again."

"I thought that kind of thing only happened in romance novels." I ran my fingers through his sandy-colored hair.

"Oh, I'm going to show you some romance." He kissed me again and I was lost.

Five Great Things About Sex

1. The fantastic feeling
2. The kissing
3. The orgasms
4. The intimacy
5. The glow

Chapter 21

Deep into that darkness peering, long I stood there wondering, fearing, doubting, dreaming dreams no mortals ever dared to dream before.

"THE RAVEN"
By Poe, Edgar Allan, 1809–1849
Call #: F-POE
Description: 1v (unpaged): ill; 25cm

I woke with Caleb's arms and one leg wrapped around me. I felt like a captured woman, as if he didn't want to let me go. I loved it.

I'd read so many books, seen so many movies with love scenes, and nothing compared to what I'd experienced the night before.

Sliding out so as not to wake him was difficult. I managed, or at least thought I had. As I reached for my robe, a hand touched my thigh.

"Where are you going?" His voice sleepy, his eyes were opened only a crack. He was sexy as hell.

"Shower, and to start some coffee."

"Want to share?"

"The coffee? Sure." I grinned.

"The shower."

My head dipped. I'd never taken a shower with a guy. It was one thing to be all sexy and exposed under the covers, quite another in the light of day.

"Baby, don't be shy. You're gorgeous. I just thought it would save us time for *other* things." His bold stare made me blush.

Those other things put me behind almost forty-five minutes and left me exhausted. I'd have to take a nap during my lunch hour or I wouldn't make it through the rest of the day.

He left a little before eight. Feeling powerful, I donned one of my Armani suits and four-inch Pradas. I spent most of my days sitting behind the desk answering questions for patrons and callers, so the shoes weren't as impractical as they seemed, and they made me feel good.

That loving high lasted until I opened the library. Everyone who walked in gave me a strange stare. It was as if they knew everything I'd done upstairs.

The gossip mill had obviously noticed that Caleb's truck had been parked in front of the library until almost eight this morning.

Around ten, I caught an elderly gentleman staring at me oddly. I decided I just didn't care anymore. It was the twenty-first century and what happened between Caleb and me was our business. The rest of the town could stick it.

The older man kept peering at me from around the rows of books.

"Can I help you?"

Turning, he looked behind his shoulder.

"Sir." I rudely pointed at him. "Can I help you?"

"Well, yes. As a matter of fact I'm looking for a Western,

written by a fella named Jimmy Butts, but I didn't want to interrupt you. I didn't know if you could see me."

I smiled, sorry that I'd been so cranky. He was probably shy. I checked the computer. "We have several. Is there one in particular you wanted?"

He nodded. "I missed *Brotherhood of Blood* if you have it."

I walked to where the book was shelved. We had several of the paperbacks, and I handed it to him.

"Name's Hornsby." He gave the book back to me to scan. I picked up the wand and put the scanned book on the counter.

"You're all set, Mr. Hornsby. You have a nice day." I smiled. He was a nice guy. I shouldn't have been so rude to him. I just couldn't figure out why he was looking at me that way.

"Thank you, ma'am." He tipped his cowboy hat and faded away.

I'd just seen a dead guy.

Thankfully, no one was in the library. It was early for lunch, but I needed a break. I locked the front doors. When I turned around the library was full of people. And a dog. The one I'd seen earlier.

The people waved.

I leaned back against the door.

Something told me these weren't my normal library patrons. The temperature had dropped twenty degrees.

A woman appeared in front of me. Well, I use the term "woman" loosely. It was actually a drag queen. She/He had to be in his early thirties and wore a beautiful green dress that looked very Jackie O. A black wig flipped on the ends, a pillbox hat, and three-inch pointy-toe heels finished the outfit. "Hi, Kira. I'm Terry." He held a tiny white dog or an end of a mop. It was hard to tell.

"Hi." It was more of a squeak than anything. "Are you a—um." I couldn't formulate words. This situation was beyond bizarre.

"A drag queen? Yes, darling, I am." He struck a glamorous pose.

Coughing, I held up a finger. "I was going to say ghost."

He chuckled. "That too. Though I'm more fond of 'spirit.' "

"Nice dog."

Terry gave the pooch a squeeze. "Isn't he just the cutest? We call him Rascal. He's actually a pal to Herman over there." He pointed to the large Irish wolfhound. I'd looked up the breed after my experience the other night. "Poor Herman's just been beside himself with worry. He didn't think you were ever going to invite him in. Rascal has been keeping him company until you came into your powers.

"Anyway, doll, I'm your spiritual guide. Or one of them, actually. You've been assigned three."

"Three?"

He sat primly on the table closest to the door and crossed his ankles. "Oh, yes. I'm sure the others will be along when you're ready."

I nodded. "I'm hallucinating. I think I should probably call my doctor."

He laughed again. "Oh, honey. You aren't hallucinating. I know this is bit disconcerting, as you could only hear us before. I'm sure it's frightening to wake up and see us this way. But it's your second week here and that's what happens.

We try to ease you into it a little at time, but the schedule works the way it does."

"Schedule?" My brain wouldn't function. I wasn't a hundred percent sure, but I had a feeling a mob of dead people stood before me.

"Yes." He smiled and his feminine black hair bobbed around his face. "They've all been waiting weeks to check out books. See, they can't do it without your permission. It's against the rules."

I raised my hands and squeezed my head, closing my eyes as I did so. It was a pose that would rival Edvard Munch's painting *The Scream*. When I opened them everyone was still there. "I need to sit down."

"As I said, it's difficult to understand. This library is a portal. We've been trying to point you to the book of rules, but it seems to have been misplaced."

There was a *tsk*ing sound behind Terry.

He gave them the evil eye. "It's not Mabel's fault she was called before her actual day. She had things as ready as she could."

I looked up at the ceiling and then back down to him. "Let me get this straight. You're dead and you want to check out books?"

He smiled sweetly. "Yes, exactly. Or at least they do. I'm your guide, here to answer any questions you might have."

Oh, I had a lot of questions. "Why are dead dogs hanging around the library?"

Terry smirked. "Honey, you find out you live in the middle of a magical portal, and you're worried about your pets?"

"I don't have any."

"Don't follow you, doll."

"Pets."

Laughing, he put Rascal on the floor. The little mop ran to me and whined at my legs. I picked him up and he snuggled into my arms.

"Looks like you do now. The animals are guardians chosen specifically to protect you. They'll let you know when shadows or demons are around or if there's bad energy in the room." Terry patted Herman on the head.

I shivered. "Demons?"

"It's all in the book, honey. It's a portal, so most anything can come through. You protect the portal, and the library. That's your job."

I squeezed my eyes shut one more time. This was one elaborate hallucination. They were still there when I opened them again. *Darn.*

"I don't understand why you need a librarian. None of this makes any sense. I know I keep saying that, but it doesn't. And you can't just take the books, I have to give them to you?"

He nodded.

I took a deep breath and blew it out. "Why?"

Perplexed, he stared at me. "Why, what?"

"Why here? Can't you just go to any bookstore or library and get what you want?"

"No," the crowd mumbled in unison.

Terry held up a hand. "You guys behave. The dead must always be respectful of the living. We come here because you are the librarian. There are only a few like you, who can see us. And as you might have guessed, this is no ordinary library."

I chewed on my lip. Over the last two weeks no one had

asked for a piece of information or a book I couldn't find. I'd spent a lot of time in libraries in college, and none of them had been as well stocked as this one.

"It's . . . a library for the dead?"

"And the living," he added.

"Oh, my." I sat back in my chair.

"You really need to find the book. It explains everything. Poor Mabel is still in holding, but I know she'll be here to help out as soon as she can. Though she isn't one of your guides.

"Unfortunately, she was taken on the wrong day. Someone up there"—he pointed toward the ceiling—"is dyslexic with numbers. So this whole thing was one big mess, since she was to have until the first of January to make this happen. It will be straightened out once Mabel is processed."

"Processed?"

"Yes. It's in the book. Now, I know you're busy, but maybe some of them could go ahead and check out their novels. You let Mr. Hornsby."

"Um. Okay." I waved toward the library. "Just take what you want." *And go away*.

"Oh, they can't do that." Terry jumped off the table. "You have to use that little wandy thing. Otherwise it's like stealing."

My head throbbed at the temples. A migraine was on the way. I didn't get headaches often, but this promised to be a big one.

"It's the energy in the room—too much all at once for you, until you learn to channel it," Terry said.

"What?"

"You're rubbing your temples and feel a headache coming

on. I'm afraid that's from us." He turned. "Some of you will have to wait until later. Those of you returning books can stay. The rest will have to go for now."

There was a low groan, but more than half the room disappeared before my eyes. The pressure in my head lessened.

"Maybe for now you could just check in the books we checked out. Mabel just waved them under that funny little thing and the computer took care of it."

I moved behind the counter, and the crowd lined up.

"So you're my guide? And I can ask you anything?" What kind of cosmic joke was it that I ended up with a drag queen as my spiritual guide?

"Sure. Well, once you've read the book. There are rules to follow. I'm a level one guide. As your powers increase, you'll move up the ladder, but I'll always be here for you." He gave me a sincere smile.

I kind of liked him.

A short, stocky man handed me a book of Frederick Seidel poems. "I'm Thomas Kinnear," he said.

I typed in his name, and sure enough it came up on the computer. I hit Next and another patron came up to turn in a book. For a half an hour I checked in each of their books and then checked out new ones to them.

A surreal event, to say the least, and as I did this, each one of them would disappear before my eyes.

Terry waited, patiently flipping through an *InStyle* magazine. "I swear, some of the things the girls wear these days. Less is more, ladies!"

"Why did I only hear you before, but now I can see you?"

A white hand flitted my way. His nails were long and

painted bright red. "I'm sure it's in the book, but I think it has something to do with the schedule."

"You think? I don't understand. If you're a guide, aren't you supposed to know?" I leaned my elbows on the cold granite counter and put my head in my hands.

"Oh. Feeling a little snippy, are we?" He pretended to be offended. "Technically, I can't help you until you read the book. But I can be here for support." He smiled.

My head throbbed again. "Sorry. I just don't understand any of this. Do you know what it looks like? This book you keep talking about."

"Not really." The corners of his bright lips turned down. "But you'll know when you find it. You'll be the only one who can read it. I'm sure this is all a great deal to take in, but you are a special woman. Without you, many of us would lose out on one of our greatest joys." He lifted a copy of J. D. Robb's latest.

"Can you at least tell me why, at this point in my life, I see dead people?"

"The veil lifted when you were sick. With your defenses down, your mind was more open to the other side. Everyone is a receiver of some sort, but adults can block the waves. It usually happens soon after your twenty-fifth birthday for the really special librarians, but you were a tough cookie. When you were ill, your boundaries finally shifted so we could do a bit of peeking in."

I made a motorboat sound with my lips. "This is so . . . I don't know. So people don't really die. Well, they die, but then they go somewhere different. Like on another plane." The words sounded ludicrous even to me.

Terry nodded and gave me a look that told me he understood. "Look, honey, I know it doesn't feel like it right now, but you are one special girl. You find that book, and you'll understand. This is a big deal and it would blow anyone's mind, so give yourself a little break. I've been here too long and my energy is sagging. We girls can't let anything sag." He winked. "I'll see you soon." He faded away.

I closed my eyes and opened them again. The library was blissfully empty. Resting my head on the cool counter I tried to think, but my brain was full to capacity. It was as if I'd just taken ten final exams in a row.

A few moments later, I lifted my head. It still hurt but the panic was gone.

I looked back at the computer and pushed a few buttons. No, I wasn't imagining any of this. I'd checked in and out almost forty books. *To dead people.*

"I'm taking the rest of the day off." I said it out loud so *they* would know. I desperately needed to lie down. I climbed the back steps. Pulling down the shades in the bedroom, it dawned on me.

"No one comes up here. No one." I yelled to the air around me. "This is my private spot. My bedroom is off limits."

Oh, God. Had they seen Caleb and me last night? Mortified, I slipped on my tank and the flannel pajama bottoms with the coffee cup print. Crawling under the covers, I pulled the pillow over my head.

No matter how hard I tried to push the thought from my mind, it kept repeating.

I see dead people. I see dead people. Crap, crap, crap, I see dead people.

Chapter 22

Fan the sinking flame of hilarity with the wing of friendship; and pass the rosy wine.

THE OLD CURIOSITY SHOP
By Dickens, Charles, 1812–1870
Call #: F-DIC
Description: xv, 732 p.: front, ill; 21cm

A few hours later I sat on the side of my bed feeling like I had the worst hangover of my life. It was the afternoon when the children came by for homework help. Otherwise I would have hidden under the blankets the rest of the day. I glanced at the clock. They would be downstairs in an hour, and I had to get everything set up and bake cookies.

You see dead people.

Shut up. I can't think about that right now.

A dull ache throbbed at my temples, but it was nothing like before. I liked fresh-baked cookies, and the Pillsbury Doughboy made them way better than I did. I cut thick slices off two rolls and put them in the oven for fifteen minutes.

While they baked, I cleaned off my face and decided not to worry about makeup except for some lip gloss and a little blush for my pale cheeks.

I hung my suit back in the closet and grabbed jeans and a sweater. While the older kids worked with the adult volunteers I usually sat on the floor with some of the younger ones, listening to them read.

By the time I pulled myself together and had the cookies and milk ready, it was three.

I unlocked the library door.

My first patron wasn't a child, she was 100 percent adult.

There had been a lot of gossip in town about a new witch who had moved into one of the gothic homes out past the highway. A high witch, which meant she was incredibly powerful. I don't really know much about the world of magic, other than that it exists. Our town was protected by a coven, and, well, magic was about the only thing that would explain what had been going on in the library these days.

The witch's name was Bronwyn, and the rumor mill said she could kill a man with a glance, and that she once took down six evil warlocks with a flick of her wrist.

Intimidating to say the least.

Caleb had done some work for her, but he didn't say much. Just that she was never home.

So when a cute little brunette with curly hair came in asking for books about herbs, I never suspected she was one of the most powerful women on the planet.

"Hi." The woman smiled when I looked up from the books I'd been lining up on the cart to shelve later. "I wonder if you can help me."

I walked to the front desk. "Sure."

"I'm trying to find out the best kind of soil for some new herbs I want to try in my garden." She paused. "Um, Mrs.

Canard, the librarian, said she'd order some books, but then I had to go out of town. I—I'm not sure if she had a chance to do it before . . . well. I'm sorry. I'm trying to find a nice way of saying it, but of course it comes out crap." She rolled her eyes.

"It's okay. If she said she would order them, I'm sure they are here. Can I have your name?" I moved to the computer.

"Bronwyn—"

At the sound of her name, my head jerked up.

She sighed. "I promise not to blow you up, or strike you dead if you can't find the books."

I laughed out loud. I knew what it was like to feel like an outsider in this town. I'd spent my entire youth trying to get away from the place for that reason. I didn't know why things were different now, but I could certainly sympathize with the witch.

"Darn. I was kind of hoping I could give you some names and you could take care of a few people for me." I raised an eyebrow.

At first I don't think she knew how to take my joke, but then she smiled. "Well, I'm always happy to help a friend in need."

I stuck out a hand. "I'm Kira. It's nice to meet you."

She shook it. "Oh, are you the one Caleb's all gooey about?"

I blushed. "I don't know about that, but we have been dating a little."

She nodded. "He's such a goober. I can't imagine what you see in him, but he's very taken with you. I've never heard him go on and on about a woman like this. And believe me, he's gone through a few." She slapped her head with her hand. "I'm so sorry. That was wrong in so many ways." She shook her head.

I giggled and couldn't stop. "Don't worry. I know, or at least I've read about some of them. He won't tell me anything."

She shrugged. "I think it's best to leave the past behind." A shadow passed over her face, and I wondered who had hurt her.

"You can totally get away with murder, because you have him well and thoroughly hooked. Geez, he's even been talking about moving here full time. Like I need that bozo hanging around."

I blanched.

She sighed. "Argh. He hasn't talked to you about it? Me and my mouth. It just doesn't stop. Please don't freak out—he's just mentioned a couple of times how much he likes it here, but it seems to happen more often since you moved here."

I cleared my throat. "I haven't."

"Haven't what?" She pushed an errant curl behind her ear.

"Moved here. I'm just helping out, temporarily, until I can figure out what to do."

"Huh. So where do you live?"

"I was in Atlanta, but I'm making a job change. I'm not really sure where I'm headed next."

"So you won't be a librarian anymore?"

I laughed. "I'm not one now. I'm a lawyer. Mrs. Canard left me this place."

Realization dawned on her. "Oh. Well, too bad. I kind of like you." She smiled. "I've lived all over the world, and I've never found a place like this one. The people, for the most part, are nice, and it's peaceful. Once in a while I get an odd stare, but most of them are pretty cool."

"That's true. It's different for me since I've been back. When I was a kid I couldn't wait to get out of here. Now I'm a little sad about leaving. But there's not much use for a corporate lawyer in Sweet."

She stared at me. "But we really need a good librarian."

I laughed again. "You've got me there. Don't tell Caleb, but I'm not sure what I'm going to do. I need some time to figure things out. There are some great job offers on the table for me, and I'd be an idiot to turn away from any of them."

"Well, I've known you for"—she looked at her watch— "seven minutes, and I have a feeling you'll figure it all out. I've found that when you let go and sort of follow your heart, and don't overthink things too much, life works like a charm. It's when we try to analyze every second of our lives and get too much into our heads that everything goes to hell."

I liked her. It helped that I discovered she's more Caleb's little sister than a former flame. There was something about her, a hardness like she'd seen too much of life. At the same time she had an incredible spirit, a positive human being who was trying to do good things in the world. You could feel it.

Tapping the keys on the computer I found the file with her name. Everything was in Box Q-4. "The books you wanted are here, back in the storeroom. The notes say she also has Carol Nols's *Book of Herbal Charms* along with *The Rose Lover's Guide*."

"God, she was a great librarian." Bronwyn's lips thinned. "I'm so sorry she's gone. She was one of the few people who didn't look at me like I had three heads when I first arrived. Well, her and the gang at Lulu's."

I'd had the same experience and understood. "Those gals are amazing. Ms. Johnnie and Ms. Helen practically raised me. If it hadn't been for them and Mr. Owen, who owns The Bakery, I probably would have starved."

At her stricken look I added, "Oh, no. My parents are great; they just like a lot of tofu."

Bronwyn made a gagging sound. "You poor thing. No child should have to eat that crap."

I knew in that moment we would be the greatest of friends. Kindred souls were we.

"Follow me and I'll get you those books."

Bronwyn hung around the library for a couple of hours, helping out with the kids and even listening to some of the youngest ones read.

"I can't help with math, but my mom's an English professor," she explained. Toward the end of the day, I assigned her to a group of teens working on a midterm paper about Charles Dickens's *A Christmas Carol*.

Everyone left at five, and Bronwyn and I decided to catch some dinner at Lulu's. She said Caleb had called and wanted to wait for a glass delivery and he'd meet me at the library at seven.

At the café, Bronwyn and I talked about everything from old boyfriends to favorite movies and food while we gulped down Ms. Helen's *special* stew. The *special* came from the half bottle of bourbon she put in each pot.

I also managed to get all kinds of information about Caleb. He never talked about himself, and whenever I questioned him, he always turned it back on me. Bronwyn said it has something to do with the journalist in him, and that he was always a really private guy.

I found out he loved old John Wayne Westerns and had a proclivity for musicals, and she'd caught him humming show tunes more than once while he'd been working on her house. She said she thinks he secretly always wanted to be a cowboy, hence the truck and the "wicked" (her word) collection of boots.

She had to leave later in the week, but we made plans to get together when she got back. I bet she'd like to meet my friend Margie too.

There was no telling what kind of trouble the three of us could get into.

Chapter 23

He has spent his life best who has enjoyed it most.

THE WAY OF ALL FLESH
By Butler, Samuel, 1835–1902
Call #: F-BUT
Description: vii, 431 p.; 20cm

riday at the library was so slow I'd thought about closing for three-day weekends for the rest of December.

My only visitors were dead. I was still trying to get used to the idea, but life was never boring.

When I wasn't helping them, I searched for the book Terry had mentioned. I'd given up looking in the library and decided to go through one box at a time in the back. I was hauling up Box L-5 to the front counter when Caleb arrived in a blast of snow and wind. "Man, it's freakin' cold out there." Leaning across the desk, he planted a big kiss on my cheek. His lips were icy. "It's supposed to die down this afternoon, which will be just in time for my big surprise."

"What surprise?" I wiped off the counter where the snow had fallen off his suede coat.

"I'm taking you on a special weekend trip. We're going Christmas shopping in Dallas," he said excitedly, his eyes bright with eagerness.

I hadn't even thought about shopping for the holidays. In Atlanta I did most of it online and had everything shipped to the recipients. This year, the list would be a little shorter since I didn't really have to worry about the people at work. Well, except for Justin.

Once I accepted one of the job offers, I'd planned to send an announcement to most of my friends and associates after the New Year.

"Kira?"

I looked up to see him staring. "Sorry. Lost in Kira's World again. I need to be back early Sunday afternoon to help with the Christmas party over at the nursing home. Margie nagged me into playing piano during the Christmas carols."

He stepped back. "I didn't know you played piano."

I nodded. "Since I was a kid. I have one at the apartment in Atlanta. It's one of the ways I relax."

"Wow. You really are a woman of mystery. So I promise to have you back by noon on Sunday. Will you come? I want to leave about four this afternoon."

"Today? I—the library doesn't close until five on Friday."

"Well, I happen to know the librarian can close up shop whenever she wants." He squeezed my hand. "Come on, it's only an hour, and I've already made dinner reservations for eight o'clock."

"How did you know I'd agree to go with you?"

He gave me a sheepish smile. "I didn't, but I made plans just in case you did say yes."

I turned to look at the big clock on the front wall. "It's

almost three. I need time to pack. Can you watch the desk while I go upstairs?"

"Sure." He shrugged off his jacket and moved around the desk. Tugging on my ponytail, he pulled me to him and hugged me.

"Your hands are cold." I could feel them through my sweater.

"I know a good way to warm them up." He glanced back at the door. "We could go ahead and lock up."

I playfully shoved him away. "Nope. A girl wants to be wined and dined before she hands over the goods." I rolled my eyes. "Or so I hear."

He laughed. "Go get ready. I'll watch your precious library for you."

"What kind of place are we going to tonight?"

"It's casual nice. Tomorrow night will be a little dressier."

I sighed. There wasn't much cause for dressing up in Sweet. I did have a cute little Diane von Furstenberg minidress. It was black and traveled well. It would be great for the casual dinner. I hunted through my limited wardrobe here at the library and wished I'd had Justin ship me even more of my clothes.

I fingered the bright blue Carmen Marc Valvo taffeta dress he'd shipped when I first told him I was spending a few weeks here. He was more than a little surprised but sent four large boxes of clothes, shoes, and other accessories. This particular cocktail dress had a layered bottom, but I didn't have any shoes to go with it.

Maybe I can pick some up while we're shopping tomorrow.

I put the two dresses in a hanging bag and threw in my makeup, toiletries, curlers, jeans, boots, and my black pump

Manolos to go with the wrap dress. And I found my black Marc Jacobs twill coat.

I slipped out of the Theory fitted jacket and pants I had on and pulled on some jeans and a red cashmere sweater.

"Don't forget your scarf," a woman said behind me. I didn't jump this time.

"I thought I told you guys not to come up here."

I turned and saw an elderly woman. She had to be at least ninety. "I'm new, dear. Didn't know the rules. Could you help me find a crocheting book?"

Do they crochet in heaven?

"Sure. Give me a minute. I'll leave it on the counter down-stairs for you. But for future reference, no one is allowed up here."

She dissipated, just as I heard Caleb's steps on the stairs.

"Who are you talking to?" He made his way to the landing.

Oh, boy. "Myself. Trying to remember some things before I leave. I thought you were watching the counter."

"I am. I had to ask you where to find *Prom Dates from Hell.* There's a young girl downstairs crying because she can't find a copy. All of her friends have read it and she'll just *die* if she doesn't get it this weekend." He said the last part with a very good imitation of the teen whine and threw his hand against his forehead for effect.

I laughed. That book was still one of the most popular among the teen set. I'd ordered three extra copies for just such an occasion.

"Under the front desk there are copies I haven't shelved yet. Give her one of those, and don't forget to run it through the computer."

He smiled and waved his hands behind him like he was

wearing Superman's cape. "I get to be a hero." And he ran back downstairs.

By the time I made it down and set my bags on one of the reading tables, he was helping the young girl check out. The thirteen-year-old was all smiles and definitely flirting with my boyfriend.

That seemed so weird. *My boyfriend*. When had I started calling him that?

He handed her the book, and she gave him another toothy smile.

After she left, he turned to me. "I'm, like, the totally coolest guy she's ever met."

I laughed out loud. "Totally?"

He nodded.

It was three thirty and the place was empty. "You want to go ahead and go pack?"

"Oh, I came prepared." He held up a hand. "Just in case you said yes. I don't suppose you'd consider closing up even earlier?"

What the heck, it's Friday afternoon. I shrugged. "Sure. I need to do something real quick. I'll lock up and meet you in the truck. Go get it warm."

After grabbing my bags, and kissing me hard, he headed out.

I went in search of a crocheting book. I set it on the counter and the elderly woman reappeared.

"Oh, thank you dear. And it has doilies—lovely." She grinned. "Martin is the last name. Edwina Martin."

I brought her up on the computer, scanned the book, and handed it to her. I still hadn't figured out how the computer could bring up dead people who had never been here before.

When I had asked Terry, he'd replied, "It's in the book." I'd
been searching for the stupid tome, but it was nowhere to
be found.

"Take care," I told Edwina.

By the time I made it to the door the book was gone and so
was Edwina. I wasn't sure I'd ever get used to it.

"You guys keep an eye on the place." I didn't see anyone,
but I heard the two dogs barking.

It would be great to get away from this surreal world and
spend some time with Caleb. When I came back, I'd search
every inch of the place for that book.

Places I Love in Dallas

1. The West Village
2. Tiffany
3. Mansion on Turtle Creek
4. Anywhere Caleb is
5. Shipley Do-nuts
6. Neiman Marcus
7. The zoo
8. Magnolia Theater
9. Tom Tom Noodle House
10. The Cheesecake Factory

Chapter 24

❦

I am never afraid of what I know.

BLACK BEAUTY
By Sewell, Anna, 1820–1878
Call #: F-SEW
Description: 232 p.: ill; 21cm

The traffic as we neared Dallas was insane. We sat in the same spot for almost twenty minutes on I-30. Caleb didn't seem stressed at all, but traffic gets on my nerves. I don't like the feeling of being trapped. It was just as bad in Atlanta, which is why I chose to live close to my office. I seldom drove, or left the comforts of downtown.

While a competent driver, Caleb was a speed demon. We made the three-hour trip in two and a quarter. And the last fifteen minutes had been spent inching forward bit by bit.

It wasn't much longer before we exited the highway. He made a few quick turns and five minutes later we were pulling into a parking garage. I'd been mesmerized by all of the shops surrounding the building and didn't get a chance to see much of it.

"We're here." He pulled into a parking spot marked 28D next to a beautiful silver Mercedes sedan.

He jumped out and ran around to let me out of the truck.

"You crack me up." I laughed as I took his hand.

"Tell me you don't like the Southern gentleman touches."

I reached up and kissed his cheek. "You know I do."

He smiled. Grabbing our bags from the backseat, we made our way to the elevator. He wouldn't let me carry anything except my purse, and he looked liked a loaded-down bellman.

"Can you push twenty-eight?" he asked as the elevator doors shut. A quick trip up, and when the doors opened it was to a long hallway. I followed him to the end.

When he opened the door, I walked through into a breathtaking sight. I took little notice of the apartment. It was the view that captured my attention.

"It's beautiful." The windows, which wrapped around the entire corner of the building, looked out onto the city of Dallas, twinkling with brilliant light.

"One of the perks of being up so high."

I nodded and moved forward. "It's a different view, but the same kind I have in my place in Atlanta. I like seeing a vibrant city out my window. It makes me feel alive."

He wrapped his arms around me and squeezed. "You are very much alive."

I turned in his arms and wound mine around him. "I feel that way when you are around."

"Oh, no. Don't move like that," he said as I pressed my hips into his. "We have reservations."

"I am kind of hungry." I licked my top lip.

He laughed. "You are a wicked woman. Come on, I'll show you the bedroom."

At my raised eyebrow he added, "So you can freshen up." I smiled and winked at him.

Before following Caleb, I spent a moment taking in his apartment. All of the furniture was low, chocolate leather, and sleek, very much a bachelor pad. A huge plasma TV, larger than mine at home, graced the inside wall over a fireplace.

He flipped the light on in the bedroom. The walls were a deep chocolate brown. A leather headboard and plush bedding made his bed irresistible looking. The lamps on the bedside tables were silver and gave off a soft glow.

"This is a nice place."

He shrugged. "Except for the artwork and photos, most of it was here when I bought the place. I built the bookcases and side tables for the bed, and painted everything. I'm not really around that much, but it's home. For now."

He pointed toward an opening. "Bathroom is in here." He set my tote bag on a large granite vanity and hung the garment bag on a hook on the back of the door.

"I'll rummage through the closet for something. Like I said, it's casual. You can wear whatever you want. People will be dressed in everything from jeans to formalwear. In the summer they wear shorts. It's that kind of place." He held up his watch. "We only have about a half hour to get ready. Good news is it's right across the street."

"Thanks." I didn't have time for a shower, but I threw water on my face and did my best to freshen up.

I removed the dress from the bag to shake it out. One thing about Diane's dresses, they travel like a dream. The taffeta hadn't fared as well. I'd have to press it before tomorrow night.

Pulling my hair out of the ponytail I'd worn all day, I fluffed it around my shoulders. The curls held tight and I decided to leave it down.

I reapplied makeup, using black eyeliner to make my eyes look a little deeper. Adding a pink shadow near the brow and gray on my lid gave my eyes a smoky look. Usually I keep the lips light, but this was Dallas. I went for the deep wine-colored lipstick.

I'd worn a black bra and thong, and I slipped the black dress over it. The clingy fabric fit my figure perfectly. It's the kind of dress that makes everyone look sexy. I pulled on black thigh-high hose, as it was too cold to go without anything on my legs, and slipped my feet into the Manolos. As high as they were, they were still pretty comfortable to walk in.

Caleb came to the door and blew out a low whistle. He was dressed in dark gray pinstriped slacks with a cream-colored dress shirt open at the neck. "Maybe we'll order in." He moved toward me.

I held out my hands to fend him off. "Nope. You had your chance, big guy. I want my night out on the town. Then, if you're really, really good, maybe we can play later." I felt flirty and fun.

He grabbed my hands and kissed my knuckles. "Oh, I promise to be very good." His voice was low and husky and it made parts of my body heat instantly.

He held out my coat and I slipped my arms into it.

The walk across to the restaurant wasn't far, but the frigid air made it seem longer.

It wasn't long before the heat of Tom Tom Noodle House surrounded me. Sleek, modern, and very Japanese, with touches of bamboo and natural fibers, it was warm and inviting.

We were shown to a booth with low seats and small, colorful pillows. It was elegant, but not overstated.

Caleb ordered us a mixed plate of sushi and I had my first glass of wine in months. It was heaven.

The restaurant was packed but I only saw Caleb.

Picking up a spicy tuna roll with chopsticks, I sighed. I hadn't been this happy in forever.

I woke up to whispering. At first I worried the dead people had found me. *Please not here.* But I soon discovered Caleb was the one who interrupted my dreams.

"Kira. Wake up. We have to go shopping." I could smell soap, as if he'd just stepped out of the shower.

I cranked open one eye. He was freshly shaven and dressed in a soft creamy sweater. "What time is it?"

"Almost seven."

I groaned. "Stores don't open until ten, Caleb."

"Oh, no, babe. It's almost Christmas. Most of the stores around here are open very early. Every place will be packed if we don't get a move on."

I was so warm and comfortable. Snuggling into him, I said, "We could just shop online."

He laughed. "What fun is that? It's not Christmas if you don't have to fight crowds, traffic, and rude salesclerks who have to deal with picky people like us all day."

"You make it sound so exciting. How can I resist?" I rolled over and squeezed my eyes closed.

"There's a big breakfast of eggs, bacon, and croissants at the café downstairs if you hurry up."

"Bacon?"

"Yep. Nice and crispy, just the way you like it."

"Give me twenty minutes."

"You got it."

I was good to my word. Twenty minutes later I was dressed and ready to go, having taken the quickest shower of my life.

It's a good thing we had a big breakfast.

Had I any idea what a shopping machine Caleb was, I might have stayed in bed. I'm fairly certain we hit every store at the Galleria.

Granted, I had no trouble finding a pair of Kate Spade jeweled pumps that matched my dress for the evening perfectly.

By noon Caleb had made three trips back to the truck to deposit our bags. Most of them were his. I didn't want to be nosy, but I couldn't help wondering whom all the presents were for.

"Do you have a big family?" I finally asked.

He shrugged. "Yeah. Why?"

I smiled. "No reason." I stared down at my three shopping bags, one of which was full of stuff for me. I definitely needed to make new friends.

I had managed to pick up Humanity jeans for Justin and

a modern silver tea set I knew Rob would love. I had no idea what to get my parents until we came across a store with DVDs. They had several seasons of *Doctor Who* and *Battlestar Galactica* that I knew my dad would enjoy. I'd dipped into his stash when I was sick and knew which ones he needed to finish his collection.

In front of Tiffany, I stopped. "Do you mind if I take a quick look?" I turned to Caleb. "I want to see if I can find something for my mom."

He gave me a strange look.

"I know she doesn't seem like the kind of woman who would want something in a blue box, but I haven't met a girl yet who has turned one away." I laughed.

"Absolutely. We can go anywhere you want." He smiled but it seemed stiff.

"Are you worried I'm going to try and get you to buy me something?"

He laughed. "Oh, no." He waved a hand. "It's just that you've talked about your mom so much and she just doesn't seem like someone who would wear jewelry."

I sighed. "True, but I saw something a few months ago when I was shopping in New York that I think she'd like. And I just wanted to see if maybe they have it here."

Caleb smiled and guided me in the door.

The place was a sea of humanity and I could barely get to the counter where they showcased the bracelets. I found exactly what I was looking for, a delicate silver bracelet with tiny butterfly, turtle, bee, and dragonfly charms. My mom loved anything to do with nature.

Finally, I had my little blue box wrapped with a beautiful red ribbon. I searched for Caleb.

Thinking he'd stepped out to wait, I made my way to the door of the store. My phone chirped and I thought maybe it was him.

"Hey."

Silence.

"Hello?"

"I'm coming for you," a man whispered.

Shivering, I held the phone away and looked for the caller ID number. It was a blocked call.

"Who is this?"

The line went dead.

Chapter 25

The venom clamors of a jealous woman
Poisons more deadly than a mad dog's tooth

THE COMEDY OF ERRORS
By Shakespeare, William, 1564–1616
Call #: F-SHA
Description: xli, 79 p.; 20cm

My stomach churned and bile rose in my throat. The crowds were thick and I leaned back against the cool glass of the Tiffany store window.

Someone touched my shoulder and my heart skipped a beat.

"Are you okay?" Caleb's worried eyes searched my face.

I stared down at the phone for a minute.

"Who called?" he asked.

"Wrong number," I said distractedly.

Chills ran up my back. I knew whoever it was hadn't dialed wrong. *I'm coming for you.*

I gave him a weak smile. "I hate to be a party pooper, but I need to rest." My hands were shaking and I tried to will them still.

He touched my cheek. "You feel warm. Maybe we should get you back to Sweet so Sam can take a look at you."

Warm? I felt chilled to my core.

"No. I just need to get away from the crowds and rest for a little bit. You can keep shopping if you want. I could just go to the car."

He ushered me toward the parking garage. "Don't be silly. We'll go home."

As we were driving back to his apartment, I closed my eyes, my mind rushing over the last few weeks. If it hadn't been for the weird letter that had been sent to my apartment, I wouldn't have taken the call seriously. But the events were too close to be a coincidence.

Back at the apartment, he pushed me toward the bedroom. "You go get in bed. I'm going to order us up some lunch."

"Caleb." I grabbed the sleeve of his sweater. "I'm okay. I just need to sit down for a little bit. I promise I'm not sick again."

His hand covered my hand. "I can't help but care about you, Kira." He leaned in and kissed my cheek. "Please, go lie down. If nothing else it will make me feel better."

I gave a soft laugh. "Okay. You win. But if you're so worried about me, can I get whatever I want for lunch?"

He nodded.

At the moment the idea of food made me ill, but I'd have to eat soon or he would get suspicious. "I want a big cheeseburger."

Smiling he hugged me. "That sounds good. I'll get one too. Now go rest."

I couldn't sleep. My nerves were a mess. When I heard

the delivery man knock, I made my way back to the living room. Clouds were rolling in and we were so high up it felt like we were a part of them.

We dined at a small table in his kitchen. He had a college football game on the plasma without any sound.

"I think maybe I just needed some protein." After only a few bites I did feel much better. "This is delicious."

His mouth full, he nodded. Then he swallowed. "Are you going to tell me who was on the phone?"

I jerked my attention back to his face.

"I saw how you looked at the store. You were scared, Kira. Not sick. I want to know what's going on. We promised to tell each other the truth."

I couldn't lie to him and I didn't want to. This was one problem I didn't want to handle on my own. I stared out the window to the busy streets below. "I don't know what the truth is." I shook my head. "I received a weird letter in Atlanta. It said, 'You're responsible and you'll pay.' That's it.

"Then, the guy on the phone said he's coming for me."

"Did you recognize the voice?" Caleb stood up.

"No."

"Get me your phone. Where's the letter?" He was picking up his own cell.

"I left it in Atlanta."

"Can you call and have one of your friends send it here? I'll give you the address in a minute."

I handed him my cell. "It's a blocked number."

"I see that, but I have friends who can trace most anything."

He punched a button on his phone. "Dave? It's Caleb." He grunted. "Yeah, man. I'm here for the weekend. Listen, I was wondering if you could run a trace for me." He gave the other person my cell phone number.

"Yep, in the last hour." He waited a few minutes. "Okay, great." The person on the other end of the line said something. "Yep. Tell Bill I'm having a letter sent to him. I need him to check it out and I'll call Tuesday and explain everything. Great, thanks." He hung up.

"The call came from a pay phone in Atlanta. Whoever it was used coins to make the call, so we can't trace a credit card. Dave is checking to see if there are any cameras in the area." He sat next to me on the sofa. "Can you think of any reason anyone would want to threaten you?"

"No." I racked my brain. "I can't. I'm a corporate lawyer. Maybe it has to do with one of the business deals we've made, but most people don't even know I'm involved." I paused and stared out the window.

"I was also involved with a sexual harassment case with a coworker, on her side of course. Things didn't go her way and justice was not done. She took her life, but I didn't have anything to do with what happened to her." At least I didn't think I did. I still couldn't remember what had happened on the roof. There were police reports, but I hadn't seen any of them yet.

"Kira, I'm sorry. That bastard should hang." I loved Caleb for believing in me. "And I didn't know your friend, but I know you, and if she took her life I know it had nothing to do with you."

I kissed his cheek. "Thank you. It doesn't keep me from feeling guilty. I'm telling you, I think whoever it is has the wrong person. Besides, if he's in Atlanta, I'm fine. Right?"

Caleb scooped me into his lap. "Yes. But I'm still not letting you out of my sight."

I wrapped my arms around his shoulders.

"Why didn't you tell me about the letter?"

I shook my head. "I don't know. I really do think he has the wrong person."

"Is that one of the reasons you were considering the job offer in New York?"

I hadn't talked to him about that. "How do you know?"

"Sam and I were talking before you and I went out that first time. He mentioned that you'd had some offers."

"Oh." Sam had a big mouth. "No. Not really. I wanted out of Atlanta because I felt like it was time to move on. I have to tell you I was a little worried at first about the letter, but I forgot about it when I arrived in Sweet. So much has happened the last few weeks, I hadn't even thought about it."

He sighed and leaned his head into mine. "Well, call and have someone send it."

I let out a deep breath. "Okay."

A few hours later we were dressed and seated at the very elegant and beautiful restaurant at the Mansion on Turtle Creek. The first course of pumpkin soup was delicious.

We talked about the Sweet Christmas pageant at the Methodist church and how Caleb had narrowly escaped having to be one of the wise men. Our salads arrived just as a beautiful woman walked up to the table.

She was dressed in a black suit, and her ample breasts were spilling out the top. "Caleb, love. I didn't know you were back in town." Her auburn hair was in an upsweep, and her dangerous red nails touched Caleb's shoulder. When she leaned down to kiss him, I wanted to rip her to pieces.

"Megan," he ground out. "Where's your man du jour?"

She winked. "Men's room. I saw you and had to come say hi."

Caleb looked uncomfortable and I knew this was one of the women from his past—and from the sound of things, a recent past.

I lost my appetite.

"Megan, this is my *girlfriend*, Kira."

For the first time she glanced my way. "So you're his eye candy of the week." She gave me a look that would freeze any heart.

Then it dawned on me that Caleb had introduced me as his girlfriend and had put a special emphasis on the word. My heart warmed in a big way.

I stuck out my hand so that she had to shake it. "You must be an *old* friend of Caleb's. It's nice to meet you." I smiled sweetly.

Caleb snorted.

A tall man walked up behind her. He had to be seven feet something.

"Oh, Dirk. You're here." She wiggled her fingers at us. "Ta ta."

I laughed as she walked away. "Do people really say ta ta anymore?"

Caleb chuckled. "She does. I'm sorry about that. She's a total bitch. Unfortunately, I've dated my fair share of women like that." He shook his head. "Present company excluded, of course.

"I think that's one of the things I love about you. You're the complete opposite of that kind of woman. You're beautiful and chic, but without the bitchy parts."

I raised my eyebrows. "You haven't seen me when it comes to business. The office had deemed me the Ice Princess of the boardroom."

He grabbed my hand across the table. "I have a hard time believing that."

It was *very* true. "Caleb, there are parts of my life you really don't know. I—I'm different with you. I've been a different person since I left Atlanta. I'm thinking that's not such a bad thing." I smiled.

He kissed my fingers.

The waiter arrived with our food, and we enjoyed our meal of baby turbot, Pacific halibut, and filet mignon.

When we left I wasn't certain I'd be able to walk to the valet stand. This time the valet brought around the silver Mercedes I'd admired the day before in the garage. Turned out it belonged to Caleb and that's what he wanted to bring tonight.

Back at his condo, we undressed quickly and I scrubbed the makeup off my face.

We were kissing when the phone rang. It was a little after midnight. He ignored it. Then it rang again.

"Hold that thought." He put a finger to my lips. "Yeah," he answered. Silent for a full minute, he grabbed a pad and pencil from the side table drawer. "Monday? Crap. Why didn't you call me earlier?" He was quiet again. "Fine, whatever. Get me on the first flight out. Oh, okay." He looked at the bedside alarm clock. "I'll be there. No, I've got it. Fax the rest of the info to the hotel. Yeah, same one." He hung up.

Sighing, he turned to me. "I'm sorry. I've got to go to Tokyo. Tonight."

I sat up. "Is everything okay?"

"Yeah. It's just a follow-up to the story I was telling you about."

"The arms dealers?"

"Yeah, turns out their funding is coming from an unusual source and there's a merger about to happen . . . That's about all I can tell you right now."

"It's all right. Is there anything I can do?"

He frowned. "You're going to have to get yourself home."

"I can have my parents come get me. It's not a problem, don't worry about it."

He kissed me hard. "Nope. I want you to take the Mercedes. I'll move your packages over from the truck and you can leave in the morning after you get a good night's rest."

I remembered that I had to be back for the nursing home gig. "I can take the truck."

"Nah. You'll be more comfortable in the silver bullet. I'll bring the truck down when I get back." He pulled me to him and kissed me for several minutes. "I don't want to go. I don't want to leave you alone."

I smiled. "I'll be fine, really."

He jumped out of the bed. "I almost forgot." He ran into the living room and I enjoyed the view. His body was strong, that of a runner's. Long legs with solid thighs and a tight butt, and the front of him with those abs was equally appealing.

Holding something behind his back, he sat back on the bed. "I want you to know how much I love you, Kira. And I know you're gun-shy about that word, but I love you and nothing is going to change that."

His lovely face was so earnest I couldn't help but believe the words. I loved him too. Saying it out loud was another story.

I leaned in and kissed him, my lips soft against his, hoping he could feel the emotion even though I couldn't say it.

He deepened the kiss and then pulled back suddenly. "Woman, you make me forget everything. Here." He held out a blue box with a red ribbon. It was long, beautiful, and from Tiffany. At Christmas they replace their trademark white ribbons with the rich red.

"Caleb?"

"Open it."

"Whatever it is, it's too much. You don't have to buy me presents." I looked from the box to him.

He smiled. "I know, baby, but I wanted to do this." Shoving the box in my hand, he tapped it. "Hurry. I now know that every woman in the world loves something in a Tiffany blue box. So I can't lose."

I picked at the ribbon, and then slid it off. Lifting the lid I saw a platinum heart charm bracelet. A tiny gasp escaped. "Caleb, it is too much. It's beautiful." I held it up as brilliant diamonds glittered on the hearts in the light.

"It's . . . gorgeous." My eyes watered and I sniffled. I bit my lip to keep from crying.

"So you like it?" He was like an excited schoolboy.

"I love it."

He took it from me and put it on my wrist. "Every time you look at this I want you to remember how much I love you."

The tears spilled over.

"Oh, baby, please don't cry." He held my face in his hands and used his thumbs to wipe away the tears. "I want you to be happy."

"I am," I said on a sniffle. "It's the most beautiful thing anyone has ever given me."

Smiling, he kissed me again. This one was slow and passionate.

"What time is your flight?"

"Three hours," he said against my lips.

My mind did quick calculations. If we hurried, he'd have just enough time to make it.

Feeling bold, I pushed him back on the bed. "I have a present for you too." I kissed his neck and nibbled at his ear. "A little something for you to take to Japan with you." I slid down his body.

Chapter 26

❧

I can resist everything except temptation.

LADY WINDERMERE'S FAN
By Wilde, Oscar, 1854–1900
Call #: F-WIL
Description: iv, 216 p.

By the time I dropped Caleb off at the airport and made the drive back to Sweet, it was almost seven a.m. I didn't want to stay at his condo without him, so even though I was exhausted, I decided to make the trip home.

I pulled up outside the library and, after locking the Mercedes, I carried the bags to the door.

Inside, the library was cool, but there weren't any dead people hanging out. At least not any I could see.

Herman and Rascal waited for me at the foot of the back stairs. "Hey, pooches. Thanks for watching over the place." They gave a short hello bark, Rascal's high and yippy, Herman's low and loud. One nice thing about ghost dogs is there are never any accidents. And I didn't have to walk them in the cold weather.

I dumped everything on the sofa, threw my clothes on

the floor, and climbed into my bed. I set the alarm for ten and slept for three hours.

I made it to the nursing home in time. I'd dressed in jeans and a green cable-knit sweater. Margie was so grateful I showed up. "Your piano playing helps drown out the tuneless crowd. Hey, what's that?" She pointed at my wrist.

"Isn't it pretty?"

She nodded. "More like gorgeous. Is that from Caleb?"

I bit my lip and nodded.

"Man, he must really be hot for you."

I smiled. "I'm kind of into him too. I've never felt this way about a guy, so it's all kind of new to me."

Margie hugged me. "Kira, I've learned when it comes to men, it's best not to analyze too much. Just enjoy your time with him."

Sam was there and gave me the third degree about my weekend. I placated my protective friend with stories about our dining experiences.

Sam groaned. "I love Sweet, but I've been missing sushi big time."

I laughed. "Maybe we can all go someday soon, after Caleb gets back."

"It's a date. You know, you seem happier than I think I've ever seen you. This thing with Caleb is going well?"

Smiling, I squeezed his arm. "Yeah. It's still new, but yes. It's the best thing ever."

He hugged me. "I'm glad. Be careful." Sam wasn't throwing doubt. He wanted me to protect myself.

"I will." After playing for forty-five minutes, I snuck out while the elder residents opened their gifts.

I picked up a meatloaf sandwich and a salad from Lulu's.

The mysterious phone call from the day before still had me spooked, and I already missed Caleb. I had to keep my mind busy. I planned to search for the all-important book Terry had hounded me about, and I wouldn't rest until I found it.

When I woke up the next morning, I'd been asleep for almost twelve hours. My plan to find the book didn't pan out. I'd lain down to take a short nap, and zonked. The good news was I felt more rested than I had in weeks. I opened my eyes to see the bracelet on my arm and my heart did a funny little flip at the thought of Caleb.

He must have been reading minds, because my cell phone rang. I ran across the cold wood floor to see his number on the caller ID.

"Hey, babe. Did you make it home safe? I know you didn't go back to the condo. I called the doorman."

I rolled my eyes even though he couldn't see me. "Yes. You sound tired. Did you sleep on the plane?"

He laughed. "Off and on. I kept having wicked dreams about a beautiful blonde driving me mad."

I wrapped the quilt from the sofa around me. "Really? Who?"

"Oh, just some girl I met. Her kisses are still making me . . ."

"Caleb! Don't talk like that. I already miss you."

He laughed. "That's what I wanted to hear. Oh, how did the carols at the nursing home go?"

"Fun. Any idea when you might be back?"

"Not yet, but I hope soon. Hold on one sec." I heard him

talking to someone. "Listen, I've got to go. I love you, Kira. Be safe."

"I will."

After we hung up, I squeezed my arms around myself. I did miss him.

"Let's see. Shower, breakfast, and then to work," I said out loud. "Maybe if I work really hard the next few days I can keep my mind off of missing Caleb."

I snorted. "As if."

An hour and half later when I opened the large wooden doors of the library, a surprise stood on the steps.

It took me a minute to recognize him. "Mr. Grayson?" He was one of the men I'd interviewed with in Atlanta.

"Hello, Ms. Smythe. May I come in?"

"Uh, sure." I backed up so he could pass through.

"I know this must seem odd." He shook the snow off his shoulders onto the mat in the vestibule, and then hung his coat on the rack there.

"Surprising, yes." I was glad I'd put on one of my suits this morning and had taken the time to apply makeup. It was kind of hit and miss with me lately. One day I'd wear jeans, the next Armani. I went with my mood. The towns-people didn't seem to care what I wore.

"Cynthia Jordan told me you were staying here through the holidays, and I wanted the chance to speak with you before you made your decision at the end of the year."

"Would you like a cup of coffee?" I offered. *This multi-billionaire had come to the middle of nowhere to woo me?* I was pleased and wary at the same time.

"That would be wonderful. I didn't realize how cold it is here. The jet had a tough time landing in all the snow and ice."

It had been snowing off and on for the last twenty-four hours. There was almost a foot more this morning than when I'd fallen asleep early yesterday.

I brought out two red mugs to the reading table where Mr. Grayson was seated. He wore a maroon sweater over a shirt and tie. "Thank you," he said as I handed him the cup. "This is a quaint town, not at all what I expected in the middle of West Texas."

I laughed. "No one ever expects the architecture. It reminds me of Prague."

He looked up at the stained glass, gothic-style windows. "It's beautiful. I can understand why you wanted to come back here to visit."

I sat back in my chair. I learned long ago to let the other person do the talking. You always find out more that way.

He leaned his elbows forward on the table. "I wanted to apologize."

I raised an eyebrow.

"I feel I came on a little strong during our first meeting." As he spoke, the room filled with people, none of them living. Terry leaned against the row of nonfiction books, filing his nails.

I tried not to notice and concentrated on what Mr. Grayson said. "We want you, and we're willing to make a deal on your terms."

"That's very generous of you." I stared hard at him. "What I don't understand is why?"

Clasping his hands together, he pursed his lips. "Money. That's the honest answer."

I liked that he told the truth.

"Mr. Grayson, any good contract lawyer could do the same for you."

"Would they be as honest or as forthright as you? Do they have your integrity?" he asked.

"What?"

"I don't want to bring back bad memories, but you stood up against your entire corporation for a woman you barely knew. You stood up for what you knew was right. I followed that case from the beginning and I know what you've been through.

"You're the kind of person I want, someone who will do what's right no matter what."

Some of the firms I'd interviewed with had used what I'd done to lowball my salary. Of course, they still wanted me to help them out. This guy saw my loyalty to my coworker as an attribute.

"I don't know what to say." I was honest. "You could have called."

He laughed. "I wanted you to know how serious we are about you. You're one of the most brilliant legal minds I've come across in years. Your instincts are some of the best I've ever seen, especially for one so young. That deal you put together between Myers and Zeb Corp. made your company more than a billion dollars. And you did it in a way that was beneficial to both organizations, made them stronger . . ." He was interrupted when the door blew open and Sam came skating into the library.

I jumped up. "Sam, what's wrong?"

He stopped so fast he almost fell over. He wore his white lab coat over a starched blue shirt and tie. "Are you okay?" He gasped out the words.

"Yes. Why?"

He took a deep breath. "Caleb called. He couldn't get hold of the sheriff. He said some guy from Atlanta was giving you trouble, and that he'd landed here in Sweet. Told me to rush over and save your—" He gave Grayson a nasty look.

It took a minute for my brain to switch into gear. I laughed.

Mr. Grayson stood up slowly, watching the spectacle.

"I'm fine. Sam, this is Mr. Grayson. He owns one of the investment firms," I cleared my throat, "where I've been *interviewing*. He flew in to talk to me personally. About a job."

Confusion ran over Sam's face and he frowned. "So he's not trying to—*oh.*"

I laughed again. "No." I turned to Mr. Grayson. "I'm sorry. I have an over-protective boyfriend who seems to know my every move even though he's on business in Japan."

I had no idea how Caleb knew Mr. Grayson had arrived, but I would deal with him later.

"Sam, you can go back to work now."

He was still trying to catch his breath.

"Oh. Yeah." He reached out a hand. "Mr. Grayson, nice to meet you. Sorry. We're all kind of protective of our Kira."

"I find that quite admirable, Doctor."

The absurdity of the situation made me smile again. "I'm so sorry about this. I couldn't begin to explain even if I tried. Do you have time for breakfast? I'd love to give you a little taste of Sweet before you go, and we can continue our talk."

He glanced at his watch, which I noticed cost more than most peoples' homes. "I do have some time."

I shooed Sam out the door. "You better call me later and tell me what the hell Caleb was so worried about," Sam whispered.

I nodded.

I took Mr. Grayson by the arm. "I think the very least I owe you is breakfast." If nothing else, the twins drooling over the handsome older man might help him forget all of this nonsense.

He'd have his hands full with Ms. Johnnie and Ms. Helen, and maybe if I was in a public place, Caleb would stop sending in the cavalry.

Cool-Looking Old Guys

1. Sean Connery
2. Clint Eastwood
3. Mr. Grayson
4. Paul Newman
5. Ian McKellen

Chapter 27

Night, the mother of fear and mystery, was coming upon me.

THE WAR OF THE WORLDS
By Wells, H. G. (Herbert George), 1866–1946
Call #: F-WEL
Description: xxxvi, 199 p., maps; 20cm

After seeing Mr. Grayson off, I called Caleb and left a message.

I was at the front desk when he returned my call. "What were you thinking?" I screamed. I seldom lost my temper, but he'd gone too far.

"You can be mad, Kira, but I'm not going to apologize. I was worried about you. The police in Atlanta have pictures from the security cameras of some guy skulking around your condo. I wasn't about to take any risks."

I blew out a breath. "How did you even know someone was here?"

"I've got Daryl out at the hangar calling me whenever visitors fly in, and the sheriff is supposed to be keeping an eye on the roads. When I couldn't get in touch with the sheriff, I called Sam."

I growled. "Caleb, common sense says some guy flying in on a private jet is not coming to kill me. You made me look like an idiot in front of a man who flew here to hire me."

"I had no way of knowing that since I'm on the other side of the world," Caleb bit out the words. "Damn. I am sorry for that. I don't want to fight with you. I'm tired and things aren't going well here. And I feel like I should be there protecting you."

I suddenly noticed several live and dead patrons trying to act like they weren't listening. I'd been so mad, I hadn't realized they were there. I gave them my best death stare and they looked down at their various books.

I made my way back to the break room and heated water for a cup of tea. "Maybe next time you could call *me* first? We'll have some kind of code word and if there's a bad guy here I'll say it."

"Hmph," Caleb grunted.

"How about, 'Sir, I'm sorry, we don't carry the Batman comics'?" I had no idea where that came from, but it made him laugh.

"I'm still not going to apologize for loving you and wanting to take care of you," he grumbled. "And I wish you'd keep your cell phone closer. If I'd been able to talk to you, none of this ever would have happened."

I smiled. "Caleb I can't be accountable to you twenty-four hours a day. Just *think* before you decide to charge in on your white horse to save the damsel in distress, or ask your friends to charge in. Now when in the hell are you going to be home? It's been almost two days, and even though I'm furious with you, I can't stand it much longer."

"I'm on my way. I leave in about an hour, and it's a seventeen-hour flight back to Dallas."

This time I was the one who grumbled. "Whatever. Bed's cold. Hurry home."

He laughed. "I'll be home to keep you warm soon. I love you."

We hung up and I carried my tea back to the front. I heard whispers as I rounded the shelves, and then a hush. The Sweet gossips, dead and alive, would have fun with this one.

Later in the afternoon I had another surprise visitor. Bronwyn was back in town. She came to return the books she'd borrowed and to check out a few more. I invited her to an impromptu girls' night and called Margie to see if she could come too.

They both arrived at seven and I introduced them to each other. We'd decided on a Mexican theme. I'd borrowed one of the cookbooks from the library and had made my first batch of chicken enchiladas. Margie brought the rice and beans and Bronwyn provided the margaritas and desserts.

I showed them to the back and up the stairs.

"What is this place?" Margie asked as we climbed the steps. At the top of the landing she said, "Oh."

"Hey, who would have known?" Bronwyn chimed in. "This is so cool."

It made me happy that they liked it.

"How did you get all this furniture up those stairs?" Bronwyn said as she deposited the margarita mix on the counter.

"I have no idea." I shrugged. "None of it's mine. It belonged to Mrs. Canard."

Bronwyn nodded. "Huh. She had really great taste. It's comfortable but kind of chic in a way."

"Yes it is." Margie pulled a Crock-Pot out of the box she was carrying and plugged it into one of the outlets on the counter.

I'd eaten most of my meals at the small table in the kitchen area, but we set everything up in the formal dining room for tonight.

By the time we had the food on the table, it was like we were old friends. Well, Margie and I had known each other forever, but Bronwyn fit right in.

"So Margie, who was that guy I saw you with at Lulu's?" I asked. We'd had two margaritas, and the giggles had already begun.

"Nosy butt." Margie bit her lip. "His name's Billy. He's a rancher and one hot kisser." She laughed. "I met him at the nursing home when he came to visit one of his old ranch hands. He's kind of nice, and not so pushy like some of the other guys in town."

I had a lot of respect for Margie. She hadn't had the easiest childhood, but she'd put herself through nursing school and carved out a life in Sweet.

"But enough about me." Margie leaned forward. "You and Caleb are the talk of the town. And when a man gives a woman a bracelet like that"—she pointed to the Tiffany hearts—"things are downright serious."

I couldn't keep from smiling. "I'm taking it one day at a time."

Bronwyn laughed. "You're full of crap. I can see it in

your eyes. You are just as sappy over him as he is over you. I think it's kind of cool."

I took a bite of my enchilada so I didn't have to say anything.

"Come on, Kira. Tell us what's really going on," Margie urged.

"I don't know. I mean, I haven't decided what I'm going to do as far as a job is concerned. I've had a couple of really great offers. One is for my dream job in New York. Caleb lives in Dallas, and I don't know how good I'd be at a long-distance relationship.

"And then there's the library. I don't know what to do about it."

"What do you mean?" Bronwyn asked.

I told them everything about the will and what had been going on, minus the dead people.

Bronwyn blew out a low whistle. "That's rough. And you haven't found any loopholes?"

I shook my head. "I'm sure Mr. Pierce came up with that will, and he's a crafty old coot. I can't find a single word out of place. It's annoying as hell."

"Man, I can't imagine this town without the library." Margie sipped her drink. "That's kind of sucky. I mean, Kira, you have to do what's best for you. Not everyone gets a chance at a dream job, but it's sad to think about this place being sold off at an auction."

The very idea made me sick to my stomach.

Bronwyn put her paper napkin on the table. "Well, one thing you don't have to worry about is Caleb. He wants to move here, but I have a feeling he's going to follow you wherever you end up. He's like a little puppy that has found the perfect master. I don't know what you did to the guy, but he's well and thoroughly leashed."

I laughed. "Don't tell him, but that goes both ways. I can't imagine my life without him. Heck, it's hard for me to remember what things were like before I met him. But it's all happened so fast." I looked at Margie. "A dear friend told me to take it one day at a time, and that's what I'm doing."

Bronwyn rolled her eyes. "I don't get what you see in him, but you could do worse. I certainly have. You guys ready for dessert?"

After serving up huge chunks of apple pie from Lulu's, we talked until almost midnight. I'd just let them out the front door into the cold December wind when I realized it was just as chilly inside.

I turned to find a mob staring back at me. Terry was once again at the lead of the pack. The dogs had materialized beside me, as if they guarded against the dead. At least the pooches were on my side.

A rose brooch had been added to Terry's green dress, and I wondered if the people on the other side had the option of changing clothes or if they could only add accessories.

"Can I help you?"

"Are you going to leave us?" His voice sounded pained.

I shrugged. "I can't stay here forever. I'm a lawyer, not a librarian."

"But if you leave, they'll sell the place and then what will we do?" He tapped his long fingernails against the back of a chair.

"Certainly there are other libraries you can go to." I refused to let them make me feel guilty. Though they were doing a pretty good job.

"No, we can't. You still haven't read the book." Terry pointed a finger at me. "You can't possibly understand the magnitude of what will happen if this place goes to auction."

Frustrated, I pulled a hand through my hair. "I can't find this imaginary book with all the answers that you've been talking about. I've looked through shelves, stacks, boxes, everywhere I could think. I haven't found any *book*."

He turned to the group. "Fan out people. You know what you are looking for, and we aren't leaving until we find it."

"What are you doing?" I crossed my arms.

The spirits spread out all over the library and more arrived. They were upstairs and down, in the break room and even under the counters.

"We're going to find that book. It's time you discovered who you really are, Kira Smythe." Terry gave me a stern look.

I didn't roll my eyes, but I wanted to. I sat down at the computer and pretended to be busy while they looked. I'd searched the place over, and I knew they wouldn't find anything.

After a half hour, a guy around forty or so whispered something to Terry.

He cut his eyes, framed with the largest pair of fake lashes I'd ever seen, at me.

I threw up my hands. "What?"

"Jack here is a detective—or was—for the Chicago Police Department. He says you need to search your apartment upstairs."

"I thought I told you guys to stay out of my loft."

Terry frowned. "You did. That's why he said *you* need to

do the searching. We've looked everywhere, and that's the only logical place left. Jack says he'd be willing to bet that it's right in front of your face."

Jack's a jerk.

Terry's eyebrow lifted as if he knew what I thought. Everyone stopped their search and turned to look at me.

I growled. "Fine, whatever. I'll go look upstairs. But no one comes up with me." I thought about crawling into the bed and pulling a pillow over my head; there was nothing they could do about it. Unfortunately, they'd probably be waiting downstairs when I woke up, so I decided to at least make the effort.

Though I'd looked through it a half dozen times, I searched the bookshelf in the living area first. There was a mixture of books from Mrs. Canard, and some that I'd brought up.

I put my finger on each spine, reading it carefully. When I ran into Dickens's *A Christmas Carol*, I picked it up. When I was a kid I read it every year around this time. The book fell out of my hands and hit the floor with a thud.

The jacket came off and the hard cover read, *Library Care for the Living and the Dead.*

Oh.

Sitting down on the floor, I picked it up and put it in my lap. It was warm to the touch. I flipped open the first page, and gasped.

Things I Don't Like About Dead People

1. They're cold
2. They're nosy
3. They always wear the same thing (I know it's petty, but it bugs me.)
4. When they want something, they won't leave you alone until they get it
5. They freak me out

Chapter 28

It's quite a three-pipe problem.

THE RED-HEADED LEAGUE
By Doyle, Arthur Conan, Sir, 1859–1930
Call #: F-DOY
Description: 101 p.: ill, 21cm

THIS BOOK BELONGS TO
KIRA SMYTHE

A headache throbbed at my temples and my throat felt dry.

You have been selected for an important position as a Seer for the Librarian of Knowledge. As you ascend to each level, your powers and abilities will grow. At the end of your tenure, you'll have full use of the Akashic Records and will use this Book of Life's power to help those around you.

In the beginning it is your job to . . .

Freaking out doesn't begin to describe what happened to me. *Powers? Abilities?*

I'm a lawyer. I can write a heck of a contract and oversee mergers, but I have no powers.

Your resources are as immense as the universe here and beyond. You have the ability to find the answer to any question, to solve every dilemma. It is a certain kind of magic that gives complete and total access to universal answers.

At Stage One of your powers you will see the living and the dead more clearly by the month's end. They will come to you with a variety of questions, and at first you may have feelings of anxiety. You may also experience nausea, headaches, and occasional blackouts while trying to find the answers. These symptoms will disappear as your power grows.

The blackouts come from your attempts to search for information in the Akashic Records beyond your current capabilities.

You are one of twelve librarians on earth with your abilities. Each is set in a specific location near a portal . . .

I shut the book. It was too much. The Akashic Records were like some metaphysical source of the ultimate cosmic library. I'd read about it years ago in an Edgar Cayce book.

This thing was telling me that I would have access to pure knowledge. It wasn't possible.

"Yoo hoo!" Terry's voice carried up the stairwell. "Did you find the book?"

I didn't bother to move. "Yes," I said through gritted teeth.

"That's wonderful. Call for me if you have questions. We'll see you tomorrow." His chipper voice grated along my spine.

Not if I can help it.

There was a simple solution to this insanity. All I had to do was leave. I could hop on a plane and go back to Atlanta or accept Mr. Grayson's offer for the New York job. I could go tonight and I'd never have to step foot in this weird place again.

I was angry. How could Mrs. Canard have done this to me? How could she think I would want to be party to this? Why me?

The book was still warm and I shoved it into the bookcase. It fell out again and I scooted away from it.

I needed to leave, but I was so tired. I looked at my watch and it was almost one. I'd been up since six. I couldn't stay here. I had to get out.

I grabbed my purse and keys, and ten minutes later I was at my parents'. I used the electronic key code to let myself in, and made my way to the room they'd given me a few weeks ago.

After a quick shower I was in bed. Someone knocked on the door. "Kira?" It was my mom.

"Sorry if I woke you," I apologized.

"Is everything okay, hon?"

"Something is up with the heat at the library. I just need to crash here for a bit."

"Oh." She didn't sound convinced. "Okay. Let me know if you need anything."

"I'm fine. I really am sorry I woke you."

"Don't worry about it."

I heard her walk away.

My life had taken a weird twist and I didn't like it. I'm a logical woman who always has a plan. Well, I had planned to stay at the library until the end of the month, but I couldn't do that now. I stared at the ceiling for hours.

I must have fallen asleep at some point, because my dad woke me the next morning.

"Kira, Mom has breakfast ready for you. And a young man has been calling the main line. Caleb? He says he kept trying your cell but you didn't answer. I told him you were staying here."

I groaned. I must have left my cell phone at the library along with all my other belongings.

"Thank you, Dad. I'll be out in a little bit. If Caleb calls again, tell him I'll give him a ring later this morning."

Splashing water on my face, I stared in the mirror.

You can't walk away.

Oh, yes I can.

I argued with myself. *Those people need you. The town needs you.*

I can't deal with this right now.

I blotted my face dry and wiped my hands on the towel. I hadn't bothered bringing a change of clothes, so I pulled on my jeans and my sweater from the night before.

My mom was in the kitchen scrambling some eggs. "Ms. Johnnie just called. She said the adult literacy team is at the diner waiting for you."

I smacked my hand against my head. "I forgot." The team worked with adults in town who wanted to develop their reading skills.

She put some of the cooked eggs on a piece of whole grain toast. "Here, eat this on the way. You're looking pale."

I kissed her cheek, and she grabbed my face in her hands.

Leaning her head to the right, she gave me the mom stare. "Hon, if something's wrong, you can tell me."

"I know." I gave her a quick hug "Everything's fine. I need to go. I'll talk to you later."

I pulled away and ran for the door, grabbing my purse as I went.

Ilooked like crap, but there wasn't time to stop by the library and freshen up. I walked into the diner to see the literacy team sitting at three tables they had pushed together.

"There she is." Travis Lyle motioned toward me. "Are you okay?" The question was kind. Travis was a substitute teacher, and when he wasn't at one of the schools, he helped out Mr. Owen at The Bakery in the mornings.

"Sorry, gang. If you want to get your coffee to go, I'll open up the library. I was running a little late this morning." I smiled.

There were some curious glances, but they followed me across the street. An hour later we had a set schedule for volunteer needs for the next six months. It felt weird talking about things for the future, when I knew I wouldn't be here. And if I didn't stay, the library wouldn't be here either.

Maybe they can meet at the high school library. I tried to console myself.

The dead mixed among the living, and before I knew it, the library was full to capacity. As I watched the masses and answered questions, I realized something important. I couldn't leave. At least, not until the New Year. I had a plan and I was going to stick to it.

But I refused to look at that book again.

Chapter 29

❧

Love has no age, no limit; and no death.

THE FORSYTE SAGA
By Galsworthy, John, 1867–1933
Call #: F-GAL
Description: xx, 715 p.: ill; 22cm

I'd shut down the computer and the library was blessedly silent. I told the spirits that they had to follow business hours, just like anyone else, and that they weren't allowed to talk to me when live people were around.

They must have finally taken me seriously. I'd been working on research for Bronwyn since the library closed at six. She'd called to see if I could find something out about golems. Turns out they are living creatures made from dirt that have no soul. They are very hard to kill because they can just patch themselves back together. To kill one, you have to etch its name in its forehead and then erase it. I e-mailed her the info, but wondered how in the world she could accomplish the task. Knowing Bronwyn, she would find a way.

A pile of books on the front desk needed to be shelved,

but it was almost nine. I decided they could wait until morning.

Rascal and Herman growled.

"Hey you two, cut that out." Pushing back from my desk, I thought I heard someone cough. The growls turned into barking. Maybe it was one of the shadows I'd heard about.

"Hello?" It seemed odd that a spirit would cough. They no longer had ailments where they were. I'd locked the door more than three hours ago. No one said anything, but I sensed some movement back by the break room. I moved around the desk to check it out, and I was suddenly plunged into an ice shield.

"No!" Mr. Greenblatt, who owned the pharmacy when I was a kid, shouted. "Don't you go back there! Someone wants to do you harm." The elderly gentleman stood two inches in front of me. "He's standing back there with a gun, little missy. You need to get out of here."

Grabbing the keys, my stomach a mass of nerves, I ran for the door.

"Don't move," a man said behind me as he poked something into my back.

Here's the thing: nothing bad ever happens in Sweet. The town is protected by a coven of witches, and not much gets past them. So the last thing I ever expected was a gun in my back. Well, at the time I didn't know that's what it was, but it felt like it.

"I don't know who you are, but we don't keep any money here. The money for the fines is deposited every day at five and we seldom have over five dollars at any given time. You can have my purse. I have a little cash and some credit cards." My voice trembled, and I tried to make myself breathe evenly. I held it out for him.

"I *don't* want your money," he spat.

Oh, crap. He's going to rape me. I couldn't keep my eyes from watering. My mind instantly flashed to the self-defense classes I'd taken in college. *Please, God. Don't let me die!*

"What do you want?"

"Answers." I heard him take a deep breath. "I want to know what you said to my sister to make her jump off that roof."

Sister? "Are you Todd? Melinda's brother?" I turned around, but it was so dark, I could only see his outline. His cap was pulled low over his face and he wore a sweatshirt and jeans. I recognized him as the man who had followed me in Atlanta.

He didn't say anything.

My mouth seemed to have a mind of its own. "She talked about you all the time. She was so proud of you." Melinda had loved her brother dearly. He'd been stationed in Iraq and couldn't come home when she was going through her sexual harassment case against her boss.

I'd witnessed her boss's touchy-feely nature and encouraged her to report it. At the time I didn't think there was any way we could lose. We had one of the best attorneys in the city and an ironclad case with tons of witnesses and women he'd manhandled before. I should have known what a lot of money could do, as well as the power of the right connections. The jerk's family was old Atlanta money; it didn't matter how guilty he might be. He wouldn't go to jail.

Todd didn't speak.

"Look, I can't even imagine what you think, but I'll tell you anything you want to know. You don't need the gun."

He moved closer and shoved the gun in my chest.

My hands shook, and I wasn't sure how much longer my knees would hold out.

Since he'd moved closer I could see his green eyes, and dark brown hair peeked out beneath his hat. He had to be at least six feet tall.

The hate rolled off of him. It was almost as if I could feel the heat of his anger.

I started to put the keys in my pocket and then thought perhaps I might need them as a weapon.

For a moment we stared at each other.

"I read the police report and the court files. The way I see it, you killed my sister."

I shook my head. "No," I whispered. But the truth is, I didn't believe it. I had been the one to push Melinda into making the case against that ass Anderson. I'd seen him pressing her up against a wall one night when I'd been working late. I'd gone to his office to drop off some files. He made light of the situation, but I'd seen her trying to push him away.

The memories flooded back and my eyes filled with tears. "Maybe you're right. It is my fault. I saw him touching her and I just . . . She looked terrified and I had to say something. I couldn't just walk away." A sob slipped out of my throat. Turning my head to the left. I tried to pull myself together. This was no time for hysterics.

I took a shaky breath and stood tall. Facing Todd I told him, "No woman deserves to be treated that way. And that jerk had no right to touch her if that isn't what she wanted. And I know she didn't. She tried to push him away before they ever knew I was there."

Todd didn't say anything and he still had the gun pointed at me. I looked just over his shoulder to see Mr. Greenblatt waving his arms in a big motion as if he was trying to get my attention.

Ignoring him, I focused on Todd. "The office was divided, and some people didn't believe her, or me, for that matter. For six months her life was . . . tough."

"I know all of this." The words weren't quite as angry as before. "She was okay. She called me after the verdict and told me what happened. She was sad and said that she'd have to quit. There was no way she could be in that building with him anymore." Shaking his head, he shoved the gun at me again. "What I want to know is what you said to her on the roof. The police report says she jumped five minutes after you arrived."

I looked down at the floor. The guilt overwhelmed me. I'd pushed all of this out of mind more than a month ago. It'd been too much. So much that my body and brain had shut down for the week afterward.

"I can't remember," I sobbed again. This time the sound was torn from my throat. Wrapping my arms around myself, I tried to calm down.

Mr. Greenblatt had moved beside Todd, and on the other side of him was a woman I didn't recognize. "Help is on the way," the elderly gentleman said. "And this woman wants to talk to you."

Why won't you leave me alone! I cleared my throat. "I was in my office on the phone when I heard the commotion out in the lobby. The police were there. I hung up and walked out. I overheard them talking to building security, saying that there was a woman on the roof."

My legs gave out and I slid down to the door in a heap.

"Stand up!" Todd yelled. He shivered. "Don't you believe in heat? It's freezing in here."

I couldn't do what he asked. The more the memories came back, the worse I felt. Bile rose in my throat and I shivered too, not from the ghosts that now surrounded us, but from my long-ago buried emotions.

"I knew when they said someone was on the roof that it was Melinda. I just knew it. At the courthouse she'd been so strong. When the Not Guilty verdict came down, she was a rock. 'I know you tried,' she told me. I cried and she gave me comfort, hugged me. She didn't show an ounce of distress."

Hugging my knees, I tried to stop the shivering, which was so bad my teeth chattered. It was as if the shock I'd experienced that day was instantly fresh in my body. "Your sister was an amazing woman. She walked out of that court with her head held high. I knew she would quit. Hell, at that point I even thought about it. Of course, they made the decision for me."

"What do you mean?"

I looked up and saw that the gun was at his side, no longer pointed at me. It didn't matter. I had to finish the story to the best of my ability.

"They fired me. Well, it was considered a layoff. But it was just as well. After what happened, I couldn't be in that place anymore.

"I told you about the police coming to the office. No one

was allowed to go up, but I thought maybe if I could talk with her, help her to see reason. They had officers posted at the elevators, but not the stairwells. I snuck past and climbed the five stories to the top of the building.

"I opened the door and there were two police officers, and that's all I can remember."

He raised the gun again. "I don't believe you. How could you forget something so important? Whatever you said made her jump."

"I don't know. I don't." I sobbed into my arm. I felt a hand on my shoulder and looked up. The woman, who had been standing next to Todd, was there. She'd moved to the other side of him so she could touch me.

"It's okay, dear. Tell him his mother is here and I want to talk to him."

I shook my head. The guy had a gun. I wasn't about to tell him that his dead mother wanted to talk to him.

"It will be okay, hon. I promise. Tell him that you see things some people don't and that Deidre wants to talk to him."

I looked to Mr. Greenblatt and he nodded.

I took a deep steadying breath. "I know you want to kill me, and I don't blame you. I'd give anything to remember what I said to her. I blacked it all out." I cleared my throat for the second time. "There's, um, see—I . . . oh, geez. I can see things some people can't." The words rushed out and I paused. Todd stared at me like I had suddenly turned into an alien.

"What the hell are you talking about? I want to know about my sister."

I held up a hand. "Trust me, I understand, but I have to

tell you this. Deidre wants to talk to you. That's why you feel so chilled. She's standing next to you."

Backing up, he looked to the left and right. "Are you crazy?"

"Yes, probably. I started hearing voices after Melinda died. Now I actually see dead people. At least I think I do. I know how it sounds. Your mother is here. She's dressed in a blue dress and black heels and she has a pink rose attached to her lapel. She wants to talk to you."

This time he stumbled back. "Hey, I'm not falling for your trick. That's what we buried her in—anyone could have told you that. Hell, Melinda could have told you."

I didn't want to argue with him.

Clasping her white-gloved hands in front of her, she nodded toward me. "Tell him when he was seven and stole the peanut butter jar, that I knew he hid it under his bed. And that when he was eleven and had the chicken pox that we made puppets out of the socks I put on his hand to keep him from scratching."

I told Todd what she said.

"It's—you can't know that. How do you know that?"

I shrugged. "She told me."

"Tell him I was on the roof that day. I know what happened to my daughter."

I relayed the message. Todd just stood there.

"After you came up, there was a bit of a scurry. The police hadn't expected you. When you explained who you were, they let you talk to her." As she explained what happened, my mind opened up.

Suddenly, I was back on the roof. It was cold being up so high, and I hadn't remembered my jacket. The wind whipped

Melinda's skirt around as she stood on the ledge. She seemed so calm for someone standing on the edge of a building thirty stories high.

Her long brown hair waved in the wind.

" 'Kira, you shouldn't be here.' She pointed toward me, her voice monotone.

"I told her that she was the one who shouldn't be there. I begged her to step down. Whatever was wrong, we would make it better.

"She shook her head. 'There are some things that just can't be fixed. You've been a good friend, but even you can't get me out of this hell,' she said. She waved some papers at me. 'He's hit me with a defamation of character suit. Can you believe that? They were handed to me as I left court.' She laughed, but it wasn't a happy sound. 'I'm sorry, Kira. I can't take it anymore. I'm at the end. I just can't do it.'

"I reached out to her," I told her brother. " 'Please,' I cried. 'If you do this, he wins. You can't let him win. I'll fight him with you. I promise, we'll see this through to the end.'

"She cocked her head and smiled, but it was so sad. 'You can't save me this time,' she said. Then she stepped back. She didn't scream. One minute she was there, the next . . ." I cried again. I couldn't help it. I put my head in my hand. "I didn't say the right things. I should have never brought *him* up."

The hand rested on my shoulder. "No dear, it wasn't your fault. You couldn't have done anything different. My daughter took matters into her own hands that day. Nothing you could have said would have made a difference."

I explained to Todd what she said. He laid the gun on the library counter.

"Tell my son I want him to get help. He's going to want to go after that man. He needs to understand that justice will be done. I won't have both of my children destroyed because of that evil. Tell him I'm with him always."

When I said the last words to him, the tears fell from his eyes and he crumbled to the floor. "I'm sorry. I'm so, so, sorry."

I scooted across to him, my legs still too weak to stand. "It's okay." He was hunched over, but I put my arms around him the best I could. He sobbed.

Someone banged on the door and I jerked up.

"Kira. Are you in there?"

It was Caleb.

"Open this damn door or I swear I'll knock it down. The sheriff's here and we know someone is in there with you. Let us in."

Todd waved a hand. "Let them in. I deserve to go to jail."

"You scared me to death with that gun, but you don't deserve to go jail. I'm not sure what I would have done if I'd been in your shoes. But you have to promise to do what your mom said and get some help."

He nodded, the tears still flowing. I grabbed the door handle and pulled myself up. Picking my keys up off the floor, I opened the door and said, "Don't worry, sir, I have some Batman comics. Everything is okay."

Things to Do When in Stressful Situations

1. Think of your favorite joke
2. Count ceiling tiles or books on a shelf
3. Think about favorite desserts
4. Make to-do lists
5. Think of how many shoes are in your closet

Chapter 30

Deep, unspeakable suffering may well be called a baptism, a regeneration, the initiation into a new state.

ADAM BEDE
By Eliot, George, 1819–1880
Call #: F-ELI
Description: 509 p.; 22cm

As soon as the lock clicked Caleb shoved through the door. In an instant he took in Todd on the floor, my tear-stained face, and the gun on the counter.

"What the hell's going on?" Caleb pulled me to his chest and then pushed me away, looking for injuries.

Before I could answer, the sheriff rushed past him to Todd. "You're under arrest . . ." As he Mirandized Todd he put the cuffs on him. The man on the floor didn't resist and stood solemnly when the sheriff pulled him up.

"What are you arresting him for?"

"Assault with a deadly weapon." The police officer waved toward the gun on the counter.

"He didn't assault me." My voice was still a little on the nervous side. I coughed. "We were talking. You can't arrest a man for just talking." If I had to, I'd pull the lawyer card.

"Are you telling me this man wasn't holding you against your will?"

I looked Todd straight in the eyes. "Like I said, we were talking. I'm not going to press charges, so you might as well lose the cuffs." I shrugged. "But I do think it'd be a good idea to have Sam check him out." I turned to Melinda's brother. "Todd, that's the local doctor here in town. He's also a dear friend. Someone you can trust. You've been through a lot and I think it'd be a good idea."

The sheriff kept the cuffs on. "This gun registered?"

"Yes, sir," Todd said.

"Well, I'll be holding on to it for the time being." The sheriff looked at me. "Are you sure about this?"

I nodded.

"I'll take you over to the hospital, we'll figure this out from there."

Todd stopped as the sheriff led him out. "Thank you for telling me the truth. I'm sorry."

I touched his arm. "It's okay."

Two cups of tea and an hour later, I had explained everything to Caleb. Well, except the parts concerning the dead people.

"That's quite a story." He sat next to me on the sofa in my living room. The night's events had left me cold. In his arms, I'd finally defrosted.

"So how did you guys know something was wrong?" I snuggled closer to him.

"The coven. Sheriff's one of the members. One of the witches said she saw trouble at the library in her crystals. I was across the street at Lulu's waiting for some takeout. I saw the squad car pull up. When he told me what was going on, I—hell, I didn't know what to think."

He continued, "You should press charges. The guy held you at gunpoint. He could have killed you." Caleb's voice dipped. "I can't even think what I'd have done if he hurt you."

I shook my head. "If you'd been there, you would understand. He's not a bad man; he's just lost so much this last year. His mother died and then Melinda. A person can only take so much."

"Yes, Kira, but that doesn't mean he gets to take his grief out on you. He could have killed you."

"No. I don't believe it would have come to that."

"You're too damn compassionate," Caleb grunted.

I laughed. "The librarian thing must really be seeping in. No one ever calls lawyers compassionate."

"Well, the story about your friend explains a lot. I could never figure out why you seemed so distant sometimes. One minute we'd be in the middle of a conversation and the next you'd be in Neverland staring out into space."

I wondered what he'd think if I told him the real truth about those moments. What would happen if I told him everything about the magical library, and the dead people?

But I couldn't do it. Not right then. I'd have to tell him the truth at some point, but my mind and body couldn't handle any more trauma. I'd been through too much already.

I sighed.

"Hey, you should get some rest. How about I run back to Lulu's for that takeout and then we'll get you to bed?" He winked. "And don't be trying to pull any funny stuff. You need your rest."

I laughed. "Food actually sounds good."

He stood and then bent down to kiss my cheek. "Do you have any idea how much I love you? I— If something had happened to you, I don't know what I would have done."

I reached up and squeezed his hand, my heart full of the same emotion. "I love you too." It was the first time I'd said it back to him.

He stared at me a minute and then kissed me hard. "Okay. I'll be back in five minutes. Don't do anything crazy like talk down a madman while I'm gone."

I laughed again. "I promise."

Sam called later, around midnight, and said Todd had agreed to admit himself into a psychiatric program in a Fort Worth hospital. The sheriff and Sam were taking him there.

"I want you in my office first thing tomorrow morning, considering everything you've been through the last two months," Sam ordered.

I didn't have the energy to argue. "Okay." I was wrapped in the quilt in the corner of the couch. I couldn't seem to get warm. "Is Todd going to be okay?"

"Yes. Eventually. I talked to him for a long time. I can see why you didn't want to press charges. This program he's going into has grief recovery as part of it. He also has some issues from his time in Iraq to deal with. A lot of those men and women are having a tough time assimilating back into their regular routines. But he's going somewhere that will give him some real help."

"I'm glad. I just feel so damn sorry for him."

"Yeah. Oh. I just remembered something. I heard you were drinking margaritas the other night with Margie and that new witch. You shouldn't be mixing alcohol with the antibiotics you've been taking."

I didn't say anything. I'd bop Margie on the head and institute a new rule for the girls: what happened at Kira's stayed at Kira's.

"You stopped the antibiotics?" Sam asked.

I sighed. "I'm so much better." Except for being beyond exhausted.

"Kira, your body fought off a major infection. You don't just stop because you feel better. No more booze, and get back on those pills."

"Yes, sir."

He laughed. "You've been through another major shock. Don't forget, eight thirty tomorrow morning in my office. If you aren't here I'll make Caleb drag you. I hear he was pretty worried about you."

I smiled. "Yeah."

Caleb walked out of the bathroom with a towel wrapped around his hips. Every nerve in my body shot to attention.

"He's a good guy."

"I'm glad you finally figured that out. The sheriff's ready to go. I'll see you tomorrow."

I clicked the off button and held up the phone. "Sam says I have to come see him tomorrow morning."

"I wish he would come tonight. You are so pale." He sat on the back of the sofa and rubbed his fingers on my cheek. So sweet and tender.

"He wants me to go back on the antibiotics."

Caleb moved away to the kitchen cabinets and pulled

down the three bottles of pills there. "Which ones are the antibiotics?"

I shook my head. "I can get them."

He waved a hand. "You stay where you are."

I kind of liked him taking care of me. "I can't remember the name, but it's the big fat white ones that start with an A."

He brought me a glass of water with the pill. "Drink up."

I did what he asked. "In case I forget, thank you for taking care of me." I winked at him.

He took the glass out of my hand. "I plan on taking care of you for a very long time, Kira. I know I said it before, but you scared the hell out of me. I can't lose you."

Scooping me up off the couch, he turned and sat down, depositing me on his lap.

His warm hands reached inside the quilt to hug me. "You're still freezing."

I leaned against his chest. "I can't seem to get warm."

"You're in shock. I'm taking you to the hospital." He started to get up.

"No!" I cried. "Please. I just need you, Caleb." I looked up at him. "I just need you."

He moved me off his lap and I worried he would make me go to the hospital. Then he scooped me up again, quilt and all, and made his way to the bedroom. "Come on, baby, let's get you warm."

Chapter 31

❧

"Some persons hold," he pursued, still hesitating, "that there is a wisdom of the Head, and that there is a wisdom of the Heart."

HARD TIMES
By Dickens, Charles, 1812–1870
Call #: F-DIC
Description: xvi, 184 p.; 22cm

About four the next morning I heard voices arguing downstairs. Caleb had me in his death grip, but I was able to slither out of his hold without waking him.

Grabbing my robe and fluffy dog slippers, I made my way downstairs.

The library was full of the dead and they bickered back and forth.

"Do you guys have to do this now? Haven't I been through enough? I mean, seriously. What's so important that you have to wake me up at this ungodly hour?"

Terry was at the forefront holding Rascal, who wore a pink bow in his hair. I wondered how the pooch felt about that. "Honey, I'm glad that man didn't do anything awful. I couldn't get here in time and I just feel so bad."

He dabbed a tissue against his eyes.

"I'm fine and I'm not sure what you could have done to help. Things were pretty weird as it was." I didn't need a six foot six drag queen dressed as Jackie O adding to that complicated situation.

"But I have a feeling that's not why you are here. So spill it."

Terry gave a dramatic sigh. "Some of us believe you should know the truth about what's going on with Mrs. Canard."

Mr. Greenblatt stepped in front of the drag queen. "Gosh darnit, woman, or whatever the hell you are, I told you, you can't say anything. It's against the rules."

"Wait." I held up a hand. "Mrs. Canard is dead and she's moved on. What could be wrong?"

"She's . . . stuck," Terry spit out—with difficulty, because Mr. Greenblatt covered his mouth with his large hand. "You can't sway her one way or another. It has to be her decision. Mabel wouldn't want you interfering with the way things are supposed to be."

Terry placed Rascal on the floor, and his hands went to his hips. "Mabel can't do much of anything right now. And I'm Kira's guide. I'm supposed to help her make informed decisions, and I can *do* whatever is necessary to help her."

I pulled myself up onto the front desk. The granite was cold even with the protection of my robe. "Guys? Where is Mrs. Canard?"

"She's in processing," Terry answered.

"Didn't one of you say she was in processing weeks ago? Does it really take that long?"

Terry shrugged.

"I'm the librarian. You have to tell me. You can't lie." My hand flew to my mouth.

274

"She read the book," Terry said smartly.

Not that part. I didn't know how I knew that.

"Until you decide for sure if you're staying, she can't move on to the next level," Terry said, his hips swaying as he walked toward me. For a guy in stilettos, he did a good job. "She's stuck in the in-between place. If you decide to stay, she moves up. If not, she becomes one of us."

Now I wished I had read more of the book. "Spirits who haunt the earth?"

He laughed. "No. We aren't haunting. We just come here for the reading materials." He paused. "And for answers."

"Why can't you move to the next level?"

Mr. Greenblatt gave me a strange look. "We don't have the power. None of us are librarians."

More confused than ever, I grabbed my head. "So if I decide to take the job in New York, not only do you lose your library, but she's stuck in the in-between for eternity."

Terry nodded. "No, she can't ascend. She'll be like the rest of us, but she won't be able to access her powers anymore."

I sighed again. "Ascend to where?"

Terry harrumphed. "It's in the book."

"Kira?" Caleb stood by one of the reading tables, wrapped in the quilt from the bed. "Honey, who are you talking to?"

I looked up at the ceiling. "Myself?"

He moved toward me. "Babe, are you hallucinating?" He put a hand to my forehead, feeling for fever.

I rolled my eyes. "I wish." I so didn't want to do this right now. If I told him the truth there was a decent chance I'd never see him again after tonight. He'd write me off as looney tunes, and I wouldn't blame him.

"Maybe you'd better have a seat." I motioned toward one of the reading chairs.

"I'm fine where I am. What's going on?"

I threw up my hands. "It's not like I asked for this."

Taking a deep breath, I told him. "I see dead people."

He was silent for a full minute. "So you are hallucinating. I'm calling Sam."

I growled. "No! Trust me. No one thinks this whole thing is more crazy than I do."

"Kira, I know you *think* you see dead people, but you're in shock, baby. It's okay. We can get you help." His patronizing tone sent me over the edge.

"Ahhhggg. I'm not crazy!" I screamed the words.

His eyes flashed and I saw the worry in them.

"This library is special. It's—I can't possibly explain this. I'm a—crap. I'm special."

He looked past me to the phone and I could read his thoughts.

"Sam's on his way back from Dallas. I'm meeting with him this morning. That will be soon enough for you to find out if I'm crazy." I jumped off the desk. "I know it's asking a lot, but I thought, maybe, you'd believe me." I stormed past him.

"Young lady." The voice was a woman's, and authoritative enough that it stopped me in my tracks. I turned to see an African American woman in a large, colorful caftan.

"Tell him Momma Grace is here."

I shook my head.

"Tell him."

She had a mean look about her and was more than a little

scary. I did what she asked. "Momma Grace says to tell you she's here." I didn't face him.

Silence.

"You tell that boy that I'll tan his hide if he doesn't listen to you."

I gave a sad laugh. "She says she'll tan your hide if you don't listen to me."

I heard one of the chairs move behind me. "How do you know about Momma Grace?"

"I don't know about her, Caleb! She's standing right there." I pointed near the Christmas tree. "She's wearing a black and orange caftan, and her hair's up in a colorful wrap."

"Momma Grace?" He sounded like a little boy, his voice a little choked. He turned to face the tree. "Ask her where she put my slingshot."

"Tell him it's in the box marked 'doll dresses' in his sister Marcy's storage unit. I knew he'd never look there."

I relayed the message.

Caleb fell back against the table and sat down. "It really is her."

"You tell him I love him, and that he found himself one hell of a girl, and you ain't crazy." She faded away.

I told him what she said.

He chuckled softly.

"So I take it you know Momma Grace well?"

Caleb nodded. "She was our nanny when we were kids. We loved her to death, but she scared the hell out of us."

"She's gone now."

He blew out a breath. "So do you see them everywhere?"

"No, not yet. I've been hearing them for more than a

month. There's a book upstairs that explains it, but I haven't had the courage to read it. They were down here this morning because they're worried, rightfully so, that I'm not staying. If I leave, the library and its contents go up for auction."

"I don't understand. Why can't you just hire another librarian to run the place?"

I bit my lip. "It's against the rules. Like I explained before, I've been given, um, powers. Not just anyone can work here."

He was quiet, letting me get it all out.

"I'm torn. I've grown to love it here, and I like running the library. But it's a big responsibility, and from the little I read of the book, it's a much bigger job than I ever imagined."

He stood and took me in his arms. "So this is the big secret?"

"What do you mean?"

He laughed softly. "I'm a journalist, I knew you had a secret. I was just waiting for you to tell me. I thought maybe you'd given a baby up for adoption or had killed someone. When I found out about your friend who died, I thought maybe that was it."

I shook my head. "Geez. You do think a lot of me."

He squeezed me. "I just knew it was big, and I didn't want to pry. Which, I might add, is not easy for the journalist in me. So what are you going to do?"

I shook my head. "I don't know. When Mr. Grayson was here he offered me the job of my dreams in New York. It would be a whole new start for me and the benefits are beyond fab. But I found out tonight that Mrs. Canard is trapped in la la land somewhere. If I decide not to do this she can't move on like she's supposed to.

"I keep asking, why me? But for someone who is supposed to have all the answers, I just don't."

Caleb kissed my head. "The whole thing is freakin' weird. I'm having a hard time comprehending that there really is life after death. This is huge."

"Believe me, I know."

He guided me up the stairs to the loft.

"There's one thing I want you to know," he said as he started the coffeepot. There was no use in either of us trying to go back to bed. "Wherever you go, I go."

I'd been getting the milk out of the fridge for cereal. "What?"

"If you move to New York, I'm coming right behind you." He leaned back against the counter. "I'm not going to be away from you anymore. I finally found you, and I'm not letting go."

I bit back a smile. It was so macho and possessive, but I kind of liked it. "I thought you wanted to move here."

"Duh. Because you're here."

I yanked on his arm, and he wrapped himself around me again. "You're stuck with me, Kira Smythe. No matter what happens, I'm here for the long haul."

I kissed him. "Me too," I whispered against his lips. I leaned my head against his chest. "Now if I can figure out what to do with the rest of my life, we'll both know what to do next."

Chapter 32

There are more things in heaven and earth, Horatio, than are dreamt of in your philosophy.

HAMLET
By Shakespeare, William, 1564–1616
Call #: F-SHA
Description: 186 p.; 19cm

I arrived at Sam's promptly at eight thirty with Caleb in tow. He wouldn't let me leave him behind. Thankfully, Sam made him stay out in the waiting room.

"You can come back after I check her out," he promised Caleb. After a quick examination, Sam said I seemed to be doing better. He was worried about my weight. I'd lost another five pounds, which explained why my clothes didn't fit.

Between the stresses of the last few days and everything that had been going on, I hadn't remembered to eat regular meals. In fact, the last time I'd eaten a real meal was with the girls a couple of nights ago. I'd had a cookie or the occasional muffin, but things had gone crazy fast.

"You're cold all the time because you aren't giving your body the fuel it needs. I'd also like to suggest taking some yoga classes out at your parents' house. I've been going out there to hike a couple of times a week, and noticed they have several classes available. That and walking are the best exercises for stress."

"Hmmm. Okay." I shrugged.

"When we did your exam in November you said you weren't on any birth control." He shifted. "I'm trying to be a good doctor and tell you that might be something you want to consider."

I laughed. "Yes, Doctor, I would like to go on the pill."

He gave a sheepish grin. "That's the only bad part about treating friends.

"And one more thing." He pulled a card out of his pocket. "I know you didn't want to talk to him before, but you should." He handed me the psychiatrist's business card again. "He's the one who helped me find the facility for Melinda's brother. I made you an appointment for eleven today."

"Sam!"

He held up his hands in a surrendering motion. "You've been through two major traumas in a month and a severe illness. Talk to him once, and you don't have to go back after that if you don't want to."

I couldn't believe he'd done this behind my back. "I'm not going."

"Um, actually, you are." Caleb stood at the door.

I crossed my arms against my chest. "You two can gang up on me all you want—you can't make me go."

Three hours later I sat in a deep leather recliner. I'd spilled it all to the psychiatrist, Dr. Redmond. I told him about Melinda, the mono, my parents, Caleb, the library, Todd, Mr. Grayson and the job in New York—and even the dead people.

Through it all he said, "Hmmm," a lot. I guessed him to be in his mid-forties, a handsome man with gray hair and a goatee. With his sweater and tie, he reminded me of a professor I'd crushed on in law school.

We were nearing the end of our hour and a half, and I had to admit, I felt better.

"So your powers are manifesting quickly?" he said once I'd been silent for a full minute.

"Huh?"

"The universal librarian powers?"

I nodded. I hadn't mentioned anything about the powers. "How do you know that?"

"I'm afraid that falls under doctor-patient confidentiality."

"Then you've treated others like me?"

He stared at me for a moment over the edge of his glasses. "We all need someone with whom we can share our troubles. Spouses, relatives, and friends can only take so much."

"So you believe me?" I didn't believe me. How could he?

"Of course. And I know that Mabel Canard believed in you."

I flinched when he said her name.

"Oh, I see. Still a great deal of guilt there. She's stuck, but you can't let that make your decision for you. If you decide to stay here, it must be of your own volition."

"Wait. How do you know this stuff? I have the book and I still don't know what's going on."

"As I said, I have my sources. Once again, Mabel believed

in you. She was—is—not the kind of person who would want you to stress over this. If you decide to leave, everything will work out as it should. You must do what is best for you."

I sat forward in the chair. "You're freakin' me out, Doctor. That's exactly what she said to me. In a dream."

He gave a sly smile. "Well, it's true. All she wanted was for you to examine your heart closely. As a lawyer you take your heart out of the equation and always use your head. She wants you to go about it in another way."

I bit my lip. "You're kind of scary."

He chuckled. "That's what *they* tell me." He said it in a way that made something click in my head.

"You talk to the dead too."

He shrugged.

"Doctor-patient confidentiality," I whispered.

He smiled. "Sweet is a very special town for a variety of reasons. Once you think you have it figured out, something else will rise out of the dust to surprise you."

A clock chimed. He put his pad of paper down and helped me out of my chair. "You are welcome to come back anytime for a chat."

"I wish I'd come a little sooner."

"I'd like to suggest that before you make any decision, you finish reading the book. You are special and you've received an amazing gift that you've barely tapped." He held up his hand. "I'm not trying to sway you in any way. I support any decision you make."

When I walked out into the small waiting area, Caleb was reading a novel by Britta Coleman.

He stood. "How'd it go? Are you still mad at me?"

I smirked. "Great, and no."

Sighing, he handed me my coat. "That's good. I don't like it when you're mad at me."

I laughed. "Actually, I feel a lot better. Let's grab some lunch. Then I have some reading to do."

He raised an eyebrow.

I nodded.

"Huh." He opened the door.

After lunch we opened the library. Caleb held down the fort while I read. Once in a while I'd get up to run down to the break room to check on him, but he was handling things pretty well, including the homework help sessions. He'd even managed to bake cookies for the kids.

The man never ceased to amaze me.

The Book scared me to death. The doctor and Mrs. Canard were right; I'd been given an extraordinary gift, one that could take my life in a direction I would have never imagined.

Boiling down seven hours of reading isn't easy, but the basic gist was that as a seer reached each level, he or she gained more power and could do everything from recalling every moment in history to jumping into alternative worlds for research.

Some of the seers/librarians/oracles were clairvoyant; others were clairsentient or had other psychic powers. No two are the same, and we each have our own approach to the occupation, following a basic set of guidelines. It was an esoteric job, as they also had direct access to the Akashic Records, which wasn't just about mystical information. It was everything that has ever happened in the universe.

Like I said, pretty wild stuff.

Once a librarian reached the top level, she was called an adept. Mrs. Canard had just moved to that level, but she didn't have to die to reach it. Until that time she was called an apprentice or chelas.

If I chose to take on the job, by the end of the month I would be able to access certain levels of the Book of Life and know what pure knowledge really meant. The whole idea of it was beyond fascinating to me.

Caleb brought me dinner and I ate while continuing to read. At midnight I finished the book.

"Wow." I sat back in my chair.

Shuffling in from the bedroom, Caleb put his hands on my shoulders. "Finished?"

"Yeah."

"And?"

I sighed. "I'm more confused than ever. It doesn't seem possible, what this says."

"Really?"

"Yes, but something tells me that every word is true. I can't explain it."

He sat down across from me. "I have a confession to make."

"Does it involve bastard children or ex-girlfriends?" I wasn't sure I could take much more excitement right that moment.

He laughed so hard he held his stomach. "No." He caught his breath. "It's about the book. I tried to read it."

I raised an eyebrow. "So what did you think?"

"That it was my favorite Dickens story."

"What?"

He shrugged. "I don't think I see the same thing you do."

I opened the front page. "Read it."

The first paragraph was straight out of *A Christmas Carol*.

"That's weird."

He nodded. "My guess is they do it that way to protect you. So that if anyone besides one of the universal librarians finds the book, they can't figure out what's going on." He crossed his arms. "Do you want to tell me about it?"

"Would it be terrible if we talked it all out in the morning? It's been a really long day, and I need some time to digest it all."

"Baby, it's your call. You don't have to tell me anything." He was sincere.

I stood and kissed his cheek. "I will tell you everything, but right now I want you to make love to me."

He bowed his head. "Oh, the things you make me do." He laughed and chased me into the bedroom.

The next morning there was freshness in the air. It was dark and cloudy, and snow fell, but everything felt new to me.

While Caleb slept, I went downstairs and looked around. Something became very clear to me.

I picked up the phone and then realized I didn't have the number I wanted to call. I raced back upstairs for my purse and dug out the card.

A few minutes later the line rang and voice mail clicked in.

I left a message. "Mr. Grayson, it's Kira Smythe. I wanted to speak with you regarding the opportunity you presented the other day. You can reach me at . . ." I left him my number.

Now all I had to do was wait.

"So you've decided?" Caleb stood near the first row of books. His messy hair made him look boyish and innocent, but he was all man.

"Um, not quite. There's one more detail to work out, and then I'll know for sure."

Caleb started to say something, but the phone rang. I held up a finger.

"Hello?"

"Ms. Smythe, you called? I hope it's good news. You're a few weeks early from the deadline you gave me."

"Yes, Mr. Grayson, I am. I wanted to propose something to you."

I explained that while I wasn't interested in working full time, I would like to do consulting for him. "Of course, I'd have to work from my home here in Sweet, but I could travel to New York when needed."

I looked across the room and caught the big smile on Caleb's face.

"That's an interesting proposition. And this would be the only way we can get you to join our organization?" he asked, knowing the answer.

"Yes, sir."

He was silent for a minute. "Can you come to the offices

after the New Year, and we'll settle on the terms? I'd like to have you on retainer if that's amenable to you."

"Yes. I'll see you in a few weeks."

Caleb ran across the room and swung me around. "So we're staying."

I kissed him hard on the lips. "Yes."

There was a cheer all around us and I looked up to see the library full of people. All of them dead.

I smiled.

Terry winked at me. "I knew you'd make the right decision."

Rascal and Herman barked.

"So did I." A woman stepped from behind him. I didn't recognize her at first.

"Mrs. Canard?" I slid out of Caleb's arms and turned to face her. "It's really you?" She was years younger. In fact she looked my age. When she grinned I'd have recognized that smile anywhere. "It is you."

"I came to wish you well, dear Kira."

"So you're free from wherever they were holding you?"

"Yes, dear girl, but it isn't as awful as you imagine. No matter what you decided I wouldn't have been stuck there forever." She turned and glared at Terry, who threw up his hands.

"Are you happy—is this truly the decision of your heart?" Mrs. Canard looked around the library as if she were checking to make sure I'd kept the place up. When she smiled, I knew I'd done well.

"Oh, yes. I woke up this morning and I knew. I felt so free once I made the decision to accept the gift."

"It's that way with all of us. But there's one thing I can't take credit for, and that's the gift. You were born with it, I only helped cultivate it."

"Really? I thought when you passed on the powers were given to me."

"No." She stood in front of me now, her hair twisted into an elegant knot. She wore a beautiful black dress in a 1950s style. "You were born with those powers." She looked up at the ceiling. "Ah, it's time for me to go, but I'll be back to visit when I can. Just remember, you will always know the answers, it's only knowing where to look." She smiled and blew me a kiss.

A tear fell down my cheek, and Caleb wiped it away.

"How did she look?"

I chewed on my lip. "Absolutely beautiful." I sniffed and turned to him. "You know what we need?"

He wiggled his eyebrows.

I rolled my eyes. "Besides that, silly man."

"What?"

"We need a Christmas tree for the loft. I want a fresh one. And presents. Ooohhh and I want to invite Justin and Rob to spend the holidays with us. They can stay out at my mom and dad's. And . . ."

Caleb grabbed me from behind and whirled me around. "I love you." He stared at me hard.

I wrapped my arms around his neck. "I love you too." I patted his butt. "Now let's go find me a Christmas tree."

Candace Havens is a veteran entertainment journalist who spends way too much time interviewing celebrities. In addition to her weekly columns seen in newspapers throughout the country, she is the entertainment critic for 96.3 KSCS in the Dallas/Fort Worth area. She is the author of *Charmed & Dangerous*, *Charmed & Ready*, *Charmed & Deadly*, and the nonfiction biography *Joss Whedon: The Genius Behind Buffy*, as well as several published essays. Visit Candace at www.candacehavens.com.